THE GUILTY GIRL

RUTH HARROW

INKUBATOR
BOOKS

Published by Inkubator Books
www.inkubatorbooks.com

ISBN (eBook): 978-1-83756-377-7
ISBN (Paperback): 978-1-83756-378-4
ISBN (Hardback): 978-1-83756-379-1

PROLOGUE

Daddy is very angry with me. He must be. Why else would he look so upset? His eyes are filled with tears. I've never seen Daddy cry before. It's scary.

He sent me downstairs after it happened. The house is strangely quiet without my mummy moving around it. She is usually here making me drinks or pulling a jumper over my head if I'm cold.

Goosebumps spread up my arms now; I rub at them with my fingers.

I miss Mummy. A funny feeling tells me she isn't coming back from where she has gone. Daddy says she has only gone away for a little while. I know he is lying. His voice sounded strange; high-pitched and choked like he was trying not to cry too much.

I've been sitting in front of the TV for ages now. Strange noises keep coming from upstairs. I look up at the smooth white ceiling feeling scared again.

I pull Bunny closer to me, inhaling his special smell. His fur is soft. He usually makes me feel all better.

But not today. Today there's a funny cold feeling coming from inside me. It makes me shiver. There's a cool breeze coming in through the windows too. I can't reach them to stop it. Not that I'm allowed to touch the windows anyway.

Outside, the wind blows across the water of the marina at the end of the garden. The boats are bobbing about scarily this afternoon.

I wish Daddy was here to hug me. Daddy's always so nice and warm. He usually tells me I'm the light of his life. Will he ever say that to me again after today?

Everything has gone so wrong. Badly wrong. That's all I know.

Where is Daddy anyway? He has never left me alone for so long. Peppa Pig has been playing on a loop for ages. I want him to wrap his big arms around me and tell me everything will be okay. He has to really mean it this time though, not like earlier.

I uncross my legs and hop off the sofa, scooping Bunny up in my arms. He is scared, so I hold him close.

The bathroom door is open when I get upstairs. This is where it happened. Mummy's screaming was so loud. I had to cover my ears after a while, not able to bear it anymore.

Now the bathroom is quiet. I look around for Mummy. She isn't here, of course. She has gone. I won't ever get to see her again.

My lip wobbles. I want to tell her I'm sorry for what I did to make her go away.

I stare at the scary bathtub in front of me. There are red streaks all over it. It's over the sides and in patches on the floor too.

If I hadn't been here earlier to see, I might almost be able to pretend it was paint; huge areas of poster paint like Mummy got me for my birthday.

I can't pretend though. Not after what I saw. Anyway, there's the funny smell. Like metal. I crinkle my nose and cover Bunny's nose too. I don't want him to be scared.

I reach for the handle and close the door on the scene of horror. I must find Daddy.

He isn't far. That's lucky.

He is in his and Mummy's bedroom. I blink at what is going on in here too.

Nothing is right today.

Daddy zips up a big backpack as I push the door open. He straightens up and gasps when he spots me in the doorway with Bunny.

'Sweetheart. I thought you were downstairs.' He tries to smile. It must be hard when his face looks so pale and stiff.

'It's okay,' he says as he pulls the backpack over his shoulder.

He takes hold of my hand in his big warm one. Bunny holds my other.

'Everything is going to be okay. It's just the two of us now, my angel. Mummy is gone. We have to look after each other.'

1

The clock begins ticking so loudly that I can't stand it anymore. I stand up and move into the hall next to it. My daily countdown begins. The dark timepiece dominates the cramped entranceway. This old thing is one of the tallest pieces of furniture in the house, wooden and brassy like everything else.

My heart flutters. My insides squeeze. I'm suddenly hyper-aware of everything. Like the way our house smells: must, mingled with furniture polish.

There always seems to be a fine layer of dust covering all the dark wooden surfaces and the dingy floral carpet. No matter how long or hard I clean, dirt clings everywhere. I wonder if that happens outside? Lush green plants don't seem to have to contend with the continuous grey powder I sweep from surfaces in here. But I'm not sure. I have never been outside much. I might have been when I was very small. That was a long time ago.

The minute hand nudges closer to the ornate numeral for twelve. When I was little, I used to think the ticking got louder on its approach to six o'clock. Now I know that was a childish thing to think. Nor does my heart beat in tandem with each tick as I used to believe back then.

Now that I'm older, I recognise the hammering in my chest is far more erratic than the sturdy old clock. I know my heart rate wouldn't form the perfect, uniform peaks if represented in a picture. Not like the images of a pulse in the old medical textbook in the loft upstairs.

Does that mean there is something wrong with me? I never mention these fears to Dad. He would only get upset, as I'm not allowed to see a doctor.

Dad gets unsettled a lot. I'm forever careful what I say to him. That is something I must have learned at a young age. Who knows when exactly my treading on eggshells started? I don't remember much from the time before this house.

The minute hand slides quietly closer still, straightening up. There is a little scene above the clock face. A brass full moon and stars. On Christmas Eve, I'm allowed out into the cold dark garden to look up at the night sky and see the real stars. I like that.

Distant memories of the festive season make me think things used to be different. I can't recall them properly. It's just that something tells me Christmas used to be warmer and nicer somehow.

As hard as I try, I can't make the images behind my eyes any clearer. There is a blur of colour and something that could be fun. That was before what happened, though, so I guess it doesn't matter now.

Our house isn't surrounded by others, just the crumbling ruin of an old cottage nearby. The trees have long grown over that though.

So the stars here are bright against the inky blackness,

uninhibited by lights. I just wish I could see them more often. Maybe I'll think about hinting this idea to Dad when he gets back from work, which should be any minute. I swallow hard. I'm not nearly this nervous when my father is actually here, or during the long hours he is away.

It's just the in-between that gets me. I can manage black or white, but not the grey area in the middle. Waiting for him to come back is tough. The anticipation leaves me a nervous wreck. Every day on the run-up to six o'clock, my hands are clammy, and the remnants of my lunch sit uncomfortably somewhere inside making me regret them.

All sorts of scenarios flash through my anxious mind. Every day I wonder if Dad will even come home at all. There are a ton of reasons he might not make it back from work. What if he gets hit by a car? Or bumps his head and forgets about me? Or meets a beautiful lady who enchants him like a sorceress from one of my storybooks.

I try not to think about this possibility. Or any others. Much, much worse could happen. I can't bring myself to even form the thoughts in my head.

I don't want to think what would happen to me if Dad wasn't here. Or what would have happened if he hadn't been there for me that day when I was small. I really needed him then.

So I stand and face the grandfather clock in the hall and wait.

And wait.

Eventually, I hear heavy footsteps on the gravel path leading to our cottage. Darkness creeps across the frosted glass panels of the front door and a key slides into the lock.

2

A breath of cool air rushes over my face as Dad's salt and pepper head and glasses come into view. I take a deep breath and savour how sweet and fresh the air is that he brings in with him. The musty taste from inside lingers in my throat and I swallow it down.

The muscles in my leg twitch. But I quash thoughts of running out in my socks from the polished floorboards to the stone path outside. I can only enjoy the warmth of the late September sun through the living room window each afternoon. Dad draws a definite line under these thoughts by pulling the front door closed behind him.

'Chloe.' He reaches out his arms and pulls me to him as he does every time he comes home. 'I missed you.'

'I missed you too, Dad.' I say these words every day, so many times that they may have formed a track in my mouth.

I don't resent this interaction though. The warmth of his body is comforting. It's so nice just to see another human being after being alone in the house all day.

My shoulders slump in relief as per our routine. *He came*

back. Nothing bad happened again today. We are safe. Will I be able to say the same thing tomorrow?

Probably.

I get myself worked up like this, and each time I find my foolish fear was for nothing. I wish I could relax more. It's been almost twelve years since we moved here. And no one has found us, have they? So why does our familiar routine make me so anxious? Maybe there is something wrong with me, after all.

'How was work?' I ask as I pull back from our hug.

My heart is dropping back into a more normal rhythm and my insides are calming too. It's like nothing happened. I will forget all about my nerves again until the same time tomorrow. Then the whole thing starts over again.

'Fine.' Dad shrugs as he slides his coat off and hangs it neatly on the peg. 'Same as usual.'

I nod. We exchange the same words every day. Dad doesn't talk much about his job. I never used to be quite so interested in the world outside our house after hearing how dangerous it is. But lately, I find myself wanting to know so much more.

I try and ask Dad as much as I can, but it is difficult. He doesn't like questions, especially about work. He finds his job stressful, and I don't like to upset him. So I have to be careful how much I say and when.

Sometimes, I spend weeks planning the perfect way to phrase something, like now. I want to know how much Dad earns. The maths exam Dad set me recently got me curious about money again. Sums and equations on paper are one thing, but how does that relate to our household and what Dad brings in for us?

We don't seem to have much money sometimes. I feel

like we go through phases of eating bread and potato-based foods and things from tins. Like tonight. The menu is comprised of chicken in white sauce and some waxy tinned potatoes. It's heated in pans on the stove, waiting for Dad's arrival.

My curious brain wants to drink in the real-life figures on paper and see how much we need and use each month. Or should that be each week? Or does Dad get paid once a year? Maybe that is why money seems tighter sometimes than others, because he runs out before the next payment.

I don't know.

I wish I knew more about how things worked. But my father doesn't like questions and I'm not allowed outside, so I can only guess how things like that work.

These queries burn in my brain until they are all I think about. Dad calls them "bees in my bonnet". Which I suppose is a good way to describe them.

Either way, that is what drives the words from my mouth now.

'Dad,' I say slowly, knowing there is no subtle or easy way to ease this question in. 'Can I ask you something?'

My father looks suddenly weary as he lifts his glasses to rub a tired eye. 'What is it?'

His sudden change in body language lets me know my inquiring mind is getting me into trouble again, but I'm committed to this now. Who knows? Maybe things will be different this time around?

I'm older than I was the last time I asked. Back then, Dad got so annoyed with my twelve-year-old self trying to understand economics that he set me extra maths homework for a month.

Perhaps that had been less of a punishment, more Dad's

way of answering my question in a roundabout way? I don't always understand my father's actions. I'm starting to understand that he thinks a lot more than he lets on.

Maybe too much. That might be why his rules and words seem confusing to me. But I'm getting better at understanding as I grow older.

I clasp my hands together and hope for the best. 'Well, it's just that I've been thinking a lot about money lately.'

One of Dad's thick eyebrows twitches but he says nothing and waits for me to finish.

'I was just wondering if you could tell me more about how money works. And sort of... how much you make, perhaps? Also, how much do we need to run the house? That sort of thing.'

My hopeful question is met with a tired sigh. 'Chloe, I've told you before. Money is a complicated thing. I take care of it all. It's not something you need to worry about.'

'I'm not worried. It's just that maybe I could help if I understood more about it.'

'Do you think I need help?'

'No. Well, yes. Maybe a little.' My voice trails off. I know immediately the rabbit hole of words my tongue led me down was the wrong one. A tightness spreads across Dad's face and the air goes funny like it does when I've said the wrong thing.

'I'm sorry, Dad.' I intertwine my dampening fingers in front of me. 'It's just that I'm fifteen now, almost sixteen. I thought if I'm growing up, maybe I can help out with the running of the household more.'

There is a pause. 'What do you think is wrong with our household?'

'Nothing. You do a great job. Everything is fine.' I nod my

head quickly. If my answers are quick and adamant, maybe Dad won't latch onto an idea and rant on for hours as he sometimes does when I've done or said the wrong thing.

In the recent summer heatwave, he forgot he opened the living room window before leaving for work one morning and wouldn't let me go until I had "admitted" it was me.

It was past midnight before I decided to tell him I had done it, even though I hadn't. I confessed just to break the tension and relentless questioning and be allowed to go to bed.

As a result of that incident, I'd been banned from TV time and missed the new episode of Columbo I'd been looking forward to watching for ages.

He said it was a punishment for him too, as he had been looking forward to that particular episode of our favourite detective show as much as I had.

In a way, I'm glad he didn't watch it without me. Watching videos on our VHS player is one of the things I love the most.

'"Everything is fine".' Dad repeats my words now and looks at me. I can almost hear all the options being weighed up. *Go to your room; do extra chores; no reading for a week.* The list goes on.

'I just wanted to understand, that's all. I see you going out to work, even though you don't like it. I want to help.'

'What makes you think I don't like my job?'

I open my mouth, unsure of the right route of verbal stepping stones out of danger. 'I don't know. You just seem stressed all the time.'

'I have many reasons to be stressed, Chloe. You know that.'

My eyes sting. I try to resist the urge to swallow down a

lump in my throat. I don't like admitting to having emotions as I remember the past. 'I know. I'm sorry, Dad.'

'You know the sacrifice I made for you. That I continue to make. Going to work is just another one. We both have to do things we don't like. I know you would like to go outside more, but you can't. It's not safe for you beyond these walls. That's just the way it is.'

'I'm sorry.' My words sound hollow and pathetic when I consider everything my father has done for me. Simple words for the sacrifice of a normal life seem ridiculous, but I don't know what else to say.

'Don't be. You are the light of my life, Chloe. Never forget that.'

Dad snakes an arm around my shoulders and gives me a comforting squeeze. The gesture is reassuring. At the same time, it makes me fearful. What if Dad wasn't here to do this? What if something happened to him and I was suddenly all alone?

As though in response to my unwanted thoughts, Dad continues, 'Everything is going to be all right, Chloe. We have each other. That's all that is important. Don't worry about anything else. Nothing matters outside this house.'

3

A punishment for my renewed curiosity never comes. It should be a relief, but I spend so long fretting and watching out for some kind of backlash that I don't truly enjoy its absence.

Then I wonder if Dad did that on purpose. Was the anticipation of reprisal intended to be the punishment itself? I try and shake thoughts like these from my head. They only confuse me. Dad has his moments, but I know he loves me. He seems happy enough with me today. I hadn't done anything wrong, so I don't know why I worried so much.

Our monthly outing always occurs on the first Sunday of the month. Today, I get to see what October looks like this year. It is still warm enough that I don't need a coat, which is a relief as I have outgrown the one I've had for years now.

There was a time when the green parka had hung off me, heavy and puffy and far too oversized. That was ages ago. Dad first bundled me up in it when I was nine. The last time

I tried the thing on I had to work to get it over my shoulders and it gave me pins and needles in my arms.

Dad acts like coats are expensive things to be treasured. I have no idea how much in real figures though. Are the garments a big type of expensive like when we needed a new refrigerator? Or more like the thick and heavy encyclopedias I get for Christmas? I can't tell.

I want to ask him if he will get me a new coat soon, but I don't want to stumble upon the subject of money again. Not so soon, anyway. Is he holding off buying a new one because he is struggling for money at the moment? I don't dare ask.

So for now, I enjoy the still-warm October air and can only hope for an uncharacteristically mild November ahead too. I just wish he would talk to me more about outside-world stuff.

Dad leads the way along our familiar route. We tread down a narrow country lane. Being outside is so different from staring at the inside of the cottage.

There is movement everywhere. Plants sway in the breeze, even on days that aren't windy. Shuffling sounds come from the brambles around us. Birds dart here and there with a hurried tweet. On these walks, I like to try and identify them from my books at home. It's fascinating to see them in real life.

I trail behind Dad, dodging blackberry brambles. They stretch across the ground laden with dark, overripe fruit. Not many people drive down here, only occasional lost tourists. They soon realise their mistake and turn back when the thorns scratch against their shiny car windows.

The next time I will tread along this path, all the juicy berries will be gone. What the robins and blackbirds leave behind will have shrivelled up and spoiled. The leaves will be shrinking back too.

Memories float back to me of a game I had used to play in my head. I would pretend this overgrown lane was a route through a jungle I had to journey through. Dad was my only travel companion then too. I had used to imagine I was venturing through the ancient forest of Fangorn like in *The Lord of the Rings*.

I'd forgotten about that little scenario I'd dreamed up. I must have been much younger then to play a game like that. I definitely must have been smaller to still be able to fit into that comfortable coat. But those days are gone now.

What will I be like when the same amount of time has elapsed again? That would make me... twenty-one. Wow. That is hard to imagine. Will I still be ambling behind Dad like this on a monthly outing?

Twenty-one sounds really old. Would I have the authority as an adult to negotiate more than a supervised walk? Will we have been caught by then? I shudder at that last thought.

'Is everything all right, sweetheart?'

'Yes.' I realise my answer is too quick.

My father raises his eyebrows at me. Beneath them, his dark eyes I've also inherited are enquiring. 'Are you sure? Something must be troubling you. You've been quiet all morning.'

'I'm fine.'

'Just fine? I tend to find you say that when you aren't. Which means you must be the opposite at the moment.'

I can't stop a smile from spreading across my face at this. He knows me so well. Better than I know myself, he often tells me. Maybe he is right. We are alike in so many ways, it's probably like him knowing himself.

My father drops back to allow us to walk side by side. 'Tell me what's wrong.'

'Nothing exactly.' I look down at my feet as I draw level with him. I know voicing my feelings will lead to unrest, maybe even an argument. Sometimes though, there is so much going on inside me that I can't help but let some of it bubble out.

If I didn't, I think I might explode. 'I was just wondering... how much longer are we going to keep going on like this.'

He says nothing.

I don't dare look up. I realize my question was formed with the wrong words; I should have chosen some more carefully. Rough ground and countryside weeds pass by beneath my all but immaculate trainers.

Only wearing them once a month means I don't get much use out of my footwear. At least my shoe size seems to have stabilised in recent years, so the ones I've got on now don't seem so much of a waste.

We continue to walk in silence. I know I shouldn't have said what I'm really thinking but Dad has this way of drawing information out of me. Maybe I just don't know how to keep my mouth shut with anyone. I've never spoken to someone else before. Not as far as I remember anyway.

I suppose I would have spoken to Mum when I was little. Perhaps she even drew the first words from my lips as a baby, beating my father to it? I was too young to remember that now though.

It's hard to imagine anyone other than Dad. He is my world.

I take a deep breath of sweet-smelling air. Maybe this is a typical day in the countryside. It's just so different from our musty old house that my heart aches funnily. I want to stay out here all day, sleep in the fresh green grass even.

I don't feel I have enough experience of being outside to make a judgement on my favourite time of year, but this might be it. The remnants of summer warmth and the glowing orange hues resonate so deeply with me. Perhaps it is because it is such a contrast to the dark wood-panelled furniture and dusty brass ornaments of the house.

There is so much I don't understand about the world and how it works. I may be ignorant in a lot of ways, but I'm aware of just how little I know. My limited access to books and television shows has raised more questions than it answers.

For example, I've concluded that Dad and I must be poor. We often seem like we could use more money. Our small, old house is so different from the houses of the villains I see in episodes of *Columbo*. Or the grand mansions with servants in *Great Expectations*. I suppose I'm sort of like Pip and Dad is a more modern version of the guardian in the book. Only instead of being a blacksmith like Joe, Dad is a solicitor. I can surmise from this that solicitors must not get paid much.

I don't mind being poor. It's not money that I wish for when I close my eyes at night, or when I blow out my birthday candles every year. My only wish is that Dad and I could live a normal life. Maybe I will focus more energy on this affirmation in a few months when I am seated in front of my sixteenth cake.

Even as I make a mental note of this, I know that can't

happen. It's like the universe is answering the question I voiced aloud only minutes ago.

The country track Dad and I have been following starts fizzling out. The crumbling grey stone beneath my trainers turns into a smooth road surfacing. This has appeared since my last outing. Dad doesn't seem surprised. I suppose he has seen it already. The dark surface looks smart and almost menacing against the yellowing straw of the nearest field.

I guess we aren't heading up the hill to Bamford Edge today.

My father leads me around a corner and heads down the nearest snicket. This is where my stomach does a funny drop.

I expect we will follow the narrow country track past the local B&B as we have done so many times before without incident.

Today, however, two police cars are parked in this usually quiet little through route. Well, not parked. More strewn really. The wheels are stuck out at odd angles, abandoned in a hurry.

The only vehicle parked here usually is the little red car belonging to the elderly B&B owner, Mrs Turner. Most guests are backpackers looking for somewhere to stay before they set off across the hills.

Now the scene looks stopped in mid-action. It soon bursts into life as we pass, however.

Two officers emerge with a third man between them. The man has his hands behind his back. I realise why as I glance down at his wrists. They are bound with handcuffs.

In a swift movement, one of the policemen puts a hand on top of the man's head and he is tucked neatly into the car with the slam of a door.

The other officer walks around the car towards me and Dad. My feet bring me to a stop now as my fearful eyes move up to the hard face of the policeman.

My heart rages in my chest. I know any second now those steel blue eyes will lock onto mine or Dad's and that will be it. It will all be over.

Then I feel a hand on the small of my back. Dad urges me forward with a surprisingly firm nudge and we are moving again. The officer gives Dad a casual nod without really glancing at him.

Then the moment is over. The car is behind us.

My trembling legs struggle to get me over the wooden stile I've been over plenty of times before. Dad's strong hands support me as I step over and land with a crunch on the cropped straw of the field. The sharp remnants threaten to poke up through my trainers.

The engine of the police car roars into life in the quiet country lane behind us as Dad drops down into the field too.

Nothing happened. We weren't recognised. No one tried to force the two of us into the police car too.

We are safe once again.

4

'Dad, take me with you.'

My father looks at me incredulously as he pulls his coat on in our narrow hall. 'Don't be silly, Chloe. You know that can't happen.'

It's been years since I have voiced those words. When I was small, I used to cling to Dad's corded trouser legs and beg for him not to leave me in the house for hours on end alone. Sometimes, if I kicked up enough fuss, he would leave a tape in the music machine running. That was some comfort sometimes.

But even Neil Young's or Van Morrison's happy beats can turn melancholy and bleak in some of their albums. It used to scare me so much that I would go upstairs and curl up beneath my duvet with my favourite plush bunny until a happier song came on.

When I was older, I realised I could just switch it off, or press fast-forward. There are only so many times you can hear the same song over and over again though. Well, for me, anyway.

Dad loves his music. He can listen to his favourite songs on repeat for hours and not get bored. It's nice that he has passions and interests. I feel a bit vapid for not liking anything as much as him. If he likes something, he *really* likes something.

Last year I made a batch of chocolate cupcakes and, aside from the single one I ate, Dad finished off the whole lot in a few hours. He wouldn't stop raving about how delicious they were for weeks. He certainly is passionate.

I wish I could find something I loved that much. For that to happen though, I would need to be allowed to explore what is out there in the world. Or have more of the world in here with me. I've read every single book on the shelf. Dad can't buy me new ones fast enough.

'Please, Dad. I won't attract attention. I promise.'

'Won't you? You didn't do a very good job of that yesterday out on our walk. Why did you stop and stare when we neared the police car? That clearly had nothing to do with us. Old Mrs Turner has been having trouble with a homeless man stealing food from her guesthouse for months, that's all.'

He huffs impatiently. 'This area is changing. You know that because I've already told you. Wasn't there a way that you could have put two and two together quicker? Staring was the worst thing to do; you should avert your eyes when walking past people. They remember you less if you don't make eye contact. Remember that. You couldn't have drawn more attention to us yesterday afternoon if you had tried.'

I shrug. 'I'm sure I could have done.'

Dad's eyebrows dart upwards. 'I beg your pardon?'

I'm just as surprised at my unbidden words as my father. 'Sorry. I mean, I just froze. I didn't know what I was doing. I wasn't expecting there to be any police on our walk. It's usually so quiet. I thought... I don't know. I just panicked.'

'That's what happens in the real world, Chloe. The unexpected can happen at any time. And it does, believe me. That is why you have to stay here, in case another issue crops up where you panic and don't know what to do.'

'How will I ever know what to do if I never go outside? There is so much I want to know.'

'I know that, sweetheart. It hurts me more than it does you to have to leave you here alone so often. You are breaking my heart by talking like this. But there is no other way. I've already thought long and hard about it. We shouldn't be seen together if we can help it. It increases our chances of being recognised. I don't want to have to ban you from coming out for walks too.'

I cross my arms across my chest in defeat, unwilling to say anything more. The last thing I want is to be locked in this house with no chance of going out at all.

Dad sighs. 'I would have thought what happened yesterday would have reminded you why we have to stay hidden. That's how quickly our lives can be over, Chloe. The police could turn up at our door any day as we witnessed less than twenty-four hours ago. Do you want to see me shoved into the back of a police car like that man?'

'No, of course not.'

'Then let's stay safe, eh? That was less than a mile from here. Those very same officers could turn up here for us.' He turns his back to me and steps into his shoes.

'But I don't want you to go and leave me here.'

I take a step forward. My father has his sturdy walking shoes on now whilst I stand here in my socks. He is all set to get going and abandon me here for another long working day. Last week, I completed all the schoolwork Dad had prepared for me. That was the final bit of what would have been my secondary school education. I've read every book and magazine, listened to every tape and watched every video cassette in this house several times over. I feel like I would go mad if I were to sit down today and revisit any one of them.

Now there is nothing but the decor to stare at and I already know every detail: every mark in the paintwork; every indentation and scratch in the wood; every bit of peeling wallpaper and missing pieces from the ornaments. I could close my eyes and jot everything down in a massive mind-numbing list.

So now I voice what has been my biggest fear all these years. 'Don't leave me, Dad. Every day I get so frantic, as though I'm going to have a heart attack or something. Every time you go outside, I'm terrified you won't come back.'

My voice comes out louder than I expect and a little wobbly. Dad looks back at me as he lifts his keys from his pocket. 'I had no idea it was that bad.'

I shrug with my arms crossed. 'Well, it is. I don't like being left here all alone. I've told you that before.'

'I thought you had outgrown all that. Why don't I put some music on for some company?'

'No!' I say quickly as he blinks in surprise. 'Sorry, I just don't want that.'

'Chloe, of course I will return. I always do, don't I?' My father's tone softens and he rests a hand on my shoulder, which makes me feel like a tiny child all over again.

I have the sudden urge to shrug off his patronising hand. Instead, I readjust my folded arms, my last line of defence. 'I suppose so.'

'You are the light of my life, don't forget that. I will always make my way back towards you, no matter what.'

'I guess.'

'Yes. You know Daddy needs to go out to work to earn money. I wouldn't leave you for any other reason.'

I roll my eyes. 'I haven't called you that for ages. I'm not five anymore, Dad.'

An embarrassed smile spreads across my face, and I expect my father to share in it. But he doesn't. All of a sudden his lip tenses. For a split second, I think he is going to burst into tears.

He simply nods and wishes me a hurried goodbye as he heads outside. It's so abrupt that my arms are still raised expectantly for our usual parting hug when the door slams, separating us.

I stand in the hallway long after his dark shadow has gone and contemplate another day alone.

I look at the brass display of the grandfather clock. Dad was seven minutes late leaving today thanks to me. Would he get into trouble for being less than ten minutes late for work just once?

Dad is always so punctual. He has been for the twelve years he has worked at his job. Does that matter to the person he works for? Is that how having a job works? Can bosses be lenient and maybe even become friends with their employees, or are they forever strict like the mean teacher in Matilda?

That's another thing I don't know if I will ever know about. The world of work. Will I ever reach an age where Dad will allow me to go outside? A flash of a little girl pretending to administer medicines to a cluster of soft toys floats before my eyes. Was that me? I'd completely forgotten I had used to want to be a vet when I grew up.

That dream has never seemed so childish. I know that will never become a reality now.

The majority of the time we have lived in this house, I have thought work was something that only my father could do. I may not be able to have the career in animal care I wanted, but I could still find another way to earn a living.

Didn't the characters in *Little Women* have jobs to support the household? I could surely find something to earn extra money without being exposed to many people. I've passed every exam Dad has set me with almost full marks. And at the very least, I can clean for money. I know that's a job.

I hate cleaning. I do enough of it in our own house, but I would do it if it meant it would take some of the pressure off my hardworking father.

Old Mrs Turner from the B&B across the village has been "old" as far back as I can remember. She always says hello if she is outside her property as Dad and I pass on our walks and has always seemed kind.

Mrs Turner must surely need help running her business as she ages further. I could clean the place for her. Or maybe bake cakes for her guests to buy before they head off on their hikes across the hills. Dad can't be lying when he eats my food and says it is delicious. I could be Mrs Turner's chef, cooking breakfast in the kitchen at the back of the property.

My stomach bubbles with excitement when I think of the possibilities. This is something I could do. Not only would I earn money, but it would mean I could leave the house more than once a month, maybe even alone. I rush upstairs to my room and pull out the lined notebook I have used for this year's schoolwork. There are still some sheets left.

I start writing down my ideas and draw lines for the columns where I will write how much to charge per item, how many I could sell and how much I could potentially earn in a week.

I imagine Mrs Turner would still take the prepared plates of food out to the guests at their tables. That bit is easy if you aren't me. It wouldn't do for too many out-of-towners to see me regularly. Dad says I can't ever be recognised. I laugh out loud at the prospect of proposing such an idea to him.

But then my smile fades when I consider how I could realistically be a chef if I'm not allowed to be seen. What if Mrs Turner jumped at the chance to have some help? How much longer would she be capable of doing any of the work herself, even just walking back and forth from the kitchen?

And would guests enjoy my food so much that they would want to personally thank me? I've seen that done in at least one of the films I've watched before. Does that happen in bed and breakfast places or just expensive dinner restaurants? I've no idea. Maybe it's just an American thing.

The excitement fizzles out of me as quickly as it arrived. My marker pen hovers over the paper and I stare at my foolish ideas hastily scribbled down in something other than my best handwriting.

My idea about baking cakes is still surely a good one. I wouldn't even have to do the cooking over at Mrs Turner's place. I could bake batches of treats here and box them up. I suppose Dad could drop them off on his way to work. Then again, I don't want to burden him more.

I realise my enthusiasm is tainted when I consider a job

where I don't leave the house. Was that the most exciting part of the prospect for me?

Dad wouldn't approve of such a thought and that makes me feel guilty.

'Would Dad let me deliver the boxes of products myself?' I say out loud.

I glance over to my plush bunny, snuggled under the duvet beside my pillow. He never responds when I talk to him, of course. When I was little, I suppose I imagined he did answer back. Long gone are those days.

Bunny is looking very grey and dishevelled these days. It's hard to believe he was once white and plump-looking. His stitched-on mouth is fading with his flattened fur. His stuffing is gone from his neck and his head flaps about these days. Dad says I should rename him Flop.

'I need to stop talking to a toy.'

I sigh, realising I'm doing it again. It's just nice to stretch my vocal cords when Dad is away. Or else they go unused. Sometimes I put them to work just so it's not so quiet.

I return to my plans. I don't see a reason why I couldn't deliver the items myself. I could take the back roads, which our monthly walk leads me down anyway. I know that route so well. Nothing could go wrong.

The tip of my pen hovers over my hastily drawn black columns with enthusiasm once again. But now I don't know what figures to scribble in for the profit projection. How much would I charge for my bakes? And just how many could I sell?

What if the out-of-town guests don't like my food? They might be used to bigger and better things if they are from big cities.

I take a separate piece of paper and jot down all of the

things I have ever baked and how much Dad seemed to like them, giving each item a score out of ten. I'm just trying to remember the reception I got for a batch of chocolate almond bars when a sudden noise makes me gasp out loud and drop my marker pen. An erratic black squiggle appears, ruining my list.

5

The loud buzzing continues, unrelenting. Like an angry bee with all the stamina and determination of the entire hive.

I'm on my feet before I know it. My heart hammers in my throat. I wonder what to do as the sound continues to pierce the air. It's like nothing I've ever heard before. It vibrates through the thin glass and rickety old wood of my mullioned window.

This house is always silent when Dad isn't here. There is normally nothing to be heard but the ticking of the clocks, the creaking of the floorboards or the groaning of the old pipes. When I was little and scared I used to fear these noises were the work of ghosts.

This new sound is certainly not spectral, however. This exists in the real world and Dad isn't here to tell me what it is. Right now, I wish more than ever that I wasn't alone.

I creep down the varnished stairs into the hall, half-expecting to see a giant monster of some sort gnawing through the front door; squares of glass dropping out everywhere as its teeth ripped away at all the flimsy old wood.

There isn't one though, of course. Nothing seems amiss at all, which isn't the relief it should be. The same goes for the lounge and then the kitchen.

The sound seems louder at the back of the house, not as much as in my room though.

The droning continues as I grip the banister and launch myself back upstairs. The sound is urgent. It needs tending to. Somehow I know there is a climax coming, even though I have no idea what.

I suppose it is like the telephones I have seen in TV shows. A ringing phone needs to be answered with some urgency.

We have never had a phone here so I can't imagine what it might be like to need to answer a call. The noise now is giving me a taste though and I'm not sure I like it.

Everything is usually so calm and still.

I thought I hated that, but now I would give anything to make the house quiet again. It's what I'm so used to. My whole world has been quiet and still as far as I can remember, apart from that terrible day before we got here.

'What's going on?!' I call out to no one, upset to hear how small my voice sounds.

I place my palms on my writing desk and stare out the window to the overgrown garden I've begged Dad to let me tend to so many times over the years.

Weedy grass at least half my height becomes hedges and brambles. At the very end of that is a cluster of very old and tall trees. One of which is a horse chestnut, currently heavy with fruit.

Even from this distance, I can see small slits where the

shiny conkers peek out. I gave these trees names when I was little. The old horse chestnut is Old Mighty.

Beside him is his female friend with long trailing branches, whom I imaginatively named Willow. Apparently, my five-year-old self thought this amazing creativity. Then there are Bill and Ben, the tall conifers.

These trees form the barrier to my world. They block out the real one. They always have done. So when I see Old Mighty sway oddly as though dancing, I gasp in shock. It is as though the walking, talking trees from *The Lord of The Rings* have stepped out of the pages and into my back garden.

But eyes don't spring open in the crusty bark now. There is a sudden shout and the whole thing disappears from view.

6

It takes me a few moments to realise that I am standing wide-eyed with my hands pressed over my mouth. I'm staring at the scene out the window in horror. To say my world has come crashing down might sound a bit dramatic, but that is almost literally what has just happened. Old Mighty has always been there.

Now he is gone.

The terrible buzzing noise has stopped too. Something has attacked and killed Old Mighty. What could have enough power to do such a thing?

No sooner have I wondered this, then the noise starts up again. I catch Willow's sage green leaves shudder and I just know what will happen to her next.

'No!' I whisper out loud. I have to stop this.

I rush downstairs not knowing what on earth to do. I run into the living room and do nothing but wring my hands. My anxiety is the worst ever. I can hardly breathe. I check the window but it is locked up tight.

Dad has been extra careful to lock them all before he

leaves ever since his recent mistake. I think part of him knows it was his error that day. So I haven't a hope of getting out that way now.

In the kitchen, I scan around for ways out. It occurred to me years ago that if a fire was to break out when my father was away, I would have no way of getting out. This scared me. When I voiced this concern to Dad he told me simply, 'Don't allow a fire to break out.'

It's good advice, I suppose. I've always been extra careful when cooking. Dinner is always underway by the time Dad arrives home, but I never cook lunch for myself when alone, always opting for something cold. Even if that means eating new potatoes straight from the tin.

Quietly, I've thought in a total emergency, I could perhaps smash a window to escape. Dad never suggested this, but as a last resort, I might have to try it.

Is this that sort of emergency?

In the hall, my gaze falls on the door to the cellar.

I've never been down in the cellar before. It's a dark, mysterious void in my mind. Dad has always told me never to go inside. I've never had the urge to either, especially when I was little. I've heard noises coming from down there. Scratching and rattling. On the rare occasions that my father has been down there, the place has always seemed cold and dark. It smelled funny, I remember. When I was little I used to imagine there might be a monster living down there. Something with sparse hair and bulging eyes, like Gollum.

I'm not eight any longer though. What if there is a door down there? Dad might not have thought to lock it. He knows I would never go into the cellar. Not after all the times in the past I admitted I was afraid of what could be down there. He always used to laugh and pat me on the back, but never deny my fears. What if there is another reason he wanted to keep me from that room? I have the feeling I'm right.

Besides, today is different. I need to get outside in an emergency.

It occurs to me that Dad might have locked this door, but he hasn't. It creaks open without any resistance.

I stare at the darkness. Nothing immediately jumps out at me. That's a relief.

I feel weak and frightened still though. I slide out a long walking stick from the umbrella stand beside me. I've never understood why Dad has one; he never uses it.

It's thick and heavy in my hands, making a good makeshift weapon against the uncertainty of the darkness I now step into.

I descend the concrete steps. It's so different from the rest of the house down here. The walls are rough and unfinished. There isn't any wallpaper or decorative colour, however old and faded. There is just bare, crumbling stone.

I'm hit with the overwhelming smell of must and damp. I wonder if this is the source that permeates through the rest of the house. I glance back up at the door at the top of the stairs with wide eyes, as though it might swing shut and trap me down here.

The walking stick slips in my grip.

There isn't a door down here. The staircase is the only means of escape. There is a small window, however. Lucky really. It's the only source of light, allowing me to see my way around. I can immediately tell there aren't any monsters. Just some old junk.

A sudden scratching noise makes me jump. I stare down

at some old boxes in the corner. I swear I see the cardboard edge move as I turn to look.

I swallow. The nearest box is only small, containing golf balls and what look like medals. I've never seen them before. There can't be much of a monster hiding inside. Maybe it's a mouse or a rat?

Some girls are afraid of such things, but I find small rodents cute. Maybe I could capture one to keep as a pet? I can't admit to Dad I've been down here though.

There are more boxes of random objects I've never known Dad to use; old lamps, a photo album, broken furniture and a box of little animal ornaments. I'd love to explore this further, but that is not why I'm down here. Besides, Dad doesn't like curiosity.

I move over to the old cellar window. It's bigger close up. There isn't a lock as with the other windows in the cottage. This one is older, I can tell.

I reach out and lift the catch. To my surprise, the stiff window swings open with a push. Cool fresh air washes over my face.

It would be a tight fit, but it occurs to me I could squeeze through this opening.

My heart hammers in my chest harder now, and not just with fright. I'm one hundred per cent certain what I'm planning to do goes against all of Dad's rules. His voice sounds in my head sometimes, even when he isn't here. It's loud now. Something at the edge of my thoughts tells me I'm doing the right thing though.

The window opens further with a good nudge from me. Bits of paint and dust drop from the frame. I stare through the misty glass at the rough brickwork outside. Atop that is the long grass of our garden. I'm confident I could pull myself up once I'm outside.

Outside. The thought is unimaginable without Dad.

A sharp splinter slides into the pad of my index finger, but I ignore it. I'm too troubled by the size of the window in front of me. It's tantalisingly big enough to tempt me.

Can I fit through it? I'm just wondering what would happen if I were to get stuck halfway through. Or less. What if I only managed to get my shoulders through? My head would barely clear the fabric of the house and I would be stuck in the dark in one of the filthiest parts of the building with all the spiders until Dad comes home hours later. It's not even 10 a.m. yet. What if I couldn't breathe?

I put my face close to the glass and peer upwards. Willow is still shaking violently as the noise drones on. I can't just hide in here and do nothing.

The noise outside reaches a new pitch, urging me on.

I pull an old wooden stool over to the window and stand on it.

Sticky web catches on my face and I gasp and cough on years of powdery dust as I squeeze through the window. I make good progress at first.

Then I reach a point where I can't push through anymore. Panic erupts in my stomach and I realise my chest is constricted. I can't take a full breath in. My arms are pinned at my sides and I can't move.

Somewhere back inside the house, my socks slip uselessly on the old stool as it rocks beneath my feet. Why hadn't I thought to put my trainers on first? They would have given me better grip. Then I knock the stool over completely. Being stuck in the window wedges me in position.

This was a stupid idea. What will Dad say when he

catches me trying to leave the house like this? I'm breaking the number one rule: Stay inside.

What if today is the day he doesn't come home? I could slowly dehydrate or starve to death here in this claustrophobic position.

The only way is forward.

My legs flail around unseen in the cellar behind me.

After a few minutes of panic, I reach out in front of me and grab a tuft of overgrown grass. It seems to tolerate my weight as I grip it. My heart flutters with hope as my shoulders slide forward once again. Moist grass brushes my face and I pull myself up and out. I pull myself up onto the grass and scramble to my feet, grateful to be able to expand my lungs freely again.

My eyes water and I screw them up against the sudden influx of light. It is so much brighter than inside the house.

I take a few deep breaths and feel quite dizzy. Maybe it's because I'm not used to fresh air. Or perhaps because that buzzing noise is ten times louder out here. My eardrums throb.

Or maybe it is because I am going against what my father has always told me. Well, not against it exactly, just around. But when he tells me his rules, he doesn't plan for emergencies. He always told me never to let a bad situation arise. But he isn't here now. He didn't expect this strange noise to pierce the house and start stealing the barrier to our world.

I take some tentative steps forward, my socks soaking through instantly in the long grass. Why didn't it occur to me to put shoes on? Did it rain recently? Or is grass always a little bit wet? I don't have enough experience of it to know for sure.

The noise of the mystery tree killer reverberates through

my chest. Everything about it says stay away, but I can't help but hurry forward in the long unkempt grass flattened with neglect. The muscles in my thighs burn with the exertion of striding high. I stumble a few times when my toe hooks beneath unseen brambles too.

I haven't been in the garden in the daylight for years. I only get to come out here in the darkness of Christmas Eve to see the stars. The outdoor space is smaller than I remembered. Or is that just because it is so much more overgrown now? I'm bigger too.

I glance over my shoulder, as though expecting Dad to be standing behind me, ready to dish out a punishment for breaking rules.

You don't understand, I would say to him. *I had to go outside. Something was killing all the trees. I had to see what it was. I had to stop it.*

He isn't here, of course. He won't be back for hours. I can count on one hand the number of times he has come home early from work over the years when something unexpected happens.

But, Chloe, that's the thing about the outside world. The unexpected happens all the time.

I glance back at the windows in fear. They are all clear. Dad's spectacled face doesn't peer back at me from any of them.

Instead, something else happens that frightens me more. The noise comes to an abrupt end. A man's voice shouts again like when Old Mighty fell. Then Willow topples over in slow motion and joins him somewhere out of sight.

I take my hand down from my mouth again and rush forward.

Brambles tear at the leg of my jeans after a few steps,

stopping me from moving any closer. The slight incline in the ground allows me to see over the thorny branches though. I'm just in time to see the back of a man in bright orange trousers and a matching helmet walking away.

He has a dangerous-looking blade machine in his gloved hands which he places inside his white van. A pair of figures emerge from somewhere and hover near him. It seems like they are talking, but from this distance, I can vaguely hear the edges of their voices.

I watch them for a little while, wondering what they are discussing.

Are they asking the man to destroy more trees? I hope the fragrant conifers aren't next. Even as I stand here, their delicate scent fills my senses.

I shift my position and gasp out loud when I suddenly see past the leaves blocking my view. Where there was always a crumbling old cottage similar to ours, there is now a taller, smart-looking building. It reminds me of the smooth tarmac down the country lane yesterday.

Willow must have gotten bigger and broader over the years, as I used to catch a glimpse of the little abandoned house now and then when I was small. I used to want to go over and explore the place, but Dad would never let me, of course. I didn't see the harm, as there hasn't been anyone living there for years.

I guess that has changed more recently though, without me even realising. Or did I? Perhaps the sound of distant traffic and construction that transformed the building next door was closer to home than I realised. These new people certainly have made their mark on the place.

Willow's thwarted form trails over Old Mighty's

branches. I realise several horse chestnuts are strewn atop the grass around me.

Guilt snatches at my insides. I wasn't quick enough to help them. Is this it for my only friends? Can trees heal and grow once again if they were to be somehow put upright?

'Hi.'

I gasp as I spot the owner of the sudden voice. From the edge of my vision, a boy emerges. He is roughly my height and looks back at me from the other side of the brambles.

'Sorry. I didn't mean to scare you.'

He steps thoughtlessly onto Willow's fallen trunk and closer to me, wobbling in his trainers as he balances.

My mouth drops open in outrage. I want to tell him off for being so disrespectful. Willow is a living thing. How dare he?

He looks surprised at my silence. 'Do you speak English?'

'I – yes.' I tuck a strand of hair behind my ear, flustered. I'm not allowed to talk to strangers. Or anyone. Another of Dad's rules.

Now I'm really in trouble. Two golden rules have been broken and it's not even lunchtime.

'Cool.' He nods. 'How old are you?'

'Fifteen.'

The answer slips easily from my tongue. I have the feeling of sinking further and further under a blanket of trouble. What will Dad say when he finds out about this? I want to turn and run back into the house, but my legs don't seem to be responding to my command. They remain rooted in the long grass instead.

He nods again. 'I'm sixteen. I had my birthday last month.'

I don't know why, but I can't help but answer back, 'Mine is in January.'

'Cool.' He flicks chocolate-brown hair from his eyes with a toss of his head. 'Where are you going for it?'

'What do you mean?'

'Where are you going out for your birthday? Do you have any plans yet? My parents booked a Turkish villa for my sixteenth. They invited all my cousins I haven't seen for years like I'm still six years old or something. It was really embarrassing. I only see them on special occasions. It's not like I really know them.'

He scoffs. 'Mum really likes to show off in front of my aunt. Every time there is an event, they always try and outdo each other. Christmas is the worst. It just makes me want the ground to open and swallow me up. You know what I mean?'

'Um, yeah.'

'Are your parents like that? Or are they chilled?'

'I don't know. It's just me and my Dad.'

'Oh. Are your parents divorced?'

'No.'

'Oh. Did something happen to your Mum?'

Heat bursts through the skin above my cheekbones when I think of what happened to my mother. I try to word an answer. Dad's voice runs through my head again. *The unexpected happens outside all the time, Chloe. You have to think quickly. Stay inside. You are safe in the house.*

I take half a step back towards the house.

The boy looks at my watery eyes and apologises quickly. 'Sorry. I didn't mean to be nosy. I shouldn't have opened my stupid mouth.'

He makes a gesture as though he is pulling a zip across his lips. 'So how about your Dad? Is he laid back?'

'Not really.' I swallow. 'He is pretty strict.'

'That's too bad. My folks let me do mostly what I want. Apart from leaving me alone back in Milton Keynes, apparently. That's why I'm here. They don't trust me not to have a massive house party or something the second they leave for a couple of weeks.'

He nods his head behind him to the impressive new house. 'They had this house built in the middle of nowhere so they can have somewhere to escape when city life gets too much for them. Dad wants to rent it out as an Airbnb the rest of the time when we aren't here. But Mum is stressing over it, worried people are going to trash the place. She has read too many stories online about Airbnbers doing drugs or turning the place into a brothel or something.'

My brain tries and fails to process what the boy has said. He has come out with a load of words I can't understand. My only response is to shrug, which he finds funny.

'Sorry, I'm going on a bit.' He looks past me to mine and Dad's house and nods at it. 'I guess you aren't here on an online stay, then?'

I blink again, wondering why he keeps mentioning some kind of line. He speaks like it is an ordinary thing and I instinctively know to question it would make me sound stupid. It must just be something an outsider finds normal. 'I live here.'

He nods. 'Yeah, it looks like it.'

'What do you mean?'

I glance back towards the house and get a shock. It's been years since I've been out here.

The old cottage looks so much different than I remembered. I see the front of the property on monthly walks, of course.

The back face of the building seems so much more uncared for. It wasn't given the magnolia coat of paint the front received a few years ago, for one thing. Old grey stone stands crumbling and neglected instead.

Dark stains and cracks jump out at me from all over. The place looks a mess, so much further away than the nice homes I see in the movies I am allowed to watch. Dad and I must be poorer than I realised.

My face flushes with heat again as I turn back to the boy.

'Sorry,' he says quickly, looking embarrassed. 'I didn't mean it like that. I just meant, if you rented that on Airbnb, you should ask for a refund.'

He pulls a mortified face and shakes his head. 'That didn't sound much better, did it? Now I totally feel like my parents' son. Right fucking snobs they are. I'm not like that, I promise.'

I blink again. Why does this boy know so many different words than me? We are both speaking English, after all. Maybe it would have been better if when he'd asked me if I could understand him, I had told him no, or just walked away.

Now I'm more confused than ever.

The boy shrugs at the silence that has fallen between us. 'What's your name anyway?'

'Chloe.'

'That's a pretty name.' He smiles awkwardly. Now I see colour creeping up his square jaw. 'I'm Matt. Boring name, I know.'

'No, it's nice.'

'Thanks.'

A shout pierces the air and Matt looks over his shoulder.

His father makes a definite "head this way" gesture from the front of the house.

Matt groans. 'I guess I'd better go back. Dad said he wanted to take us out to the local pub for lunch. It looked pretty ancient when we drove past. Is it any good in there?'

'I've never been in there.'

Matt pulls a face. 'That bad, eh? Mum thinks the place is a tourist trap with microwaved ready meals coming out of the kitchen. Maybe she is right.'

'I don't know.'

I wish I had something better to say. I know I'm coming across as boring and for some reason that bothers me at this moment.

Matt pulls something out of his pocket tentatively and looks up at me. 'Listen, you're really cool to talk to. You're probably the only person around here my age too. Can I add you on WhatsApp or something?'

He presses the side of the flat thing in his hand expectantly. The black surface suddenly is illuminated white and green.

I open my mouth in surprise again.

Matt takes my lack of answer to mean something though. 'Sorry. I guess that was too forward. No worries. I probably wouldn't give my number out to some random guy either. Especially if they are a lanky weirdo like me. Haha. Forget about it. I'd better go. See you around, I guess.'

With that, Matt jumps off Willow's trunk and strolls off towards the newly built house. I watch him until he has slipped behind one of the tall mirrored panels on the ground floor that reflects the trees and grass around it.

The orange-clad man has gone now too. So has his van.

It's just me outside alone. It's blatantly obvious I'm breaking the number one rule. In broad daylight too. I need to get back inside before I'm caught.

7

I spear a boiled potato on the end of my fork and bite into it without paying much attention. Tonight, I've paired the bland root vegetable with slices of fried corned beef and tinned carrots.

We must be going through a hard time financially again. I don't dare say anything though. Besides, my mind has been elsewhere since I've spoken to Matt.

Mainly, my thoughts have been drifting to the end of the overgrown garden where I spoke to him and reliving the encounter over and over again. Dad says I've been quiet since he got home. He asks me what is wrong, but I tell him everything is fine. This gets me a raised eyebrow, but I ignore it and smile inwardly.

I keep thinking about how Matt said I was cool to talk to. That didn't need any translation. It makes me feel warm inside. Of course, that was before I made some kind of mistake with etiquette when Matt pulled some device from his pocket at the end of our chat.

Still, that doesn't stop me from daydreaming about when I

might see Matt again. What if I could slip out of the house and strike up another conversation with him? Is that possible? Or wouldn't he venture close to the property border again?

It's only when there is a clatter of cutlery that I am brought back to the here and now. My return to consciousness is just in time to see Dad's arm reaching out for my face.

He runs his finger along my cheek and brings it up to his glasses to examine it. 'What's this?'

'Huh?'

My father tilts my face towards the yellow glow of the ceiling light. 'What are you covered in?'

He blinks. 'You have black smears all down the side of your face. You look like you have been up the chimney.'

He twists in his chair, palms on the table, and looks towards the fireplace. There is an old gas fire that must have broken down before we arrived in this house. It still appears fully secured in place at the base of the chimney breast as it always is. This seems to satisfy Dad, but he turns to look at me suspiciously.

'What have you been doing today?'

I rub my face with my sleeve hurriedly. After I slid myself back in through the window in the cellar, I made sure I shut the stiff door securely, just as Dad had left it. I made sure the hallway floor was clean and free from mud. I knew it was vital I eliminated all evidence of my being outside.

I ruffled up the long grass behind me to cover my tracks as I went, and washed and dried my socks and outfit before Dad got back. I obviously overlooked cleaning my face. Upon reflection, that should have been my priority. I just hadn't had the chance to look in the mirror before dinner. Not that I thought to check. 'Just cleaning.'

'*Just* cleaning?'

'Yes. I was trying to keep myself busy. You know I've finished my schoolwork and didn't have much else to do.'

'Mmm. You're right. I should have made sure you were kept occupied. It stops your mind wandering to things it shouldn't, I suppose.'

Dad looks again at the fireplace before returning his fork to his crispy corned beef. 'What else did you do today, Chloe?'

Well, Dad, I made a friend for the first time in forever. His name is Matt and my brain is still buzzing with a load of new words I can't understand. Can you explain them to me?

Of course, I don't dare tell my father I managed to escape the house and spoke to a stranger.

I realise my features must be pulled into an uncharacteristically light expression so I shrug. 'Nothing much. I just did some calculations. I was thinking of business ideas I could run from home.'

'Oh? A business that doesn't demand leaving the house at all?' Dad stuffs a whole potato into his mouth. 'Did you come up with anything good?'

His interest in my idea surprises me. I expected my ingenuity to be sneered at or dismissed. My heart does a little leap. The excitement I felt before that noise started this morning returns. It is hard to believe it is still the same day I sat at my desk and dreamed up ways to earn money. It feels like a lot has happened since then.

'Actually, there are a few things I thought I could do.' I tread carefully here. Maybe I can ease my dad into the idea of my leaving the house to cook for Mrs Turner?

'You love my baking. I thought maybe I could bake cakes

and biscuits and things and the local guesthouses could sell them to their guests.'

Dad nods.

'I wouldn't have to leave the house for that,' I add quickly. 'You could take a box over there on your way to work. Or someone else could pick it up and distribute the products. There are lots of ways the business could work.'

'Ah. That would mean more work for me, going back and forth all the time.'

'Not necessarily. We could get a courier. Or, maybe I could do it.'

Dad looks at me sharply. 'You would be seen!'

I sit up earnestly in my seat. 'No, I wouldn't! I would take our usual route over to the B&B. We hardly ever see anyone along that way. I would only see Old Mrs Turner, and she knows me.'

'No, she doesn't.'

'She always says hello if she sees us.'

'Oh, Chloe. That's not *knowing* someone. She is just being polite. Mrs Turner says hello to everyone. I don't think she recognises you.'

'She doesn't?'

'No. She sees so many guests and tourists coming and going. She can't remember everyone she comes across.'

'Well, so what if she doesn't know me? I can make friends with her. I would only see her briefly whilst I am dropping my products off.'

'Why would old Mrs Turner agree to such a deal? What would be in it for her?'

'She would get a cut of the profits, without having to go to any extra effort herself. I would be doing the hard bit by baking the goods.'

'Then it sounds like a lousy deal for you, sweetheart.'

'It isn't. I've worked out how much I can make. If I sell fifty cakes a week I can make fifteen pounds.'

To my surprise and dismay, a laugh bursts from Dad's lips. It's not forced. He seems genuinely unable to contain his amusement, which causes anger to stab at me.

'Oh dear, Chloe. For a moment, I thought you were onto something when you said you had been brainstorming business ideas.'

Heat rises in my face. 'That's only if I charge one-fifty per item. I didn't know how much that sort of thing would cost to buy or to make. I could maybe make two or three times that much. Or sell more of each item.'

I swallow down the foolish feeling in my throat. 'I don't know how much the ingredients cost. I have no idea how it could work out because I'm not allowed outside!'

Dad doesn't detect the rise in my tone. He is still chortling to himself over my stupidity as he cuts a stack of sliced carrots in half in the fiddly way he always does. I've never found his habits more annoying than I do right now.

'Probably just stick to what you know.' Dad speaks around his food, making the irritating mouth noises I'm so accustomed to hearing every time I'm not eating alone. 'So-called *businesses* where you have to scramble around and do all the work for others don't earn enough to be worth your time. I've seen it before. You are best off safe in here, not selling ungrateful tourists novelty snacks for pennies.'

Tears well in my eyes. I blink them away angrily. 'Don't be such a fucking snob!'

This time, my father's cutlery makes an even louder clatter on his plate. It makes me jump.

'What did you just say?'

'What?'

'Chloe, where did you hear that word?'

My mouth runs dry. I've completely forgotten about my dinner and I'm surprised to see a fork still in my hand. 'What word?'

'You know exactly which one I mean! Where would you have heard something like that?'

'I – I don't know.' I realise I've accidentally repeated what Matt said earlier about his parents. 'Did I say something wrong?'

'The f-word is swearing, Chloe. I can't understand where you would have heard such a thing. Tell me where you learned it.'

Did Matt use a bad word? I've heard of swear words but never known any. Matt had let the word slip so casually from his mouth, and about his parents too. Why would he use bad language in such a friendly conversation? Maybe it wasn't as genial as I thought. Could Matt be a bad person?

'I heard the man say it,' I say, thinking fast. I just hope Dad buys it.

'What man?' Dad asks sharply.

'The man that we saw arrested at Mrs Turner's guest house. He said it to the police officer as he was taken away.'

Dad looks away and stares at the faded floral wallpaper ahead of him. He is watching the incident we witnessed yesterday on the reels of his mind. I just hope his recollection is more fuzzy and confused than mine was. Could he have been so focused on getting us out of there that he could believe my lie now?

'I don't remember him saying anything.' Dad's voice is low as he looks back to scrutinise my face.

'He did.' I nod imploringly. 'He was muttering in a low

voice though. I don't think the policeman noticed either. He ignored him. The guy being arrested wasn't making much sense.'

Dad watches me for a moment with a look of concentration on his face. 'No, I suppose he wouldn't. I'm sorry you had to witness that. What a shame we chose that moment to walk past. We couldn't have timed it worse.'

'I know. I'm sorry too. And I'm very sorry for using the f-word. I didn't realise it was bad. He... I heard him say it so casually. It didn't sound like it meant anything bad. He said something about his parents, so I didn't think it could be anything wrong.'

My father takes a sip of water from his glass. 'Mmm.'

Silence falls as we start eating again.

'Dad, why would anyone use a bad word about their parents? I don't understand.'

Dad's eyebrows move in surprise, but he doesn't glance up from his food. 'The world is full of bad people. Immorality will be tied to a lack of respect for parents. Just look at the man being arrested. He was a common thief. It doesn't surprise me one bit that he would swear when talking about the people he should respect most in the world. He must have been tainted through and through. We have to be extra careful to stay away from people like that.'

My dad looks across the table at me. 'You don't have to worry about a thing, Chloe. You are safe in here. People like that can't get to you from outside these four walls. I have made sure of it. I'll always be here to protect you.'

8

It is daylight the next day before Dad notices something is amiss. He is filling the kettle for his morning coffee when I hear a strangled yell.

'Chloe!' he shouts from the kitchen.

My senses immediately are on high alert. He must have noticed the cellar door has moved, I think. I cleaned too well, or not well enough. He has noticed something is off in the hallway.

I rush down into the kitchen to find Dad staring out the window at the back garden, kettle still in hand.

I follow his gaze to the end of the overgrown grass. It's immediately obvious how much more light there is in the kitchen. The heat of the morning sun is pleasant on my face.

Dad has clocked it almost straight away. It was darkening when he arrived home from work last night and I don't recall him venturing into the kitchen at all. It was left to me to cook and serve dinner as usual as he sat at the dining table in the living room.

Now my father is seeing the scene outside for the first

time. He looks as shocked as I must have been when it was happening yesterday.

'The trees are gone,' he mutters. 'When on earth did that happen?'

'Oh, that.' I shrug in what I hope is a casual way. 'The horse chestnut and willow tree were cut down yesterday.'

'Yesterday?' Dad shoots me a sudden look. 'You didn't say anything. Why not?'

'I don't know. I was busy thinking of ways to earn money. Besides, I couldn't do anything about it from in here and I didn't want to upset you after you had been at work all day.'

I shrug again. This must be the default move of liars, I think. I make a mental note, if ever I speak to another human being that isn't Dad again, to look out for this vital sign. Didn't Matt shrug a few times yesterday? Was he lying to me during our conversation?

Dad slams down the kettle, causing water to slosh over to the worktop. It dribbles down the cupboards and onto the floor. 'They've ruined our privacy!'

'Who?' I ask with as innocent a look of surprise as I can muster.

'Those ruddy outsiders! They have torn down that character building for their modern monstrosity and now they do this. How dare they encroach onto the border of our property? What makes them think they have the right?'

'What monstrosity do you mean?' I ask, keeping up the pretence that I was inside behaving myself as always yesterday.

'I didn't tell you, did I? Some grubby property developers have built a modern house where that old cottage was next door. A townhouse they call it. They've ruined the area. And now they have done this.'

He gestures stiffly to the scene out the window.

I fold my arms nervously. I've never seen Dad this angry before. 'Weren't the trees on their side?'

'Whose *side* are you on?' he snaps angrily, blinking at my apparent audacity.

I open my mouth, but Dad gets there first.

'I'll tell you which side you are on. This side – with me! I won't stand for this.'

Dad knocks into me on the way out of the kitchen. I lose my balance and end up putting my sock into the cold wet puddle on the floor.

I am about to follow my father out into the hallway, but he is already storming back with his shoes on. He pulls out a key and slides it into the back door lock.

This door is so rarely opened that my father takes hold of the little handle in both hands to give it a firm tug, fighting against the warped wood.

The kitchen is flooded with fresh air as well as sunlight. I feel like I'm in a dream, blinking in the warm golden rays uninhibited by glass. I look down at my hands, seeing all the details I normally wouldn't; faint moles and the colour of my veins.

I move to the back door and drink in the fresh air as my father struts angrily through the grass. Despite his large frame and height, he looks small now. As though he is the one now trudging through the jungle from one of my storybooks.

He stands with his hands stiffly on his hips as he stares through the newly created gap. I know what he is seeing; the modern build I spotted yesterday. I wonder if anyone is up at this hour and enjoying the sunlight in their garden too. Can Matt spot my father from where he is now?

Dad turns on the spot and stares back to face the house, glancing over his shoulder a few times, as though trying to decide how much our new neighbours would be able to see from their perspective.

Apparently, too much. Dad shakes his head and storms back to the house. He shoos me back from the doorframe and throws his weight against the stiff back door, turning the key in the lock with a loud click again. He shoves his weight down on the handle to test if it is locked.

'This area is changing,' he mutters again to himself as he thuds upstairs.

I call after him. 'Aren't you going to work? What are you going to do?'

He ignores my questions, as he often does. Ten minutes later, he emerges from the loft. A bundle of old cardboard and some wooden panels are tucked under his arm as he marches towards my bedroom.

I screw my nose up as a particularly bad waft of damp stings my nostrils. 'What are you doing with that lot?'

'Take back our privacy.'

Dad busies himself taping scraps of flattened cardboard to my bedroom window. Any light I thought we had gained yesterday is now blocked out with old food boxes. He runs out partway across and hammers nails into a strip of wooden board. The wood is like a wooden cake, I think. Lots of pieces all mixed up and set hard. Like one of the collages I used to make sometimes when I was younger, glueing overlapping pictures.

'This is crazy.'

'Don't name-call, Chloe.'

'I'm not.'

'Don't answer back.'

'I wasn't.'

'You are doing it again.'

I sigh and fold my arms. 'This is over the top. It would be fine just to leave it for a day or two until we can sort something else out. It looks so dingy in here now.'

'It's better that it is slightly darker than have strangers gawping in here.'

'But they are so far away. I don't think they can see anything from their house anyway. Their house has some kind of mirroring on the windows. It might inhibit their view.'

'And therefore, inhibit their light too. So you won't mind if it is a little dark in here. It's just the same as being over there. Nothing to worry about.'

I'm losing sight of Dad in the darkness as he nails the final piece of board.

'Dad, I don't want–'

'There are a lot of things I don't want! They happen, however, regardless!'

I blink in the dim light. 'It's so dark though.'

'Don't argue with me!'

I watch him work with disappointment. I had been planning on sitting at my desk for most of the day with an uninterrupted view of the adjoining garden, hoping for a glimpse of Matt.

Then I'd maybe happen to slip out into the garden at the same time and accidentally start talking to him again. My stomach had been twisting knots all last night when I had thought about it. Instead, I'm left reading the same words over and over again on an old Walkers crisps box.

Thankfully, the bathroom window has frosted glass and Dad doesn't deem it necessary to board it up too, so it provides a little daylight. He applies the same treatment to the kitchen window downstairs, however.

'It's just temporary,' he tells me. 'Until those newcomers can provide a more satisfactory solution. I wonder how long it would take them to realise they have besmirched established trees that would have shielded us from their prying eyes?'

Dad sets off for work in a slightly better mood than earlier, leaving me in a gloomier-than-ever house. It's so much darker now that the morning sun can't get through at all. I keep out of my bedroom, the darkest room in the house.

Dad's room doesn't seem to have had the board treatment. His curtains are pulled over aggressively, I see when I push his door open a crack.

I don't dare step inside though, not when Dad is having such an episode of suspicious thoughts. Certainly not when I have a guilty conscience about breaking a rule yesterday. I can't take the risk of disturbing anything. Dad would notice. He is good at spotting things like that, especially in the space that is exclusively his.

I spend the morning in the living room with a book, feeling defeated. At least it's brighter in here. This room is front-facing and hidden behind a hedge at the dead-end of a country lane no one ever ventures down.

My annoyance with Dad only grows throughout the morning. He didn't have to board the windows up. That's a step too far, even for him.

I wonder if Matt's parents would have done the same if the situation was reversed. I've never met the people, but somehow I just can't imagine they would react in the same way. Does that mean my father isn't normal?

Fury bubbles inside me as I consider how Dad has ruined my secret plan for today. It makes me think of what he said to me over dinner last night too when he had laughed at my business plan. He didn't have to be so rude.

I so desperately want to speak to Matt again. I liked talking to someone. It staggers me how I managed the interaction without making too many mistakes. After all these years with only Dad to talk to, I feel proud of myself for conversing with another human being.

Especially Matt. He keeps sneaking into my thoughts, even when they are elsewhere. He makes me feel warm inside.

Maybe Dad is too critical? I feel like Matt is nice, despite the fact he used swear words. Maybe he is like me. He doesn't understand what they really meant. I know I have to see him again, if only for a few minutes.

At lunchtime, I take my time spreading cream cheese neatly into the corners of some bread, the same way my father likes it. When you don't have much to fill your time with, you have to pace the day.

Later in the afternoon, I close my book, having re-read the same line over and over without taking it in. I stand up, as though following a plan I've been subconsciously concocting instead of immersing myself in *Anne of Green Gables* for the millionth time.

I've now moved beyond Anne's age. When I'd first read the book series, she had been an older girl to me. Like a friend, or older sister who allowed me to join her adventures. Now she seems a tad childish. As though I'm the elder sibling.

Nevertheless, I leave the book angled on the coffee table next to my glass of water. When Dad comes home, it's a good idea to have clear evidence that I've been kept occupied in a permitted task. I'll have to check myself in the mirror too this time. I can't afford to make a mistake like I did yesterday, leaving dust on my cheeks.

It doesn't seem as dark in the cellar today. I open the window as far as it will go and push myself out. I do it with more grace this time, knowing which way to twist and turn at the right moments.

Cool air touches the gap between my socks and hem of my favourite jeans as I clamber up onto the grass of the garden; I'm getting quite tall for this pair these days.

I've matched the dark blue denim with a black t-shirt, factoring in my slip outside as I'd dressed today. Guilt has been eating at me since last night as I considered this bit of rule-breaking, but I feel Matt might be a good friend. Maybe even something else...

Dad would be furious if he found out what I am doing. I don't like to think of his reaction if I were to get caught. It's almost unimaginable.

9

Today, it seems as though I am truly breaking the golden rule. Yesterday had felt like an emergency as I made my escape. I could justify it. This time, I've squeezed myself outside for fun, I suppose. A weak stab at a social life, simply because I have the urge to do so. I know it's wrong. I glance back down at the window. Maybe I should turn back? I could slip back inside now and Dad would never know.

My palms sweat as I wade through the long grass. There is a rush of something else inside too.

Exhilaration, maybe? Is that what the funny feeling is when I think of Matt?

I've always done what Dad has told me because it has been the right thing to do. Now defying him feels good.

He has been so unreasonable sometimes. Like boarding the windows up this morning. I also can't get the thought of his amused face out of my head as he noisily chewed dinner and laughed at my business ideas. Should he be the one to judge whether I should be confined to the house save for a few hours a month? There is no one else to look out for me. He has exclusive decision-making abilities regarding my life.

I know my father has my best interests at heart, but I know he has his own too. He pretends he does everything to protect me, but he is preserving himself just as much. Maybe even more so.

He was the one who committed the crime in the first place, after all.

I didn't kill anyone.

Therefore I believe it isn't unreasonable that I should be allowed out to the garden once in a while, especially after so many years of behaving myself. I'm sure I can justify this.

The air is cool as it brushes over my face and hands and I regret not thinking to put on a jumper before coming out here. Or would I not look as cool in a jumper in Matt's eyes?

Disappointingly, there is no sign of him as I reach the bramble border at the end of our respective gardens. It was a slim chance, I suppose. He might be off somewhere doing something exciting, eating a meal out or participating in an activity I don't understand.

The thought of him got me out here. Now that I am, I find I don't want to go back indoors, despite the fact I feel so small out here alone. I turn my back to the border of the property and face the house. It's a more grim picture than yesterday. The mismatched wood and cardboard blocking the windows make the place look abandoned.

From here, there is no sign anyone lives inside the building at all. My presence and thoughts have filled the rooms every day for twelve years without anyone other than my father knowing.

A funny feeling catches in my chest when I think of the little girl I used to be. It might be grief. There is no sign that girl existed at all. I must have been so small when Dad brought me here all those years ago. If something were to happen to me at some stage, no one would even know I was ever here.

That was the point, I guess. Dad is right – I certainly am well hidden. Only now that I see our home from an outside perspective, I realise what he means. If only it didn't have to be this way.

Dad was the adult. He made the decision for us to move here and hide. He says we stand out more, the two of us. It's the couple of us together that makes us conspicuous, he tells me. That's why we are allowed out together so rarely. He is far less recognisable going out alone. I'm told he has changed his appearance.

'I wouldn't leave the house at all if I didn't have to, Chloe,' he says often. 'You know that, don't you? I don't like leaving you all alone. It breaks my heart. Every moment spent away from you is unnatural. Our time together is so precious. I wish it could never end sometimes.'

I was too young at the age of four to even know what was going on, simply going along with it, I suppose. It wasn't me who picked up a blunt object that day. I didn't use it to put an end to Mum's life.

'Chloe.'

I spin around, away from the sad sight of the cottage that stole my childhood.

It's Matt on his side of the bramble border. 'Sorry. I didn't mean to scare you again. I keep doing that, don't I?'

I swallow and will my heart to calm. It throws out some discordant beats, warning me of my wrongdoing. I shouldn't be out here. 'That's okay. I thought you were my dad for a second.'

'Oh, great. Thanks for that,' he says sarcastically. Then he grins and I find my face reflecting his instantly. His smile is so warm. It makes his blue eyes shine.

I wonder what he thinks of my brown ones. I don't dare ask him. 'Sorry. I just thought... well, no one else knows my name.'

'What do you mean?'

'I mean, you know, I haven't met anyone else here before.'

'Oh. I thought you were a proper local. I noticed you didn't have the local accent. How long have you lived here?'

'Twelve years.'

Matt's eyebrow shoots up quizzically. 'And you have never met anyone else outside of school?'

I shrug. 'I don't go to school.'

'Wow. There's not even a school here? This place gets better and better. Talk about being in the middle of nowhere. Are you homeschooled then?'

'I was. But I finished my studies recently. Dad hasn't found me any more work to do. I suppose I've graduated early.'

I can't help but throw in this little comment, thinking Matt will be impressed or find it "cool". But he doesn't seem to. His reaction is quite the opposite. His gaze rakes over me, as though he is re-assessing his opinion of who I am. I hope I haven't messed up again.

'So it's just you and your strict Dad?'

'Yeah, it is.'

'I bet that's cosy. I'm bored of being in our holiday house all day. We can't even get 4G with those hills in the way. There's no TV signal either. The engineer hasn't turned up

to install Wi-Fi yet. Dad says we should enjoy the area whilst
we are waiting.'

I'm getting used to the fact that I don't understand everything Matt says. I think I do a good job of acting like I do get
what he means.

I nod. 'I know. We can't get a television signal here either.
If you want to watch anything, you have to get the videos.'

'Is the Wi-Fi speed decent?'

'I don't know. My Dad buys the video tapes. We play
them on our VHS recorder.'

It's Matt's turn to look confused. He blinks. 'Tapes? You
don't mean those old box things with the black plastic reels
in them?'

'Yeah, that's right.'

'For fuck's sake. This village is worse than I thought. It's
like it's stuck in the eighties. Video tapes are so ancient.
When I was little, Mum wanted to get rid of Dad's old collection she found in the loft. He didn't want to let them go, so
she upcycled them. Wove them into baskets.'

Matt laughs at the memory. 'It was a disaster, because
Mum can't do arts and crafts to save her life. So Dad agreed
to chuck the lot in the end.'

Chuck the lot? My face reddens. Dad buys us a tape here
and there as a treat when he has saved up enough money. He
has the entire collection of *Columbo* up in the loft somewhere and brings one out once every three months for us to
watch together. I so look forward to those occasions. It's one
of my favourite things to do.

Yet Matt's family treat the things like old rubbish. Maybe
Dad was right when he said these newcomers are destruc-
tive. They've already pulled down two trees and a cottage
that was in some way a piece of history since they have been

here. They are the reason my bedroom window is boarded up. What will they ruin next?

Matt looks at me tentatively. 'I didn't mean any of that in a nasty way. I mean, if you can't get any signal out here, then I guess you are limited to what you can do. Maybe DVD's and Blu-rays haven't made it over here yet either. I don't know.'

He shrugs. 'Where do you go for fun around here, anyway?'

'You mean outside?'

Matt grins. 'Yeah, outside.'

'There's not really anywhere to go. I mean, Dad takes me for walks sometimes. That's quite good... ' I trail off.

Matt seems to have glazed over at my answer. He shakes his head. 'I was kind of hoping there was a hidden retail park or cinema or something we missed on the way over here. That pub we had lunch at yesterday was a total dive, and not in a good way. I'd even kill for a McDonalds right now. Just something normal, you know?'

I nod, wishing I knew that he was talking about.

Matt shrugs and kicks at something at his feet. 'We should get out of here. Go and explore a bit. What do you think?'

'What do you mean?'

'I don't know. Maybe we could go on one of those hiking trails I've seen people going off on. Casually, I mean. Not with all the goofy gear on and walking for miles. I've seen loads of backpackers wandering off for the hills. Dad wants to take me. But it might be more fun if we went together. You know, the two of us. Just for a laugh.'

Matt trails off now and I notice a flush spreading up his cheeks. 'It doesn't matter if you don't want to. I just thought it would be cool spending time with someone my age.'

'It would be,' I say quickly. 'But I can't. I know the trails you mean. My dad has the routes on some leaflets in the house. I've seen them so many times I think I know them off by heart.'

'Would you be my guide then? Show me the area?'

'Sure, I'd love to.' A sinking falls through me. 'Dad will be back soon though. He gets back from work at six.'

'Aren't you allowed out on your own?'

'Not much. He doesn't like it.' I shrug, trying to seem normal, like my life is a more casual arrangement than it is. Something deep down tells me it's important to do that.

'What about tomorrow then? We could head out earlier if you want. What time does your dad leave for work in the morning?'

'Eight-thirty usually. He was delayed this morning though because he wanted to board the windows up.'

Matt blinks and looks back at the house behind me. He uses the f-word again. 'Why did he do that?'

'Oh, he was annoyed about the trees being cut down. He was worried the gap took away our privacy.'

Matt looks between me and the windows of the house a few times.

'Okay,' he says slowly. 'That's a bit weird, but whatever. My parents didn't realise anyone lived in this house. They were under the impression there was an old guy living here when they bought the house. Since we got here and saw it though, they assumed he might have been moved into a home or something. They were surprised when I said I'd spoken to you yesterday.'

My insides clench uncomfortably. Matt told his parents I

was outside talking to him. What if that gets back to Dad? He was on the verge of storming over there this morning. He might already have done that on the way to work for all I know. What have I done?

'Matt, have you met my father?'

'No, why would I?'

'Just wondering. I hope he didn't go over to your house and complain or anything. He didn't, did he?'

'Don't think so.' He shakes his head and flicks his hair back in a way that makes my stomach do something funny. 'Look, I can talk to Mum and Dad. They can sort something out if your dad is upset. They wouldn't want to piss the neighbours off as soon as they arrive. They usually wait a bit longer in a place before they do that. Haha.'

'No – don't!'

Matt looks at me quizzically.

'I mean, no, thanks. It's all right. Dad might get over it by himself in time. Please don't say anything.'

'Why not?'

'I'm not supposed to speak to strangers.'

'A stranger? Thanks. Never been called that before. I'm not thirty with a dodgy beard.'

'Sorry. I didn't mean to be rude. It's just that Dad wouldn't understand. It's best if he doesn't know we have spoken at all.'

'Oh, I get you. No worries. I won't mention it.' Matt does that zip motion across his lips again and glances back at my house. 'So are we on for tomorrow morning?'

He looks at me hopefully and I don't have the heart to say no. So instead I give him a surprisingly confident, 'Sure. It sounds like fun.'

'Great. I'll knock for you at nine and we'll head off.'

It occurs to me that I won't be able to open the front door to Matt. Dad locks me in every day. The back door is very rarely opened either, certainly not by me. Though I can't explain this to my new friend.

I can't very well let him see me crawl out of the window in the cellar. 'You best meet me at the end of the lane.'

'Oh, sure. Yeah. I'll see you there then. Cool.'

Matt smiles at me and then disappears back into the shiny new house in the distance. I don't think the place is the monstrosity Dad described it as. I think the building is a nice addition to our corner of the world.

10

W hat was I thinking? I'm so stupid. Why did I agree to leave the house with Matt? I'm blatantly breaking the key rules. What if I get caught?

My insides squirm worse than ever as I get dressed for the day. It's way past sunrise, but I'm having to get ready by lamplight. The windows are still boarded up, blocking the warming morning sun.

It's not just nerves making me uncomfortable. It's another thing too. Something about the way I feel when I think of Matt. Together those elements make quite a cocktail that bubbles inside me. It makes it hard to eat the toast I prepare for breakfast. I try and swallow it down with my morning orange juice, hoping it will make up for my lack of saliva.

It wasn't easy to decide what to wear, despite my limited wardrobe. I've gone for a black glitter top; it's the nicest thing I own, even if it seems a little childish. The tag has a younger age on it, but it still fits.

I'm so caught up in my own thoughts that I don't notice Dad hasn't touched his boiled egg. It's only when he sets down his spoon and inhales loudly through his nose that I look up from my own plate to find him watching me closely.

I jump a little at the unexpected action. Dad is upset. 'What's the matter?'

He leaves a dramatic pause before he answers. 'I don't know, Chloe. Why don't you tell me?'

'I don't understand.' My heart suddenly changes rhythm. It doesn't slow or quicken, it just does something funny in my chest so that I feel lightheaded.

Dad knows, I think to myself.

'Tell me why you went outside.'

A sweat breaks out around my temples. How could Dad know? I covered my tracks so well. There is no way he could know what I have done.

I open my mouth to protest. 'I – I haven't.'

'Don't lie to me, Chloe.'

Some part of me marvels at my ability to tell the untruth. 'I'm not lying. I don't know why you would ask me that. I never go outside. I know it's against the rules.'

'Come with me.' Dad slides his chair back from the table. The carpet is so well worn from this action that the floorboards are visible beneath the pile.

I follow him whilst shaking, feeling a little like I'm being led to my doom. Dad is about to point to the door leading to the cellar and watch me for a reaction. I know I will crumble when he does.

Instead, he sails right through the hall and into the dark kitchen. He stands beside the back door and flicks on the light switch to substitute the blocked daylight.

'Well?'

It's now I spot what has got him so worked up. Slotted neatly into the back door is a small silver key. I'm so unused to seeing such a sight that it looks strange.

My mouth drops open. 'You left the key in the lock.'

'Yes. I must have overlooked it when I went out to see how the tree felling impacted our privacy. I'd had a shock. It wasn't my fault. You took advantage of my slip though, didn't you?'

Relief flushes through my system. So much so that I feel like laughing; I work hard to keep a straight face.

Dad doesn't know I went outside at all. He is just fishing; testing me as he often does. He wants me to prove myself yet again. Simply assuming that I wouldn't break a rule is above my father, despite all my years of loyalty.

Although for the first time ever he is actually right, there is no way I will tell him this. 'It's okay, Dad. I didn't go outside.'

'No? Are you sure?'

'Positive. I had no idea you left the key in the door. I didn't notice, I swear.'

'Then how do you explain this?' He moves dramatically over to the window and pulls down the hastily taped card-board. The kitchen is flooded with daylight. It makes my eyes water.

I open my mouth, but my question is answered as my eyes are drawn to the end of the garden. A concertina row of tall sage-green panels has been erected at the end of the bramble border.

Immediately, I know Matt must have said something to his parents about the trees. Or did they simply notice the boarded-up windows of our house themselves?

'What's the problem?'

'It's a bit coincidental, Chloe. I got upset about the inva-
sion of our privacy on the same day that I accidentally left
the keys in the back door. Then all of a sudden, the gap has
been blocked up. Strange, don't you think?'

I hate Dad when he is like this. I've come to think of him
as having two faces. Like one of those creepy old dolls. One
side is happy and the other is something else. He can spin
from one to the other and back again so quickly. Part of me
believes he can't help it. It's like a condition.

The only thing I can do is wait for him to switch back to
the parent I love and trust.

'It's not strange. Maybe those people realised they had
done something wrong when they saw boards go up at our
windows. That might have been a clue.'

'Don't get cheeky with me.'

'I'm not. It has to be a coincidence. I haven't been outside.
I didn't even notice the key was left in the door.'

Dad makes a noise of dissent. 'Likely story.'

'Honestly, I had no idea the key was in the lock.' Otherwise, I would have gone out the door instead of squeezing
myself through the cellar window with all the bugs and dirt.
How silly of me not to notice Dad's mistake. It's probably
better I didn't. It makes it easier to lie now.

'Of course I didn't go outside. Anyway, the door is too
stiff for me to move.'

'Aha! So you did try it then?'

'No. I saw you pull it open yesterday with two hands. You
are so much stronger than me. I wouldn't be able to do that.'

Dad seems to lift his chin at this compliment, his
thoughts running inwards. 'Yes, I suppose I am.'

He flips off the light now that daylight pours again into
the kitchen. It's a relief to have the board down. He pockets

the key and gives the back door handle a firm tug until he is satisfied it is secure. Then he moves systematically around the house, checking the windows are shut and locked.

I glance at the clock and get a fright. It's eight forty-five.

Dad is normally long gone by now. Matt is supposed to meet me at nine. Why did we set the time so early? Why didn't I interject with the suggestion of ten? That would have been much better, allowing more room for error. Will Matt arrive at the meeting place early in anticipation? Or might he not turn up at all?

Will Dad pass him on the way out to work? What if they start talking and my lies are exposed? Dad will never trust me again. My insides writhe with guilt. Should I be lying to my father like this?

The way he tried to catch me out in the kitchen just now on a whim stings me, however. He has done it too many times over the years unsubstantiated. I know I'm doing the right thing. 'Aren't you going to be late for work?'

He peels the corner of card from one half of my bedroom window and checks the lock. 'You're right. I'd best be off.'

'Great. I'll take the boards down whilst you are out.'

'Eh?'

'I'll remove them. What should I use to remove the sections with nails?'

Dad blinks. 'Don't touch them. I'll deal with it later.'

I get a sinking feeling. 'You are going to take the boards down from my window, aren't you, Dad?'

He pulls on his coat and slides himself into his shoes before he answers. 'With all these newcomers around, it's best not to. We need to keep you safe, remember? That's my number one priority. Don't worry any more about it.'

'But it's so dark. I never go outside. You have to let me

have some daylight. The medical textbooks I read emphasise the importance of vitamin D.'

'You can do that in the rest of the house, sweetheart. Look on the bright side, you will get to spend more time in the house with me when I get home, instead of shut away in your room as you do sometimes.'

'But—'

'Don't touch those boards, Chloe.'

The front door shuts in my face and Dad's mosaic figure quickly disappears with the fading sound of gravel.

The way something inside me rages now, I'm delighted to be about to not just break one of Dad's rules. I'm not sure that's the right way of phrasing it, as I'm not just breaking the rule, am I? I'm smashing it to pieces.

11

A fter that stressful breakfast with Dad, I don't exactly feel in tip-top condition to meet Matt. I wanted to arrive more composed. Not that I wanted to arrive late for our secret outing.

Or, rather our date. Might this be an actual date, dare I say?

Matt didn't describe our meeting as anything in particular. So I have no idea. The spirit of rebellion courses through me though as I squeeze through the window in the cellar. I brush myself off before moving to the front of the property.

It is now that doubt hits me. Hesitation forces me to a standstill. Now I'm in uncharted waters. Dad has always been here to lead me from the house and onto land that isn't exclusively ours. He is at work, oblivious to what I am doing.

I feel weak and small as I force myself to walk across the crumbling concrete driveway at the front of the property. I take little steps, as though wading through something thick and viscous. I have an almost overwhelming urge to turn back. This fear comes out of nowhere and hits me like a train. I had it all planned. I know the route. What's the problem?

My conscience is the issue, I think. I hadn't banked on that. This is new territory, leaving our patch of land for somewhere else. I'm misbehaving terribly. I shouldn't be doing this.

I'm shaking as I force myself to step into the public domain. The country track is deserted. There isn't any traffic, no one to witness me.

Good. If there was anyone else around, other than Matt, I would probably turn back.

I need to meet him. I told him I would be at our agreed place. And I want to see him, don't I? I take a breath and push forward.

I've arranged things with Matt already. What if he came looking for me later and ran into Dad on his way home from work? My lies would unravel.

I'm committed now. Besides, I really want to see Matt today. I've been excited about this outing all night.

It feels so good to stretch my muscles once I get going down the lane. I usually only get to do this once a month. How naughty to do this at will, without permission? I feel like laughing. I'm not sure whether it is through happiness or hysterical fear.

Well, if Dad wanted me to do everything he tells me, he shouldn't be so unreasonable, I think to myself.

But it's only sometimes, isn't it? Most of the time he is nice. The problem is, you never know which side of Dad you are dealing with. You never know which side of the doll will be facing in your direction.

These thoughts are pushed completely out of my head

when I venture further down the lane, my ponytail swinging behind me. There is no sign of Matt anywhere.

He's changed his mind, I think. Or he has forgotten. Then again, was Matt clear about where I suggested meeting?

Or maybe this is a trick. A prank. A cruel something or other designed to hurt my feelings. Why would he do such a thing? Maybe I was wrong about him.

Then I round the corner and my stomach does the flip it does every time I have laid eyes on Matt. He is there. His jeans are the opposite of my flared ones, tapering down his leg, making him look extra tall.

'Hiya,' he says as I arrive, giving me a quick glance. 'You look nice,' he mutters.

'Thanks. Um, so do you.'

He grins and shrugs. 'Shall we get going then? Which way is it?'

'The nearest hike starts this way.' I point in the direction of the route Dad and I always follow together. This is the first time I have trodden along this path without him. My insides squirm at my audacity as we start walking. I glance around, as though Dad might suddenly appear to punish me.

Matt glances at me as he walks next to me, hands in his pockets. 'Did you notice the new fence panels my parents put up? At the border of your property?'

'Yes. You didn't tell them we spoke, did you?'

'No. I just pointed out that there were boards put up at the windows after we cut the trees down. So I suggested perhaps the neighbours were upset by that. Don't worry, Chloe. I didn't tell them we talked. I told them I was going to explore by myself this morning. Your dad won't know you are sneaking out with a scoundrel like me.'

He laughs and I smile too. I wonder if he is truly joking or not. Maybe it's like an inside wisecrack, or Matt is trying to tell me something about his personality. Is he a good guy or not? I quash down the thought that he is anything other than good. Matt is nice. That, I'm quite sure of.

I don't have enough experience to make a judgement either way. I wonder what my father would make of Matt? He carries a great deal of experience in the real world. Sometimes he tells me little snippets. I just hope it isn't as bad as he makes it sound. It should be safe here in the village and surrounding hills though. It's nothing like the big cities and towns I see in the videos I'm allowed to watch.

Dad isn't a massive fan of other people, that's for sure. The main person in particular Dad has spoken negatively about is Mum. I'm too young to remember her though.

Other than the odd flash of memory too vague to examine of being cared for, I only remember the day she was killed.

And out of that, the main thing I remember is the blood. So much of it. It stained the white bathtub in our old home. I don't remember the rest of the house much, just that room. There is no way that image will be erased from my memory, no matter what I do.

Dad had stepped in that day and saved me. Mother was having one of her episodes. She flew into violent rages often, Dad told me as I got old enough to understand.

That day I would have been the target of her fury if it wasn't for my father. He stopped her from hurting me at the expense of her life. And ours to almost every extent. I've been locked up in the cottage ever since. Is this life any better than the consequences of being caught?

Dad says he would go to prison if he was captured. I can't

be taken away from him, he says. I would never survive being raised in the immorality of the real world, he tells me.

We have been in hiding for twelve years. If Dad's physical appearance has changed enough to allow him to go to work every day, then mine certainly has. I was a small child when we arrived here, barely out of toddlerdom. I'm not a child anymore. I must look completely different these days. Matt hasn't noticed anything. I'd know by now if he had recognised me.

Right now is the first taste of real freedom I have ever had. I'm certain it must be safe in our rural little corner of the world.

I walk along the country lane with Matt excitedly.

I am Cinderella for the day. Instead of midnight, I have to be back by five thirty to be safe for Dad's return from work. I explain the time constraint to Matt.

He nods. 'That's cool. My mum would probably fret if I hung out until it was dark anyway.'

'Would she? I can't imagine what normal parents are like.'

'Yeah, your father does seem a bit too strict. Hopefully, it's not so bad now he has taken the boards down from the windows. That was a bit over the top if you don't mind me saying so.'

I watch my trainers thumping against the cracked surface of the lane. 'No, it's fine. I know my dad is very protective of me. Sometimes he can be pretty intense.'

Matt glances at me. 'He has taken the boards down, hasn't he?'

I shrug, as though it makes what I say next not so bad. 'Most of them. Just not the one on my bedroom window. He's worried about people seeing me.'

'Why?'

'He's just really protective. It's been just the two of us since Mum died. We're pretty close. He worries about losing me. It's this way.' I point towards the stile as we pass Mrs Turner's guesthouse, glad of a change of subject as Matt looks at me enquiringly again.

A group of hikers sit on the low wall outside, tying their laces and sliding water bottles into their backpacks. One, I notice, has one of those flat objects Matt had in his hand the other day when he asked me for my number. This guy seems so engrossed in staring at the illuminated face that he looks almost comical.

I keep my gaze averted from the group as we pass, remembering what Dad said about avoiding eye contact.

My heart hammers with nerves at being so defiant, at being outside without Dad and being alone with Matt. Together, it's all quite a heady mixture. The thought of it all makes me dizzy. I realise the cottage is my anchor, and when I'm out on my usual walks with Dad, he becomes the centre of my world instead.

I feel the lack of the old building as though part of me is missing. It's my shield against the outside world. I feel so much lighter without it, yet at the same time, it's terrifying.

We walk in silence for a little bit across the straw field before Matt talks again. 'Hey, Chloe. Do you have anyone else to talk to? An aunt or uncle that visits or something?'

'No. Like I said, it's just me and my dad in the house. I don't have any other relatives.'

'I can't imagine only having one person to talk to. And no internet either. That must be tough. I've been without it since we got here and it's been a nightmare. The days seem to last so much longer. I can't check anything or chat with my friends.'

I nod and try and look sympathetic, but then I decide to just bite the bullet. I'm desperate to know what this boy could be missing so much. 'Matt, what's internet?'

He laughs. Then his face falls when he sees my serious expression. 'You're joking, right? You must be pranking me.'

'No, I'm not.'

'I feel like there must be hidden cameras in this village somewhere.'

'I don't think there are.'

'Well, probably not. I was sort of joking.' He watches me in puzzlement for a moment. 'I can't figure you out, Chloe.'

'What do you mean?'

'You can't have been living in that little house with only your dad for company since you were little.'

I shrug. 'Well, I have. I've been kept busy, with school-work and stuff.'

'It's just so hard to imagine. I would have gone a bit bonkers if I'd had to live like that.'

'You're lucky you haven't had to live my life then.'

'So what exactly did happen to your mum?'

I look away towards the large white wildflowers growing here and there in the hedgerow. 'She died.'

'How?'

'She had an accident one day. In the bath.'

'Oh, I'm sorry. How old were you?'

'Four. I don't remember her much.'

'What was she like? Was she nicer than your dad?'

'I can't remember.' I search for a distraction. Something to steer this conversation in a different direction.

Heat is erupting all over my body and I'm not entirely

sure why. I thought I had accepted what happened to Mum. I suddenly long for the protection of the cottage walls. No one ever got inside to ask me difficult questions there.

Maybe I haven't forgiven Dad entirely. Perhaps that's the problem? And on some subconscious level, I blame him for protecting me. If he hadn't subdued his wife, then would she be alive today instead of me? Would that be a worse situation than the one surrounding me now? I wonder sometimes if Dad would prefer things to have played out like that. Is that why he can be so hard on me sometimes?

Matt's voice interrupts my thoughts. 'I don't mean to be nosy, you know, Chloe. I just want to get to know you. You're so interesting.'

'Oh.' Heat rushes to my face so fast it feels almost cold.

'I mean it. I've never met anyone like you before.' He adds quickly, 'In a good way.'

We follow the well-trodden route through the grass.

Matt proceeds to explain the concept of the internet to me, taking my mind off my aching leg muscles. I'm not used to exercise.

I listen in fascination as he speaks. All the while, he pauses and gives me glances, as though expecting me to call out, 'Gotcha!' at any moment. From the questions I ask I think Matt understands my ignorance is genuine by the end of his explanation, which seems to confuse him more.

'I can't believe your dad didn't tell you about something so major. What does he do on his phone?'

'We don't have a phone.'

Matt shakes his head. 'Neither of you have one? That's crazy.'

He pulls out the flat black device he carries around in his pocket and presses something on the side. An image of a colourful nebula appears, with the time overlaid on top. 'I can't imagine living without a phone. You need one to exist these days. I've always had one. Ever since I was little.'

'It's not that we don't have the money for one,' I say quickly. 'Dad says we don't need to talk to anyone.'

'That's even worse.'

'Is it?'

Matt glances at me sideways as we walk on. 'Does he ever hurt you?'

'No, of course not. He's my dad.'

'Parents can hurt their children too, you know. They are just people.'

'Oh.'

I'm unwillingly reminded of my mother again and the episodes she used to have. I don't remember them, but Dad has filled me in. They sound terrible. I'm genuinely relieved I have only snatches of memories of her. Especially on the day the worst happened. Her screams echo in my head sometimes. Usually late at night, when I've woken from a nightmare alone in the darkness of my bedroom.

I glance at Matt. 'Do your parents hurt you?'

'No. But you hear about what's happened to other kids on the news. They used to talk about it at school sometimes too. I guess you missed that if you were homeschooled. I think it happens all the time.'

'That sounds horrible,' I say as I think about this. 'My dad isn't like that though. He can seem a bit over the top when it comes to security. He wouldn't ever hurt me. He loves me. My father only does it all because he thinks he is keeping me safe. He puts a lot of energy into protecting me.'

'You live in the middle of nowhere with your bedroom window boarded up and only one person to talk to. How much more protected do you need to be? It's like he is hiding you.'

'We're not hiding,' I say quickly. Probably a little too fast.

There is a flicker around Matt's eyebrows. 'I didn't mean it like that.'

We push our way through a wooden gate at the end of the field. This is the only path I've taken my whole life. The surroundings are so familiar, yet it feels distinctly different today.

We cross quite a distance with my feet leading the way on autopilot. We talk about our favourite things. I tell Matt about my ambition to be a vet as though it might still happen. As though Dad would ever allow it. Then Matt talks about his parents. And their determination to force him into a career in dentistry, and not his own choice of art.

'Dad's a dentist. So was my grandad. They just expect me to carry it on, you know? Family tradition and all that. Dentists get paid loads, obviously. I know that because we certainly aren't poor. I just don't want to spend my life with my hands in random people's mouths. It's gross. And that's before you even have to do any treatments. That's when it gets messy.'

He shudders. 'You wouldn't believe the horror stories Dad has come back from his practice with over the years. Like telling me all that is going to make me want to go into that field. It was every bit as bad as he had said when I turned up for work experience. Maybe even worse. I don't know. Have you ever had to have anything done at the dentist?'

'No.'

'My dad got braces fitted on me as soon as I was old enough. You can imagine how popular that made me at school. Again, I suppose you can't if you were home-schooled. Did you ever need braces?'

I shrug. 'No. My teeth are naturally straight, like my mother's apparently.'

'Cool. You just get the six-monthly checkups then? You're lucky.'

'I've never been to the dentist at all. Dad says I have great teeth.'

'What, you've never had a checkup ever?'

I shake my head.

Matt's mouth drops open. 'You must have been at least once.'

I laugh at his surprise. Matt's father must put too much emphasis on teeth in his house. 'No. I told you. My teeth are fine.'

Matt seems overly focussed on my mouth as I speak now and it makes me purse my lips self-consciously. 'Is there something wrong with my teeth?'

'No,' he says quickly. 'It's just that I was surprised. All kids get a free checkup twice a year. Dad takes them seriously. You can just imagine, can't you? He does mine way more often at home too. It's important to spot potential problems before they come up.'

Matt pulls an embarrassed face and groans. 'I sound just like my dad now. Maybe he is just obsessed with teeth. Yours are perfect, by the way. All I meant was that you are lucky.'

My face feels warm again. I hope Matt will just think it's from the steep incline we are both struggling against.

We don't talk much as we pant our way up the slope. This is the toughest bit of the walk. My legs burn. Matt's long ones seem to take him more effortlessly up the rugged terrain. He catches himself when he realises I'm starting to trail behind and falls back a bit. He doesn't seem quite as breathless as I am. I feel like an old lady struggling to keep up.

Walking this route once a month must not be enough to keep fit. I make a mental note to tell Dad this, but have no idea how to argue my point without telling him the truth.

Relief floods my muscles along with the renewed flow of oxygen once we level out at the top. I take deep breaths as we follow the footpath to the summit.

Matt puts a hand awkwardly on the small of my back. 'You all right?'

'Yeah, fine,' I gasp.

He grins. 'I thought you would find that easier than me, being a local and all.'

'I just don't do it very often, that's all.'

'I didn't realise. It sounded like the main bit of time outside you get is up here.'

I clutch a stitch in my side. 'It is.'

Matt looks at me with curiosity again. It worries me I can't tell what is going on behind his bright eyes.

Luckily, we reach the part of the walk where the rocky outcrops form a more dramatic natural feature, Bamford Edge. Our trainers hit the dark stone of the ledge that sticks out like a diving board. The dark rock is like a stoic guardian of the rolling hills below.

The sudden impact of the view elicits an obligatory, 'Cool,' from Matt. His glassy eyes reflect the clouds in the sky as he takes it all in.

Excitement bubbles inside me. I'm so naughty be out here with Matt, doing something fun and taking in this beautiful view without permission. It's hard to believe all this still exists when I'm facing the four walls at home.

There are tourists milling around, taking it all in too. I worry they will spot me without Dad, my protective guardian. He always knows how to keep his distance and make it look casual.

But I needn't worry. No one pays me any attention. All this has been passing me by when I've been studying or reading and wishing I could take big lungfuls of air and feel the warmth of the sun on my face without the barrier of a window.

October sun breaks through the clouds here and there. Glowing rays highlight the mass of dark green; it could pass for broccoli reaching for the heavens at this scale. The light falls on the nearby Ladybower reservoir making it glow with sapphire tones.

Once I've got my breath back, I point out some landmarks to Matt. As I'm showing him the ominous Win Hill opposite us, he does something that makes me forget what I'm saying.

He takes my hand in his and my heart does a happy little dance as we stand and look across to the horizon together.

12

I lose track of how long we stand at Bamford Edge and enjoy the beautiful scenery. I was right, this trip is nothing like the ones I have taken with Dad. I feel like I'm stepping into completely uncharted territory, despite the fact the familiar rocky terrain looks superficially familiar.

Matt pulls the phone he carries from his pocket and raises it, arm outstretched in front of us. His other moves over my shoulder and I see the two of us looking back from the screen. My look of confusion is reflected at me before Matt tells me to smile.

The image of the two of us smiling as a happy couple freezes for a moment and turns into a miniature version in the corner of the screen.

This must be how rich people take their photographs, I think. All Dad can afford is the heavy old camera that takes snaps Dad develops himself in his dark bedroom. Nothing to do with the internet or email. It certainly doesn't have a colourful screen either. You have to raise it to your face and look through the viewfinder, inhaling musty metal. The times it has been used I can count on one hand.

A grey-haired couple in full hiking gear appear nearby and Matt asks them to take our photo. My insides squeeze with nerves, but neither of the pair does more than glance at me. Matt hands the woman his phone and she takes a few steps backwards, walking sticks tucked under her arm as she raises it.

Matt takes my hand and leads me onto the hanging ledge. We both settle into a seated position, our legs dangling precariously over the drop below, and smile for another photograph.

He thanks them as they pass his device back and he examines the shot. It's another beautiful image.

'They've come out great. I don't suppose I can email you these, can I?'

I shake my head. Matt explained to me earlier how people send messages instantly to each other. Dad has never mentioned such a concept to me before. We certainly don't have an email address.

'Maybe I can get them printed for you instead?'

'I'd like that.' Then my heart sinks as I ponder how I will get the photos past my father. Then there is the issue of Dad potentially stumbling upon them in the future even if he did. How could I keep them hidden from him forever?

Other hikers appear now. They hover nearby and throw glances in mine and Matt's direction, which makes me nervous. I realise they probably want to have their photos taken in this spot too. This area certainly makes for stunning results.

Eventually, Matt asks if I want to move on as a large

group of hikers can be seen in the distance making their way up the hill. I'm glad it is his suggestion and not mine. I don't want to give him the idea that Dad and I are in hiding, even if it is true.

As we start our descent, however, my heart sinks a little at the thought of him taking me back to my stale cottage prison. I'm thoroughly enjoying myself out here today, holding hands with Matt and breathing the fresh air, feeling the sun on my skin. I don't want to go back yet.

We trail through the woodland I had used to pretend was the forest of Fangorn. I ask Matt about books he likes. It sounds like he hasn't read many, whereas I feel like I've lived a thousand adventures in various places and times. Often the only thing I could do to vent some frustration was to live vicariously through familiar characters. All of it seems quite petty compared to actually being out and doing real things. There is so much going on out here, I just want to stay atop this hill and take it all in.

Matt talks now about holidays abroad and an extensive list of places he has been. His tone is casual, bored even. I struggle to imagine what it must be like to get on a plane and fly off somewhere. I try and convey this to Matt whilst trying to sound normal. I realise just how much life experience Dad has kept me from.

We come to a stop on the bridge crossing the reservoir. I look across the water hand-in-hand with Matt. My calf muscles shake beneath me from traversing the slopes. I don't care. It is such a novelty to be breathing in the outdoors. The weak October sun warms my face and arms. It feels glorious.

The water before us is alive with movement, slopping noisily against the concrete edge. I want to bottle all this. I know I'm soon going to be back inside the four walls that have been my entire existence. How amazing would it be to come here whenever I felt like it?

I sigh. 'What time is it?'

Matt pulls out his phone. 'Just past two. We've still got ages to get you home. Don't worry.'

We are prompted to move on again by the sight of the group of hikers we saw earlier. They emerge from the woodlands behind us. Matt seems almost as keen as me to put distance between our two parties. It's as though he enjoys us being alone too.

It's unsettling to be aware of such a large group of people on our periphery. Dad always makes avoiding tourist groups effortless somehow. He is quite skilled at it. I get a flutter of anxiety as I realise he isn't here to protect me. Matt doesn't understand the connotations.

The group seems to have a different collective agenda to our desire for solitude, moving on promptly from the reservoir, despite the photo opportunities. I recognise some raised arms and quick snaps being taken before the distant leader figure hurries them on.

Matt and I can take a quicker pace as a pair than a whole gaggle with heavy boots, coats and backpacks, however. As a result, we lose them in the next stretch of woodlands.

'That was weird,' Matt says, looking over his shoulder with a smile. 'It felt like they were following us a bit.'

'Do you think so?' I look over my shoulder too with a frown. 'I kind of felt a bit like that too.'

'Do you know any of them?'

'No. They couldn't know me. I only know my Dad, but he is at work. Those people looked like tourists. All of them would be strangers to me.'

I get a shot of panic at the thought of being recognised.

Dad always says I should keep my eyes averted and my head
down. What if I am caught because I was foolish enough to
sneak out without Dad's permission? What would he say if
he found out?

13

M att seems to sense my anxiety. He gives my hand a comforting squeeze as we walk. 'I was probably just imagining things about those tourists. So, where to now?'

I indicate towards the gravel path Dad and I always take. 'It's this way.'

'What's down there?'

'It takes us back to where we started.'

'Oh.'

'There's an old mill on the way.'

'What does it do?'

'Well, not much. It's pretty scenic around it though.'

Matt shrugs. 'I'm kind of hungry after all that walking. I think we should find somewhere nice for lunch. Where can we go?'

'Oh, I think there is a cafe in the garden centre nearby. I've never been in there though.'

'I bet we could find somewhere more interesting. Isn't there a castle near here?'

'That's in Castleton, I think. It's pretty far. I've seen it on the leaflets Dad has in the house.'

I think of the stack of tourist leaflets I found Dad had slotted in the magazine rack a few years ago. I'm not sure what he got them for. At first, I had high hopes Dad would take me to some different places on our monthly outings. That fizzled out.

All the hours I had spent poring over the maps inside each one seemed wasted.

When I asked Dad about them one day, he was vague. Then they disappeared after that. Goodness knows what that had been about. Dad does random things like that sometimes.

At least I can put that knowledge to good use now. 'Castleton must be at least an hour and a half's walk from here. Maybe we could go that way another time, head off first thing.' I add this hopefully at the end, wondering if Matt will want to have another outing with me. A second date, dare I even wish for it.

We venture further down the country lane beside the dry stone wall.

Matt points to the nearest signpost where a pair of chunky-looking bikes have been rested. 'I think we can make it over there today if we take these. Look, they are electric. We can be there and back in no time.'

I watch anxiously as Matt disentangles one bike from the other. 'What are you doing? I don't think we can just take those. They don't belong to us.'

'We aren't taking them, Chloe. We are just borrowing them. I thought you wanted to get out more, have an adventure?'

'I do.'

'Then what's the problem? Or are you so desperate to be locked back in that tiny little cottage by yourself? I thought we were having a nice time.'

'We are,' I say quickly, not wanting Matt to think I don't like him. 'It's just that we would be cutting it too fine if we walked to the next village, and we can't just steal someone else's bikes.'

'*Borrow*,' Matt emphasises. 'I bet the owners won't even notice. We will have them there and back before they even realise. They've probably gone off for a pint or five at the local pub. It will be hours before they get back. We can return them in time, I'm sure.'

Matt blinks suddenly, as though he has been struck by an idea. He leans the bike away from him at arm's length, examining it. 'Actually, I just remembered my parents said they were going on a bike ride today. These are probably theirs. They said they would hire some.'

'They are?' I glance around, as though my question might be answered by an emerging couple nearby. But Matt and I are quite alone.

'Yeah, I'm pretty certain these will be theirs. They said at breakfast this morning they might head this way. Come on, Chloe, hop on.'

I look at him uncertainly. 'Won't they mind you taking them?'

'No, not at all. Dad lets me borrow his stuff all the time. We are pretty much the same height now.'

I look down at the bike as Matt swings his leg over. He is right – the seat is perfectly adjusted to his height.

He jerks his head. 'Are you coming, or what?'

'I can't.' I fold my arms across my chest. 'I don't know how to ride a bike.'

Matt swears. 'Your dad has a lot to answer for. It's lucky these are electric. There's nothing to it.'

Matt runs through the controls. To be fair, it all seems easy enough, but I'm too scared to try. What if I fall off? There aren't any helmets.

In the end, Matt helps me climb onto his bike behind him. I feel wobbly and foolish. The feeling triggers an unexpected flash of memory; pink tassels and an extra set of wheels. I must have ridden a tricycle when I was younger.

That must have been before we came to Hope, when Mum was still alive.

We leave the second bike behind, leaning against the post. I suppose that will work better for Matt's mum and dad when they return. They can always ride together on the same bike back to their house or wherever they were going, just like Matt and I are doing now.

I keep a firm fistful of Matt's hoodie in my grip, terrified I'll fall off. He seems quite adept at riding though, so I feel secure enough.

The feeling of the wind in my hair is incredibly freeing. Unfamiliar roads and fields blur by in a haze of green and grey.

It takes us hardly any time at all to reach Castleton. It's a relief to get off the bike in the end, as the fresh wind I was enjoying has now caused goosebumps to erupt over my skin.

Matt notices this and unzips his dark green hoodie, wrapping it around me before he finds a lamppost in the centre of the village to lean the bike against.

I slide my arms into the sleeves of Matt's jacket, appreciating the residual warmth left behind in it. It's big for me and long in the sleeves, but I'm grateful.

It feels like sliding into a hot bath after experiencing the wind chill. 'Do you think it's okay to leave the bike there?'

Matt shrugs and glances around. 'There are quite a few people about and it's the middle of the day. It should be all right. I'm starving now. Let's find somewhere to eat.'

My stomach does a flip as Matt takes my hand again and leads us to a nearby cafe. I've never eaten anything other than at home before. What on earth should I expect? I instinctively know I can't explain this to Matt, or ask him what to do. He strolls up like it's the most casual thing in the world; as though this place is an extension of his dining room. These surroundings couldn't be more alien to me.

My companion makes a big show of comedically pulling out a chair for me at the table and chairs outside. It makes me laugh and for a moment I forget my nerves at never having been to a cafe before. I feel lucky Matt is opting for seats outside.

It seems informal enough though, I realise after watching a man feed his dog some ice cream at a nearby table. Everything seems normal and I can even pretend I am too. Other than Matt, no one pays me the slightest bit of attention. I feel so much more free than I expected.

A waitress arrives. Matt asks me what I want and he makes the order. He taps his phone onto the device the waitress hands him and there is a beep.

Matt smiles when he sees my expression; I hope it doesn't look too clueless.

'That's how I usually pay for things,' he says. 'It's easier than carrying money around. For some things, you just have to have a smartphone. I don't know how your dad could manage without one these days. He must need online banking, for example. How does he do it?'

'I don't know. He doesn't talk about finances with me. Look, I'm sorry I don't have any money on me.'

'That's okay. I kind of assumed you wouldn't have an allowance if your dad doesn't let you out much.'

'We aren't poor, you know.'

Telling Matt this seems important. Even with my limited world knowledge, I know that having money is the thing to do. It puts you into some sort of scoring system in the view of others. For some reason I can't explain, I don't want to be seen on the bottom rung, especially not in front of Matt, who seems to exude wealth.

'Don't worry about it. I'm happy to pay.'

'Thank you so much.'

'It's just lunch.' Matt's cheeks grow warm looking now and he seems relieved by the distraction of the arrival of our food.

I ordered a cheese sandwich thinking it would be something familiar. But what arrives is nothing like the simple slices of cheese I put between two uniform slices of bread at home. The bread is special and it's presented nicely on the plate, with a side salad and tiny tubs of chunky chutney and mayonnaise. It's the nicest sandwich I've ever eaten. I know it isn't just the fact that I'm eating something someone else prepared.

Afterwards, Matt orders us a lemon cake to share and that is wonderful too. It makes me doubt my baking abilities. Maybe Dad was right to laugh at my idea to sell baked goods myself, especially when I realise I was way off with my pricing strategy. If only he had just told me.

When we have finished eating, Matt checks something on his phone and I'm alarmed to see it's now past 3 p.m.

I must look worried because Matt says quickly, 'It's okay,

Chloe. We've still got hours before you have to be back. I'll make sure you're on time. I promise. It only took us half an hour max to get here on the bike.'

'That was from the woods near the reservoir. It's an hour's walk at least from there.'

He shrugs. 'Don't worry. If we run out of time, I'll ride you straight back to your house and I'll return the bike to where we found it on my own later.'

'Won't you just take it back to your house? Your parents might have taken the other one back by now.'

'What?' Confusion knots his dark eyebrows for a second. 'Oh, yeah, probably. Anyway, we can't leave this place without seeing the castle.'

So we spend the rest of our time together exploring what is left of Peveril Castle. It turns out there isn't much to it, which disappoints Matt. Just being outside and somewhere different is enough for me. Everything feels so fresh and different. I can't tell Matt this, however. I want to give him the impression that I'm not as sheltered as I've accidentally let slip. Matt enjoys the views of the surrounding hills, especially from the bench we settle on for ice creams. It's quite an experience for me to see distant landmarks from a different perspective.

The only thing sullying it is the fact time is ticking away until we have to leave. I never thought I would be so disappointed to go home.

Before we get up to leave, Matt leans in and tentatively presses his lips against mine. There is a pleasant fluttering in my chest. I don't think I have ever been so happy. Not like this.

Matt grins when he pulls back. 'I didn't think you would appreciate that if I did it outside your house.'

'No, probably not.' I laugh. 'Thanks.'

'For what? The kiss? You don't have to thank me for that, you know. Any time.'

I smile. 'Not just that. I mean for today. And for being so understanding. I've had a great time.'

'So have I. We should do it again sometime.'

We hold hands again on the way back to the village square to retrieve the bike. I've never felt so lighthearted and contented. For the first time ever, I understand the phrase, 'having a spring in your step'.

We've walked right up to the lamppost Matt leaned the bike against earlier before we realise something is wrong.

The bike is gone.

14

Dread fills me. The image of Dad walking into an empty house takes over my thoughts. He will see the cellar door and window have been pushed open, evidence of my treachery. There will be no way he won't realise what I've done immediately.

I'm going to be in so much trouble.

Matt uses the f-word. I feel like using it now too in its true context. That bike was my ride home. We will never make it back on foot in time before my father gets home. I convey this to Matt.

'Don't worry about that. We'll have to call an Uber or something.'

'A what?'

'It's like a taxi that takes you where you want to go.'

'Will it get us back in time?'

'Probably.' Matt taps at his phone with frustration. 'I just can't seem to get a signal.'

I cross my arms across my chest. 'Wasn't there one at the cafe?'

'No, I was using their Wi-Fi, not my data. They will be shut now though. Maybe we should try to find somewhere else with some Wi-Fi.'

We try the nearest pub, but they tell us minors aren't allowed in without an adult.

Matt shakes his head angrily. 'We just want to use your Wi-Fi for two minutes. Why can't you let me have the password?'

'Sorry. Rules are rules,' the bartender says as he ushers us out the door.

We step back outside feeling flattened.

My hands are cold and clammy now and that erratic heart thing I get is acting up like crazy. 'I don't know what we are going to do, Matt. What time is it now?'

'I don't know, Chloe. About five minutes after the last time you asked! Just don't worry, okay?'

His answer is snappy and he looks noticeably agitated as he scans the area. 'I've got bigger things to worry about than your dad. Who do you think took the bike?'

'I don't know. You didn't secure it. Neither did your parents, which I think was a bit silly. Anyone could have taken it.'

'Yeah, well, someone was stupid enough to leave it without a lock in the first place.'

I stare at Matt. 'What do you mean, *someone*? Your parents left it, didn't they?'

'No. I knew it wasn't theirs. I just said that so you would ride on it with me.'

My mouth falls open. Matt lied to me. 'How could you do that?'

Matt shakes his head dismissively, still looking around as though the bike might just reappear at any minute. 'It should have been fine. I was going to take it back where we found it. I just wanted you to have a nice time, that was all.'

'My idea of a nice time doesn't involve stealing things!' My lip trembles at the thought of what might happen now. 'Do you think the owner took it back?'

'I don't know. Maybe. Perhaps we should move on, just in case. We might be able to find a ride somewhere else.'

'Just in case what? Do you think the owner called the police?'

Matt shrugs. 'They might have. Let's just go, okay?'

He reaches for my hand, but I snatch it from his grip.

'Chloe, calm down. It's no big deal. We just need to not be here if the police are looking for whoever took it, that's all.'

The memory of the man being shoved into a police car outside old Mrs Turner's place is too fresh. His crime had simply been stealing food. What do the police do when they find someone who has stolen an expensive-looking bike?

And what if that person had been on the run for twelve years? They will find out about Dad if I'm caught. He will be taken away and I will never see him again. Why have I been so reckless? Matt was bad after all. I made a poor judgement.

I feel I might be sick. I retch into a nearby bin.

Matt pats me awkwardly on the back. 'Chloe, it's okay. I can still get you home. We might just be a little later. I'll come over and explain to your dad. I'll tell him it's my fault.'

I wipe my mouth on my sleeve. 'It is your fault! I'm stranded here because of you. I should never have trusted someone so obviously immoral!'

Matt's confusion seems to root him to the spot. It gives me the chance to turn and run in the opposite direction.

Dad always told me if you realise someone is bad, you

should get away from them as soon as you can. I wish I had never stopped following his advice. He was right. The outside world is dangerous.

Now he is going to be unbelievably angry with me.

15

The journey back home is a nightmare. I think I hear Matt call my name as I race from the village, but I'm not sure if I am hearing things above the wind rushing in my ears.

I lose my breath before I even reach the winding expanse of fields that stand between here and home. I can only hope I set off in the right direction. I've never been this far from home before and it's terrifying. I'm only going off the landmarks in the distance and the vague journey over here. I pointed Matt in the right direction on the way over here atop the bike. Then he seemed to follow the road signs dotted here and there. I don't have time to stop and study any, however.

There is less than an hour to complete the walk I know takes much longer than that, according to Dad's hiking leaflets. We don't have any other maps in the house, so I found them fascinating, despite how simple they may have been. My only prayer is taking some of the trek at a run will cut down the journey time.

I'm sweating and shaking all over in no time, and not just from the physical exertion. What will Dad do when I get back?

Is there still time to beat him home?

The uncertainty is killing me. My heart delivers some threatening missed beats. It turns out I can't run for long at all. All I manage is an intermittent feeble jog peppered with a brisk walk. I'm just so unfit from the confinement of a lifetime.

Will I even be allowed to go home? What if the police catch up with me first? Are they out looking for me at this very moment? Every time a car passes by, I panic.

I should probably get off the main road just in case, but I fear I would get even more lost.

I finally see a signpost for Hope and could almost cry with relief. The name has never seemed more apt than it does right now.

I've never entered this part of the village before. It's a lot busier than our quiet corner.

I pass a college, a sports club, and a caravan park. Dad has mentioned the park before, complaining it brings too many people into the area. I didn't know where it was until today though.

I make it past the railway station and finally tread some familiar ground. I'm so close.

I wonder what time it is. Have I made it back before Dad?

I race up the lane that leads to our house at a run, despite the fact my muscles are trembling beneath me.

When I round the corner onto our property, my mouth opens in disbelief. The lights are off.

Dad isn't home yet. I can't believe it. I made it!

Tears of relief run down my cheeks now. I throw all my

energy into running to the back of the house where I made my escape earlier.

It's only once I have squeezed myself awkwardly back in through the cellar window and rushed up the concrete steps, that I realise that the door leading to the hall is jammed. It won't budge.

I'm trapped down in the cellar. Dad will be home any minute and I can't get back into the area of the house where I'm permitted.

16

T his can't be happening. I shove myself against the door, coughing on dirt and debris that fall down from overhead

'Come on!' I say in desperation as I try to force the door. How could it be jammed? It opened easily the first time I tried it.

I must had knocked something over in the hall in my haste to get out to meet Matt. I was too giddy, not paying attention to what I was doing.

Now I'm paying the price. I'm trapped down here in the musty cellar and Dad will be home any minute.

'Please!'

I give the door another good shove. To my utter amazement, the wood gives and I'm standing in the hallway

The old brass umbrella stand lies on its side at my feet. A long golf umbrella was rammed lengthways against the door. How stupid of me not to notice on the way out this morning. That mistake could have cost me. I don't even remember knocking into it.

I waste no time in shoving the door shut and returning the umbrella stand to its upright position. I'm sweating and panting as I do so, hardly daring to believe my luck that I managed to shove the umbrella out the way. If it was lodged an inch or so more at a certain angle, I might never have been able to get out. I would have been forced to wait down in the damp and dark for my father to rescue me. He would have come home for dinner and had the shock of his life.

Dinner! I haven't started cooking yet.

I race into the hall and return my shoes. They are a little muddy, but I don't have time to deal with that now. Wasn't the ground a little damp when Dad took me out last? The dirt could have attached itself on that outing for all he knows. There is always the chance that he might not notice too.

The grandfather clock tells me I have no more than four minutes before my father usually appears. I race upstairs and stare at my reflection in the mirror.

I'm alarmed to see my wild eyes and desperate expression. I'm red in the face and my hair is wet around my temples from my exertion.

My face is filthy from the crawl back into the house too.

I snatch my sponge from the side of the bath and start rubbing hurriedly at the dark spots. The cold water is welcome. I grab a towel and frantically dry myself, bitterly regretting ever speaking to Matt.

I take a few deep breaths to try and return my breathing to normal.

Then I hear keys in the front door.

My father is home.

I take a deep breath before descending the stairs.

Dad is in the hallway, shrugging his coat off and hanging

it on the peg as usual. It's a normal day. Nothing out of the ordinary has happened. I made it. I'll never do anything so stupid again, as long as I live.

Dad slides himself out of his shoes. 'Oh, there you are. I was beginning to think you weren't home.'

He chuckles to himself.

'I was just using the bathroom.'

'All the lights were off. Have you been sitting in the dark? I can't smell dinner either. Are we not eating tonight?'

'I was just about to start it. It's just tinned stew and potatoes. It will only take a few minutes to prepare.'

'That's not like you, Chloe. You always have it ready for us to sit down and eat by now. '

'I know. I just didn't get around to it. I'm sorry, Dad.'

He reaches out a hand to my forehead. 'Are you feeling well? You look very flushed.'

'Er, I don't know. Maybe I am feeling a little funny. I might have a lie down after dinner.'

'I'll get you a glass of water in the meantime. Have a sit down in the lounge. I'll bring it through.'

'No – that's okay!' I say hurriedly, thinking of the trail of evidence I might have left on the kitchen floor. Dad notices little details like that.

He raises an eyebrow.

'I mean, I'll just get a drink when I'm making dinner. You've been at work all day. You are the one that needs a sit down. I'll make your coffee.'

'All right. If you are sure you're okay. It almost looks as if you were the one that has been out all day.' He chuckles again and moves through to the living room.

I return to the kitchen to empty the contents of some tins into pans hurriedly and put the kettle on. At the same time, I try and sweep the kitchen quietly, peering around the doorway to check Dad won't appear at any moment.

My father is quite particular about the temperature of the things he consumes. He likes his food to cool to almost tepid but demands hot drinks just the safer side of scalding.

The food will take a while to be the way he likes it. He will know if I have tried to cool down the potatoes by running them under the tap. They don't have that steamed-dry quality my father insists upon.

I serve the food hot on the table along with the coffee where Dad is seated as usual.

He looks at me intently as I sit too. I hope he is purely checking for signs of illness and nothing more.

'You look a little less flushed now. Did you get a drink in the end?'

'Yes. I feel a bit better now. The water helped.' I take a sip from the glass on the table to demonstrate this, but then I realise just how thirsty I am. Today I've run further than ever before in my life. My muscles are shaking and I'm exhausted.

I glug more down, almost finishing the glass. The last thing I drank was the tea with Matt at lunch.

'Steady on. You will make yourself sick if you have a bad tummy.'

'Sorry. It's just I didn't realise how thirsty I was. Maybe I'm just dehydrated.'

'You can't be too bad unless you've been exerting your-self. Have you been cleaning? Is that why you are so tired?'

'Yes. I did quite a bit of house work, actually. It's really worn me out.'

'Really?' Dad runs his fingers along the backs of the chairs at the table and rubs the grey film between his finger and thumb. 'You might want to revisit it tomorrow. You certainly have missed quite a few bits.'

'Yes, I will. Sorry, Dad.' I face my plate of food to avoid his searching gaze. I scoop and swallow a spoonful of tinned stew. It's far too hot and it burns, but I go right in for a second one. Dad is suspicious, I can tell. I just need to hold my nerve.

The heat of the food works its magic quickly. Warmth spreads through me and I quickly get uncomfortably hot.

I immediately realise why when I look down. I'm still wearing Matt's hoodie.

I chance a glance up at Dad. He is forking at his piping hot food with distaste, spreading it around his plate in an attempt to cool it faster.

He doesn't seem to have noticed I'm wearing Matt's over-sized hoodie. To be fair, I do have one quite similar, except mine is jade green and a close fit, not khaki and obviously too big.

I wonder if taking it off will draw more attention? Or can I get away with it until after dinner and switch it? Will Matt realise his mistake and knock on the door for it later?

My insides squirm at the last thought. It suddenly makes it tough to eat the dry potatoes in front of me.

I think of an excuse to go into the kitchen and take this thing off before Dad notices. 'I might just go and get some bread. Do you want some?'

'No, thank you.'

In the kitchen, I quietly unzip the hoodie and stuff it in the back of the cleaning cupboard behind the ironing board. Dad never does ironing. Or any kind of house work for that matter. It will be safe there until I figure out how to return it to Matt. It's a good thing my t-shirt is black. Dad can't see the moist patches under my arms and up my back in this dull light.

He looks up at me curiously as I place a plate of buttered sliced bread on the table. 'So what have you been up to today, other than half-hearted cleaning?'

'I just did some reading.'

'Anything good?'

'I read *Anne of Green Gables* again.'

'Again? I thought you were tired of that. You said you've read it too many times.'

'I was.'

'What changed?'

'I don't know. I don't have anything new to read. And those books were my favourite when I was little.'

Dad chuckles. 'When you were little. You speak as though you are an adult.'

'I'm not exactly a child anymore.'

'No, I suppose you are quite grown up now, aren't you? Anyone would think so, the way you blatantly walk around the place in your boyfriend's jacket.'

I stare at my father in horror. 'What?'

'That jacket you were wearing a few minutes ago is his, isn't it? You've taken it off now. Did you hide it somewhere in the kitchen?'

Dad blinks at me from behind his glasses. The hand gripping his fork is too taut, the knuckles white.

He hasn't been fooled. I didn't get away with anything. He knew all along.

17

'Did you really think you were going to get away with it, Chloe?'

I shake my head. It's all I can do in my defence, being lost for words as I am. Dad knows what I have done.

He pulls the plate of bread towards him and tears off a large chunk. 'Where have you been?'

I watch him as he scoops up his stew erratically, sending some slopping onto the tablecloth. He stuffs it into his mouth roughly, leaving butter and gravy on his chin in his fury. It would be comical if I wasn't in so much trouble.

'I – I went outside.'

'Aha! I knew it. I knew you had been sneaking out of the house! I've known for months.'

I shake my head earnestly. 'No – today was the first day I've been outside our property.'

'Liar!'

'It's true, Dad! I've been out in the garden twice. And then outside properly today for the first time ever.'

'I don't believe you. I caught you that time when you sneaked out the window!'

'That wasn't me! You left the window open that day. I didn't sneak out then, I swear!'

'You're lying to me!'

'I'm not!' I start full-on crying like I haven't done for ages, not since the open window incident when I was innocent. These are guilty tears now. This is the first time I've ever actually been culpable of what Dad is accusing me of.

I wipe my eyes on my napkin. 'I swear I've only left the house three times, and all in the last week.'

'Where did you go?'

'I – I just went on our usual walk.'

'With that boy?'

I nod, not daring to look at my father at all. 'His name is Matt.'

'I don't care what his name is! How did you meet him? Did he come knocking at the door?'

'No. We met accidentally. At the end of the garden when the trees were felled. He has been staying at the new house with his parents.'

'I knew outsiders coming here would lead to trouble. All these property developers need to get what's coming to them! How did he get you out there?'

'He didn't. I went out there.' I shake my head. 'I didn't mean to. It was an emergency. I was scared and didn't know what to do. All of our trees were disappearing. I found I could squeeze through the window in the cellar.'

I expect an explosion of fury at my discovery of an escape route. But none comes. 'You already knew how I got out, didn't you?'

'I saw you on your travels. I thought I must have been

seeing things at first. When I came home to check on you, however, you weren't here. I pieced things together when I saw that the door to the cellar was open.'

I think of how the cellar door was shut and blocked when I got back. 'You jammed the door with the umbrella stand before I got back? Then you pretended to come home as normal.'

'I wanted to see if you would lie to me. And you certainly did, you devious little witch! If I didn't know any better, I would think your behaviour was becoming deviated like your mother's. This is how she started too. All the little lies here and there.'

'No!' I look at him imploringly. 'How could you have seen me outside, anyway?'

'I saw you with that horrible boy at the reservoir – far from where you were supposed to be!'

'What?'

'Imagine my downright shock when I was at work and saw my daughter frolicking about with some stranger! Hand in hand with him too, like a trollop! I was secure in the knowledge that you were safe at home.'

'You don't work at the reservoir.'

'No, I do not! So I bet you thought you were fine to go parading around in broad daylight where you thought I wouldn't catch you.'

'How did you find out?'

'I bet you're keen to know, aren't you? I was leading the group of hikers you seemed keen to scurry away from on that reservoir bridge! I thought you had seen me and that's why you hurried away.'

Fuck. I knew something was off about that group of hikers. 'No, I didn't recognise you from a distance. You're a solicitor. I thought you were at work at the firm. Why were you with some hikers instead?'

Dad returns to his food, stuffing several large mouthfuls thoughtlessly down again before he answers. 'If you must know, I've left my job at the law firm.'

'What? Why?'

'They wanted me to do longer hours and I couldn't commit to that. Not with a child to look after. And you certainly do need looking after, don't you? My goodness. I can't leave you alone at all if you are going to misbehave so badly when I'm away!'

'I'm sorry, Dad. It won't happen again.'

'It certainly will not!' He slams his used cutlery down, leaving more mess over the tablecloth. 'Where did you disappear to after you ran from me, Chloe? I lost track of you after you left the bridge. I even left my group behind to try and find you, but you were gone. How did you disappear so quickly?'

My stomach churns anew as I remember the stolen bike. How much does Dad already know? Should I tell him I suspect the police might be out searching for me? Or should I leave him to find out for himself? What if the police finally catch up with him because of me?

I burst into new tears again, feeling like the stupid child I am. 'I'm so sorry, Dad. Matt stole a bike. We used it to go to Castleton. I didn't know he stole it until later.'

Dad's lips grow very white. 'You did what?'

'I'm sorry – it wasn't me. I didn't realise until it was too late. I left Matt behind when I found out he had stolen someone else's property. I'm so sorry!'

A lot is going on behind Dad's taut face. He finally speaks. 'Did anyone see you?'

'I don't think so. But the bike was gone from where we left it. I don't know if the owner took it back or someone else got hold of it.'

'Did anyone call the police?'

'I don't know. I didn't see any. I ran away.'

'Straight back here?'

I nod, wiping my face on my napkin again.

'Did anyone see you?'

'I don't know. I just ran as fast as I could. It was so far, Dad.'

'How did you find your way back? You didn't follow the main road, did you?'

'Yes. I didn't know any other way.'

Dad's shoulders slump. 'You've made a massive mess of things, haven't you?'

There is nothing else I can do other than apologise again. I have nothing else I can say in my defence. Dad is right, I have messed up. I can only wait for the punishment and hope Dad doesn't suffer for my misdeeds today.

I convey this to him. 'I'm so stupid. I just wanted to go outside and do normal things.'

Dad puts his face in his hands. 'Why now?'

'I was frustrated at being locked up in here all the time. When you boarded up the windows, I thought you had gone too far, blocking even the daylight out.'

'It was all to keep you safe. Don't you see that? I thought you knew all this.'

'I did. But I thought I could go out by myself. It was only Matt who saw me close up. I thought it would be okay until he got us into trouble by stealing that bike. I've changed so much since I was little. Who would recognise me after twelve years? And the police are mainly looking for you. Not me. I thought it would be okay, I swear.'

I think of Mum and the way she died with Dad protecting me from her as she lashed out. 'I never wanted you to get into trouble because of me,' I say quietly. 'I'm sorry we don't have a better life. And I'm sorry you saved me that day all those years ago.'

When Dad's face emerges from behind his hands, he has a grimace beneath his red and watery eyes. 'Oh, Chloe. I should have told you sooner, shouldn't I?'

'Told me what?'

He sighs deeply. 'It was never me the police were looking for. I didn't kill your mother that day. You did.'

18

I let my forgotten fork thud onto the table at Dad's comment. I must have misheard him. 'What?'

Dad winces. 'All these years I've tried to protect you from the truth. Perhaps you are old enough to deal with it now.'

'What are you talking about?'

'You killed your mother, Chloe.'

'No, I can't have. It was you.'

Dad nods slowly. 'I've let you think that for years, sweetheart. I didn't think a young child could handle that sort of fact. But like you said, you aren't a little girl anymore. You should be told the truth now. I owe it to you before you do anything reckless. Although, it might be too late. I should have told you sooner.'

I stare at my father in shock. 'It was me? How could it have been? I was just four years old.'

'I know. It took me by surprise too. The last thing I expected when I got home from work was to find my wife dead in the bathtub and my daughter standing over her.' Dad's voice breaks.

'I don't understand.' Memories flood to the surface of my mind. The blood all over the bathtub. Red on white. The house still and quiet.

My chin wobbles again. 'How did I do it?'

'I'm not sure, as I wasn't there when it happened. I'm guessing you were having one of your tantrums. You had so many back then. I knew then you had inherited your mother's mental health issues, but I ignored them. That turned out to be a mistake this one day when I came back to that horrible scene.'

Dad takes a long shuddering breath to steady himself. 'I'm guessing you threw one of your toys at your mother as you so often used to. Your toy cash register was lying on its side in the middle of the hallway with the drawer open; the toy coins were scattered over the carpet. You used to have such bad tantrums. If I was there I could have calmed you down, as only I could. You used to find my presence soothing. You still do. Your mum had a bad gash on her temple when I found her. She must have gone upstairs when she started bleeding, perhaps in an attempt to staunch the flow, but it must have been too much for her. She suffered from a bleeding disorder, but the medication she regularly took only did so much. I imagine she got lightheaded and collapsed. She never left the bathroom.'

There is silence as we both contemplate that day in our heads. I want to tell Dad he has made a mistake, but it all seems so clear now. All the little pieces of confused memory are slotting together in my mind, completing the puzzle.

Now it finally makes sense. A sour taste rises suddenly in the back of my throat. I clasp my hands over my mouth.

Dad is right. I killed Mum. My father wasn't even there at the time. He was at work, of course he was. I remember now.

It was just the two of us in the house. Me and Mum. I have inherited my mother's temper. Is that why I went from zero to furious so quickly with Dad for laughing at me the other day?

Dad seems to read my thoughts now. 'I know you have resentment towards me, Chloe. Especially lately. You don't know how much that hurts me. I've only ever tried to keep you safe. I love you. I did what I thought was best to protect you. I whisked you straight out of the situation that very day. I brought you here away from it all.'

He runs a hand distractedly through his hair. 'Do you have any idea what the authorities would have done to you if you had been in that house to face them? Given your history of outbursts, you would have been, at the very least, monitored for the rest of your life. Medicated too. It would have destroyed you, turned you into a zombie. I couldn't let that happen to my little girl. Here you have had the chance for a peaceful childhood. Quiet and secluded, yes, but away from anyone that would hurt you. I know you didn't mean to kill your mother. It was an accident. You just lost control of yourself.'

'I didn't mean to.' I'm feeling dizzy. Numb. I'm even angry at Dad for keeping something so big from me.

'I know that. I believe in you, even though no one else would. So now we live here, away from the outside world and all its evils.'

Dad sighs again and stands up. I hear him in the hall. When I round the corner, he is pulling his coat on.

'Where are you going?'

'I'm going to see what damage you have caused. Can I rely on you to stay in here and not leave whilst I'm gone?'

'Yes, of course.'

'You understand the consequences better now. They will be more dire for you than they would be for me, Chloe.'

I nod.

'Where is that boy's jacket? I'll return it on my way.'

I grab Matt's hoodie from where I stuffed it in the kitchen cupboard earlier. 'Here. I'm so sorry, Dad.'

'I just hope the police haven't clocked who you are.'

Dad shakes his head to himself as he shuts the front door behind him. There is the familiar click of the lock. This time, I'm glad to be locked in the sanctuary of the house.

It turns out it wasn't the prison I thought it was after all. Rather, these four walls have been keeping me safe from the outside world and those who would want to harm me.

Dad was right. I'm safe in here.

19

Dad is gone for the rest of the evening; all night too. I start panicking that he has been picked up by the police.

I've been lying in the blackness of my bedroom for hours, fully dressed atop the duvet in case the police arrive any moment, banging on the front door.

The windows are boarded up in here, so I don't even have the moon or stars for company. It's just as well really. I feel more secure now with an extra layer of defence.

It's a little silly to think that. It's not like anyone was going to break in through the window. Not when there are two doors downstairs to be compromised. Neither of them is in good condition. I wonder how long it would take for someone to break their way inside if they wanted to.

I keep my ears pricked, listening for any little noise. I don't want them to take me by surprise. I don't know why. It's not like I am going to resist arrest. That would only prove I am what they think I am – a disturbed young woman.

I've been going over all the times I've been unduly angry

over the years, especially lately. I've hated Dad for the simplest of comments or actions. That must be what he was talking about this evening. Maybe I am like Mum?

My chin trembles again. What am I going to do? Maybe I should be locked up and medicated. What if my anger for Dad spills over into an unexpected violent act? I might not be able to help it. Was I not close to striking out at him recently for laughing at my business ideas?

I could end up all alone in this house for the rest of my life.

It turns out he was justified in finding them amusing. Now I know a little of how much things cost in the outside world it seems I was naive. My stomach swooped when I caught sight of the screen as Matt had paid for lunch earlier.

Now it seems Dad left his beloved job because of me too. It's all my fault. I have messed everything up for us both. Dad is in hiding because of me. He doesn't deserve to live like this.

I roll over onto my side as more tears leak from my eyes. I'm now face to face with threadbare old Bunny. The last remnant of my childhood. In a sudden act of anger, I snatch him up and throw him across the room.

My behaviour immediately scares me. What's going to happen to me if I can't control myself?

Sounds come from downstairs suddenly. My body stiffens, eyes wide. Is that Dad returning? Or is someone else inside the house?

I creep onto the hallway, blinking in the bright light. It's just Dad, however.

'You're still awake, I see.'

'How could I sleep?' I take a seat on the highest step, while Dad positions himself on one a few below me.

He is still wearing his coat and shoes, which is against his rule of taking them straight off at the door every time. The world feels like it has been turned upside down.

It's almost 1 a.m. according to the stoic grandfather clock.

'Well, it doesn't look like anyone saw you.' My father looks as exhausted as I feel as he takes off his glasses and rubs his eyes. 'I'll keep my eyes and ears open when I go out to work tomorrow.'

'Is that it? The police don't know who took the bike, then?'

'A bike like that would cost a lot of money, Chloe. The police are looking for someone. They just haven't figured out who yet.'

'What do you mean?'

'I spoke to the boy you were with. I gave him back his jacket and had a word with him.' Dad sighs heavily. 'Who actually stole the bike, Chloe?'

'Matt did. Why?'

Dad looks at me intently. 'Are you sure?'

'Yes.'

'Did you put him up to it?'

'No, of course not! I know stealing is wrong. You know I would never do that.'

'I'm not sure what you are capable of any longer, to be honest, Chloe. You continue to surprise me.'

He shakes his head sombrely. 'This boy is saying it was you that committed the theft. He said you took the bike and gave him a ride on the back to Castleton.'

'That's not true! It was the other way around.' I shake my head in disbelief. 'How could he lie like that?'

'That's what outside world people do, Chloe. They lie and do wrong and it's always the good people that have to face the consequences. I believe you, of course. The closest thing to a bike you have ever ridden is your toddler tricycle. You wouldn't be confident enough to ride a standard bike alone. But other people don't know that. They would just assume you capable. You had better hope the police don't catch up with this boy, or he will send them straight over here and they don't know you like I do. They won't be so lenient.'

I burst into fresh tears. I had believed in Matt not even twelve hours ago. We had a nice time. I told him loads of personal stuff, completely trusting him.

I've wasted my first kiss. My stomach does another flip as I realise that was probably my only ever one.

'People are cold in the real world, Chloe. They have no use for beings of integrity like us.'

I look back at Dad as he rubs my knee soothingly. 'What are we going to do now?'

'What we have always done. Stay hidden. Stay safe. There might be a chance that we have been lucky this time. We have to make very sure there isn't a next time.'

20

Since I got back, Dad has been looking at me differently. I fear I may have damaged our relationship forever. Is he considering the possibility that I may be turning into a product of the outside world?

I never considered the idea that I might change as I grow older. Would Dad reject me in that case, if I became bad?

He pressures me into recounting my outing with Matt to the very last excruciating detail. He seems to ride waves of fury throughout as I speak but manages to keep his temper from boiling over. That's something to be grateful for.

It seems he is on high alert instead, on the lookout for the arrival of potential consequences of my stupidity. Especially if any come knocking on the door.

My father takes the rest of the week off work to be with me. I don't dare ask how this will impact us financially. I'm just grateful he is still on my side. It's hard to say whether this is to make sure I don't slip out again or whether Dad thinks we will have any unexpected visitors any time soon. It's reassuring to have his company. Until the last few days, I had no idea I was the one who got us into this mess in the first place through my actions as a child.

Dad always told me he had prevented my mother from attacking me. I've spent my childhood thinking that he had saved my life that day; that he had no choice. But now it sounds like Mum died because of my anger. I'd lashed out at her, not the other way around.

Poor Mum. Everything is my fault. I'm so sorry. I wish I could go back and stop myself.

Dad tasks me with giving the house a thorough clean for the next few days. I know he is just trying to keep me occupied. I'm grateful for something to take my mind off my sickening guilt and fear of what might happen next.

Despite everything, I can't help myself wondering what Matt is doing right now. Has he thought of me at all? Is he as bad as Dad tells me? He had been so convincing.

When I'm doing laundry one afternoon, it occurs to me that Matt's break with his parents won't last forever. For all I know, he has returned to his home and studies in Milton Keynes already.

The good thing about wearing myself out with chores all day is that I am truly worn out. So when I collapse onto my bed at the end of the day, I'm asleep within minutes. I do the same thing on Saturday night.

It isn't until I open my eyes and can't make anything else out in the blackness that I realise it must still be the middle of the night. The determined sun usually glows a little through the panels still up at the windows in the morning.

My heart pounds as I close my eyes and try to will myself back to sleep. Then I immediately realise something has woken me.

A clawing noise comes from the window. I sit bolt upright, gathering my duvet around me.

I can't see a thing. The noise happens again. It sounds as if there is a large rat on the other side of the window.

I'm sure it is something far less friendly. Besides, could a rat climb its way up to a first floor window? I'm not sure.

I adopt the actions of my younger self and scramble out of bed, rush down the hall and bang on my father's bedroom door.

Obviously on high alert already, he whirls open the door. He is pyjama-clad and groggy-voiced. 'What is it?'

'I think there is something outside my window.'

I hate how small my voice sounds. Does that voice belong to someone responsible enough to go outside without her father?

'Wait here and don't move!' Dad hastily shoves me inside his room while he rushes off to investigate.

The blackout curtains are shut and I'm just as unseeing in here too. I try and feel my way to the window to peer out, but hit my foot painfully on the metal bed frame.

I sink atop the mattress finding comfort in Dad's residual warmth.

I would like nothing more than to curl up and pretend everything was like it used to be. The reality is that I'm so anxious I could almost throw up.

I don't know if it is my imagination on fire or not, but I'm sure I can hear strange noises coming from outside and from my room too. How far is my imagination stretching?

There is a bang then all is quiet. For a while, I wonder if Dad is hurt, but I'm too cowardly to leave his bed.

He returns five minutes later.

'What was it?' I fire at him as soon as the light from the hall illuminates his figure.

'Nothing. Fox, probably. They have become brazen lately with all the visitors in the village. No doubt our neighbours have left them a good deal of food in the bins. Tourists are wasteful. They take two bites of takeaway and throw out the rest. It has likely attracted the attention of wildlife. Nothing to worry about.'

'Why were you gone so long?'

'I wanted to make sure the animal didn't disturb you again. I've made sure it won't. It's safe to go back to your room now. Goodnight, Chloe.'

21

'A re you sure you're going to be okay by yourself?'

'Yes, of course, Dad. Just go. I promise I will be fine. Honestly.'

'All right. But remember, you aren't to go outside. No matter what. If anyone knocks on the door you are not to answer it.'

'Yes, I know. And if there is an earthquake I will stand in the corner of the room,' I laugh.

My attempt at humour does not go down well with my father, who looks back at me stony-faced and serious. I guess there is no lifting the mood this morning.

It's the first day I will be left unattended since I left the house to meet Matt. Dad's fingers must be sore from checking the locks so many times.

He finally seems satisfied enough to leave me alone, locking the door and checking it twice behind him. I feel quite anxious again at the thought of being left alone.

Luckily, I have plenty to keep me occupied. Dad has bought me some A-level books for me to start work on. I'm keen to show him that I want to work hard and behave myself from now on.

Dad hasn't been gone all that long when something happens that makes my stomach constrict. Someone rings the doorbell.

I freeze at my desk, panic fluttering in my chest. Who could that be?

It can only be the police, I think. Matt must surely have left for home by now with his parents. Very few people have knocked on the door over the years, and so rarely. Then it was just a lost tourist or someone selling something. It's too much of a coincidence that this is happening now after what happened last week.

The thought fills me with dread, but I get up and creep halfway down the stairs. The mosaic outline of the visitor is just feet away from me. It looks like there is only one of them. What do I do?

Dad briefed me for this all day yesterday. All I have to do is pretend not to be here.

I'm about to creep back up the stairs again, but then the sound of my name makes me stop in my tracks.

'Chloe?'

It's Matt. I thought he had gone home already. Dad did too. There is no way that he would have left me alone in the house if he thought Matt was still in the village.

What does he want? Dad already returned his jacket.

'Chloe, I know you're in there. Please open the door.'

I immediately break one of Dad's reinforced rules by shouting back a response through the front door. 'Go away! I'm not allowed to talk to you.'

'I know. Your dad came to see me that night. He wasn't very happy. He gave my parents an earful too. They're mortified. They thought they were doing so well on the village relations front up until that point. Are you okay?'

'Not really. I'm in the most amount of trouble ever because of you. You shouldn't have stolen that bike.'

'It wasn't exactly stealing. I was just borrowing it. But you are right, I shouldn't have done it. I'm sorry I got you into trouble with your dad.'

'And the police.'

'The police? What do you mean?'

'You know exactly what I mean, Matt. The police are out looking for the person that stole the bike.'

Matt laughs out loud. 'No, they're not. I ran into the bloke who owned the bike on my way back that evening. I saw him with the bike as he headed back to Hope. We got talking. He was annoyed, but he hadn't called the police. He was just glad to have retrieved his bike. It was he who took it from where we left it. He and his wife were on holiday in the area. I don't think he wanted any trouble.'

My mouth opens in surprise as I stare at the patchy varnish of the front door. What Matt is saying can't be true. Dad specifically told me the police were out looking for the perpetrators.

'Chloe? Are you still there?'

'Yes.'

'Look, can you open the door so we can talk properly? I feel like I'm just having a conversation with your letterbox here.'

'You'll have to stay that way. I won't be opening the door to you.'

'Please, Chloe. Don't be like that. Mum and Dad are driving me home in less than an hour. I wanted us to make up before I left. I feel really bad about how we left things.

I've been waiting for your dad to leave all week. Hasn't he been into work since we went out together?'

'No, he has stayed home to look after me. Just in case the police came by.'

'I don't know what your dad is talking about there. No police are out looking for you, Chloe. Or me either, for that matter.'

'How do you know that?'

'I told you, I spoke to the guy who owned the bike. Mick, his name was. He was so nice about the whole thing. He was just happy he stumbled upon his bike in the village centre and it wasn't damaged. He was worried some junkie had stolen it to sell or something. We walked a bit of the way home together. He started recounting all the scrapes he had got into when he was young. Mick was sound. There is no way he would have called the police.'

'You can't know that for sure.'

'I'd bet money on it. Trust me, Chloe. I bet your dad is just trying to scare you.'

I'm quiet for a moment as I contemplate this.

'Can you please open the door? I'd love to see you. I've really missed you.'

The last bit seems quite mumbled, but it makes me smile. 'I've missed you too. But I still can't open the door. Dad locks me in and I don't have a key.'

'What? That's crazy. Wait – how did you get out when we went out together?'

'I found a way out through the cellar window. It wasn't locked like all the others in the house. I wasn't supposed to sneak out that day and that's a big part of why I am in trouble. It wasn't just the stolen bike thing.'

'I didn't know that. You should have said something.'

'How could I? It sounds silly when I say it out loud.'

'It does. So what does that tell you? Don't you think your father is being too overprotective?'

'I know he can be sometimes. But it's only because he cares about me. It's sweet really.'

'I suppose you could look at it like that.' Matt pauses. 'Speaking of overprotective parents, my mum just texted me to say we have to leave now. I have to go.'

I peer through the textured glass panel on the front door but catch only a glimpse of a mosaic of dark hair. 'Will you come back?'

'Yeah, of course. I'm not sure when. Dad wants to do some more work on the house when he comes back up here next. It will probably be a weekend sometime. I wish I had a way of talking to you until then.'

'Me too.'

The letterbox opens without warning making me jump.

'Here,' Matt says. 'Something to remember our first date by.'

I take hold of the small rectangle Matt offers me. It's one of the photographs he took on his phone, capturing the moment when the two of us huddled together atop Bamford Edge. The sky is a perfect shade of blue.

I smile as I remember how happy I was that day. 'I thought I would never see this picture again. Thanks so much.'

'No worries.' There is another pause. 'Stay safe, Chloe.'

22

'Did anyone come knocking today?'

'No.'

'That's good. I was worried when I saw a police car in the village. We can only hope they still aren't sure who they are looking for in connection with the stolen bike.'

I nod and stare instead at the bulging bag of shopping Dad has brought in with him.

Matt's words about Dad just wanting to scare me into behaving myself come back to haunt me. It makes sense. It's not like my father needs the drama surrounding the stolen bike to frighten me. Not now that I know the crime I'm truly guilty of.

Dad starts unpacking his bag and loading groceries into the fridge. 'I have a surprise for you.'

'Oh?' I say, wondering what Dad could think I deserve at the moment. 'What is it?'

He waves the pack of eggs in his hand. 'I bought some

extra ingredients. I thought you could give your baking business a try.'

I blink. Dad had outright laughed in my face at that suggestion. 'I thought you said it wouldn't make enough money.'

He pulls a face, as though cringing at the memory of his blunt remark. 'Maybe I was wrong. You are a very talented young lady, Chloe. I think you are wonderful. The light of my life. Don't ever forget that. Who am I to tell you what you can and can't do? It's about time we saw what you are capable of achieving.'

'Are you serious?' My father's abrupt change of heart makes my chin wobble. I fight hard to keep the rest of my face from giving in too. 'Thanks, Dad!'

I throw my arms around his neck and hug him tight.

His glasses get caught in my hair and he laughs as he detangles us, looking a little embarrassed. 'You're welcome. I wish you all the success in the world, sweetheart. I only want you to be safe and happy. I think I thought as long as the world couldn't get to you, that you would be fine. I hadn't thought about you getting so bored and lonely you would take dangerous risks and wander out yourself.'

'I won't do anything stupid again, Dad.' I try to shake away the fresh memory of being just inches away from Matt earlier, or the feeling of his fingers brushing against mine as I took the photograph from him. 'I promise.'

'I hope so. I don't want you to risk the freedom we have both sacrificed for.'

I help Dad unpack the rest of the shopping. There are heavy paper bags of flour, several cylinders of cocoa powder, slabs of chocolate and butter, dense packets of sugar of various types and good-quality vanilla too.

He has bought everything I need to get started on our favourite recipes. In my head, I'm already doing the calculations of how much money I can make. I know how much I need to charge now to compete with other local suppliers.

I'm determined to prove myself. I so want Dad to be proud of me, to be able to trust me again after all this.

MY WISH for it to be like the old days again seems to come true. For the next few weeks, everything between Dad and me is wonderful. I'm busy in the kitchen all day, not only baking but also with the immense cleanup afterwards. Batter and bits of chocolate seem to get everywhere.

When my creations are cool enough, I package them up. Then it's up to Dad to deliver them to Mrs Turner's B&B, along with some other local businesses he has spoken to on my behalf and who have agreed to stock my homemade cakes and treats.

In total, three places now stock my range of wares. I know it's not much, but it's a start. I'm determined to make it work.

I must be doing something right. It's arranged that I will be paid the profits of my venture at the beginning of each month. The first month's payment consisted of just a week or so in earnings. Even so, business seems to be going well.

I stare at the money in my hands. It isn't just coins and small change but significant paper notes. It's the most amount of money I've handled in my life.

'That's yours to keep. Aside from what it costs for the ingredients. I'll just take some out now to account for that.'

Dad shuffles through the cash and hands me the lion's share back.

'Pure profit!' he smiles. 'Yours to spend on what you wish.'

'Thanks, Dad. Thanks for believing in me.'

'Don't be silly. I'm just grateful to have such a talented daughter as you. You make each day a blessing.'

All sorts of possibilities run through my mind about what to spend the money on. I don't know where to start. After a few minutes, I can't come to a conclusion. 'I want to spend it on something nice for the two of us.'

My father's eyebrows hover above his glasses. 'Spend it?'

'Yes. On something we both will enjoy. After all, you are working hard to make all those deliveries.'

Dad shrugs. 'Don't worry about all that. And don't be too quick to go spending all that money either. Money is precious. You should try and save it as much as possible. Make sure you put that lot somewhere safe. Always keep money out of sight. Just in case anyone comes looking in through the windows. You know the rule.'

'Always keep valuables out of sight of would-be thieves.'

'That's right. Do it now before you forget.'

Taking Dad's advice, I jog upstairs and pull out the tin from the bottom of my wardrobe. I take a glance over my shoulder to make sure Dad hasn't followed me upstairs, then I take the lid off. Inside are all my most valuable possessions. It's nothing but an old and rusted toffee tin that I don't even remember acquiring.

The familiar metallic smell fills my nostrils as I carefully lift out the contents.

There is a beautiful picture of Mum holding me as a baby. She leans her head tenderly into mine as she is seated beside our decorative fish pond in our old house. The years have tarnished the photograph a little but it's still beautiful. It's a glorious midsummer day and the image has always brought some comfort from that sunny afternoon to me.

Now that I look at it, however, a rush of anguish rises in me and I can't bear to look into my mother's beautiful face. I try my best not to look at the dark blonde hair framing her bright blue eyes and neat round features, or the look of love and adoration she has as she holds me close to her.

As though all this isn't burned into my memory already. The scar I've always had on my wrist catches my attention as it has many times lately. I've always thought it was a battle scar from her attack on me that day.

Now that I know the full horror of the truth, I realise it must be the residue of a defensive gesture from her. Or I hurt myself accidentally in my own rage. When it catches the light, I can see it as a scratch from a human fingernail. A small one though. Perhaps it was self-induced, after all.

I don't remember specifically when I got it. I just remember Dad patching me up afterwards with a plaster and some antiseptic cream. I think we were even travelling as he did it. I squeeze my eyes shut. Were we on a train at the time? I can't quite remember.

At the very bottom of the tin, I have stashed my recently procured photograph of myself and Matt, our faces close.

New shame twists my stomach at the thought of Dad's disappointment and anger if he ever saw this. Not only that the photograph was taken, which I conveniently left out of my recollection, but also the fact that I lied to him about Matt coming to visit me so soon after promising that I wouldn't misbehave again.

The only thing stopping me from confessing this sin is

the fact that Matt was the one who came to see me, not the other way around. And I technically didn't open the door or any window in response. I simply spoke to him through the door. That's not too much of a crime, is it?

I carefully stash the money away and secure the lid tightly on the tin before returning it to its hiding place.

When I get downstairs, Dad is waiting for me in the living room with a big smile on his face.

'What is it?' I ask him.

He nods his head towards the dining table. 'I got you a little present.'

I spot a package wrapped in pink and gold paper with a kind of marble effect. It's topped with a shiny gold bow.

'Wow, but it's not even my birthday yet.'

'That doesn't matter. I just wanted to get you something as a reward for all your hard work. Also, because I feel you deserve it. I'm so proud of you, Chloe. I know I don't tell you that enough.'

It seems a shame to tear open such a beautifully wrapped gift, but my fingers make short work of it. Curiosity won't allow me to simply just stare at it.

My heart leaps. It's a book. The first new one in ages. 'Rebecca.'

'I've been thinking about getting you this one for a while. It's a classic. I thought it might be too grown up for you before. I have to admit you're probably mature enough for it now. Especially since you are so much more intelligent than other people your age.'

I can tell from the ornate foil lettering on the front cover that this isn't a children's book. 'Thanks so much. You are spoiling me at the moment.'

'You're worth it. I hope you like it.'

I beam, excited to have such a grown-up book in my hands. It's not just the book itself I'm so excited about. It's a sign. My father is finally starting to treat me like an adult for once and it means so much to me. More than any physical gift.

23

'Mrs Turner wanted you to know that the coffee and walnut cake isn't selling as many as you seem to think.'

'Really? I thought that would be the more popular one.'

'Don't shoot the messenger.' Dad puts a free palm up in front of him. His other uses his spoon to bash away at the boiled egg in front of him. It's breakfast time on Friday morning and he seems in a good mood. 'I'm just passing the instruction along.'

'Oh, okay. Maybe I'll make more of the bakewell slices then to compensate.'

'I don't think you need to do that. It looks like she has plenty to sell as it is. It's only a sideline to her business, remember. She doesn't want people filling up on cake. She has to make money selling the breakfasts to go with all those beds.'

Dad chuckles to himself.

'Will the basket look full enough with just the bakewell

slices and the chocolate muffins? I thought a rule of three was good.'

'It is, I would have thought. But there's no point in making things that people aren't eating. There is no profit in that. Mrs Turner is being very generous already if you ask me. Best to not push your luck. You've got your foot in through the door. Be thankful you are having the success you are.'

'I suppose.'

'You can use the spare time you would have spent baking on your studies instead. I want to give you a maths quiz later. If you do well, I have a little treat for you.'

'Really? What is it?'

He winks and smiles. 'We might get a second visit from Detective Columbo tonight if you play your cards right.'

I grin. 'I'd like that. I'll get full marks.'

I genuinely mean it; it's both mine and Dad's favourite show. I must admit, though, that during last weekend's episode, I found myself quite distracted. The instalment heavily focussed on dentists, which led my thoughts to Matt throughout.

I've started to wonder if he has forgotten about me. Granted, Matt has no way of contacting me from another part of the country.

It's just that since he left, it's like he doesn't exist. It's almost like I imagined him. I only have the photograph as evidence he was here at all. I take it out and look at it by torchlight when I'm sure Dad won't appear in the doorway to mark my work or wish me goodnight. Sometimes I fall asleep looking at it. I think I did so last night.

The one good thing about Matt and his family's absence

is the fact that Dad has deemed it safe to remove the boards
at the windows now.

It's so nice to see daylight in my room once more. It's
something I will never take for granted again, I think, as I sit
at my desk and revise for the test Dad says he will set for me.
It's nice to be studying again. I thought I would never have
the opportunity to do this after I completed my schoolwork.
It's nice to have a purpose again. Along with my new business, I have a lot to keep myself occupied.

I find my mind wandering to my business when
someone knocks at the door. It's such an unusual occurrence
that it makes me get right to my feet. I relax when I hear
Matt's voice on the other side of the door.

'Chloe – are you there?'

'Yes, I am. You came back.'

'Of course I did. I've been trying to get my parents to
come back for ages. Dad's just been really busy at work these
past couple of weeks. I managed to talk him into driving over
a day earlier than he wanted to. That's the best I could do,
sorry. My college lessons finish early on a Friday afternoon
and I knew my only chance to see you would be while your
dad was at work. So how have you been?'

'Really good actually. My dad has let me start college
work too.'

'What, from home?'

'Yes. He buys me books and test papers. But it's better
than nothing. I enjoy the work. It's basically the same as
going to college.'

'Except that it isn't. You aren't going out and seeing
people, like you would if you actually went to a college. I
mean, there's one in the village. Why wouldn't your dad just
let you go to that one?'

I shake my head, a pointless gesture since Matt can't see me. 'I told you, he is just very protective. He worries about me.'

'A little too much, if you ask me.'

'Don't worry. My father loves me. He might not do things the way other people would, but he is only trying to protect me.'

'From what?'

I shrug, which again Matt can't see. 'All sorts. The world is a dangerous place.'

'He can't keep you locked up forever, though, can he? I mean, what will he do when you have to go to uni? You can't very well do that from home. I looked into it at my college. The careers adviser told me to be a vet you have to do all sorts of real animal work experience as well as the biology and chemistry A-levels. And then what about when you qualify as a vet? You'll have to go outside to do your job.'

'Dad doesn't want me to do biology A-levels. He is only letting me do maths and English.'

'Why?'

'He says I should focus on being something less specific. He wants me to keep my options open.'

'It sounds like he doesn't want you to do anything to me.'

'Don't be silly.' I feel uncomfortable when Matt talks like this. Deep down I know there is an element of truth in it. On the other hand, I don't think Matt is giving my father enough of a chance.

He doesn't see him the way I do. He doesn't know how hard he has worked to keep me safe, and the full circum-stances. Even I didn't realise the full extent of it all until recently.

I hear Matt's groan of frustration through the door. 'Why

else would he stop you doing what you really want when you already know what career you want to pursue? My dad has always drummed into me how important it is to have a clear goal in mind when it comes to careers and studies. It's competitive out there; you can't afford to be vague.'

'But didn't you say being a dentist was his idea? Maybe it's *your* dad who is limiting *your* career path. Not the other way around.'

'I don't think so, Chloe.'

'What makes you so sure? Why are you so determined to find fault in my father?'

'I'm not. Look – my parents want you and your dad to come over for dinner this weekend. Do you think he would be up for that?'

A laugh escapes my lips at this. I mean, the idea is ridiculous. Dad would never allow such a thing. Doesn't Matt understand how much of a private person my father is?

Matt doesn't understand my amusement. 'What is it? I thought it might be a good chance for someone to speak to your father. You know, on a casual basis.'

'What does that mean?'

'I mean, social services would probably be interested to know how you live.'

'What's social services?'

'It's like a thing that exists to keep children safe. If they think there is a problem inside someone's home they can go around and visit and check everything is okay.'

I don't like the sound of that at all. 'Dad would hate that. He doesn't like people meddling in our business.'

'That's what I thought. So why not talk him into having dinner with my mum and dad? What's your dad's name, by the way?'

'Albert.'

'Albert Morris?'

'Yes. How did you know?'

'I think my parents saw it on some records when they bought the house. You should give them a chance, Chloe. Maybe they can talk your father into letting you have more freedom?'

I sigh. There is so much Matt doesn't understand. I can't explain the full picture to him. Certainly not now I know everything.

Matt reads into my uncertainty. 'It isn't right, the way your dad has you living, Chloe. You know that. He needs to let you out more. He will ruin and control your whole life if you let him.'

Something about Matt's words tugs something deep inside. For a moment I feel I'm going to burst into tears. It's not like Matt can see me, but I know he'll get the idea if I do. I don't want to embarrass myself in front of him again.

Matt has condensed the complexity of my feelings about my situation into a few simple sentences. He really does understand me. Dad has spent the last few weeks badmouthing him in front of me. Everything he said Matt is I don't believe to be true.

I want to convince Matt that everything is okay. I know my dad can be controlling but that doesn't mean all that much, because Matt hasn't seen the good side of him either.

I try to convey to Matt how much more freedom I've gained since the last time we spoke. I tell him about the business I have started. And how my father is supportive of it.

'That's not your dream job though, is it? You told me you wanted to be a vet. There's nothing wrong with that. It's a good job. Especially if you are passionate about it. Any father would want to encourage that. Yours shouldn't have you wasting your time with a small business instead of pursuing a career you really want.'

I draw myself up higher. 'I don't consider it wasting my time. I've made real money doing it. I've only just started, and three local businesses are supplying my products.'

'I'm probably going to sound like my dad here, but it's not a job for life.' Matt groans. 'Yep, I did sound just like him. Cringe.'

'I know you mean well, but I've worked hard at this business.'

'I know. I bet it's awesome. I'd love to try some of your stuff. Can I?'

I glance down the hallway towards the kitchen. 'Sorry. I've run out. Dad took the latest batches with him this morning on his way to work. You would have loved the coffee cake.'

'I'm sure I would have done. What places stock it?'

'Mrs Turner should have some left. She runs the B&B near here. The last one before you get to the wheat fields.'

'That's funny. I was in there with my mum earlier. She wants to introduce us to the locals and show them that they aren't the greedy property developers they definitely are. She took a fruit basket over there. They only had a box of flapjacks for sale on the front desk though. Are those yours?'

'No.'

I sense Matt's shrug. 'Anyway, I didn't realise you loved baking so much that you would consider doing it as a business over your dream job.'

I sigh, thinking of the amount of work involved. Much more than I thought it would be. 'To be honest, I enjoyed it more as a hobby. It's a lot of work. It's just one of the only things I can do to earn money without leaving the house.'

I realise the ridiculousness of the words as they leave my mouth and fall on Matt's ears. Suddenly, I see my world from his perspective.

Matt can't understand my life entirely. He is free to come and go as he pleases. He has a phone and spending money and liberal parents. I imagine it's the same for other people my age. As this thought hits me, I experience the biggest pang of regret I have ever felt.

Never have I felt more sorry for myself than I do right now. I can't explain to Matt why. I wish I could. I know that if I told him the full truth right now he wouldn't be so sympathetic.

Not if he knew exactly what I had done. I caused the death of my own mother. What kind of a person does that make me? Certainly not one worthy of Matt's affection and attention.

'I wish I could see you, Chloe.'

'Come to the living room window.' I point in the direction of the lounge but realise it's useless as Matt can't see my hand.

He is there before I am, however. He smiles at me when I pull the net across the single-glazed window.

'You look nice,' he says.

In truth, I don't know what I look like. I haven't thought of my appearance since the day I went out with him on our date. It doesn't seem to bother him.

He presses his hand to the glass. I raise mine to meet his. Aside from the small amount of warmth reaching my fingers, he feels a million miles away.

A moment is short-lived, however. A flicker of movement behind Matt sends my stomach plummeting through the ground.

Dad stands on our driveway looking at the pair of us, a mixture of horror and fury on his face.

24

Dad is home early. Fuck.

He is never home early. Why is he home early? These are the thoughts my mind is stuck on. I can't even begin to process the amount of trouble I'm in right now.

That's nothing compared to what happens next though.

It all seems to happen in slow motion. Yet I am unable to do anything about it other than watch the scene in horror.

Dad storms straight over to where Matt is standing and shoves him with seemingly all his weight.

Matt falls to the ground with a crunch upon the gravel. He only turns his gaze away from me at the last second. Too late to save himself.

Dad's face is an alarming picture of fury. I've never seen him so angry. His eyes are glazed over scarily. He looks possessed, even.

'What are you doing on my property?!' he yells at Matt. 'I told you never to come here again!'

He delivers a kick to Matt's ribs, causing him to wince in pain.

At this point, I realise I am screaming too. I bang on the glass, begging Dad to stop. I'm locked inside the house, and I can only watch as my father continues his frenzied attack, delivering various kicks upon a helpless Matt. He rolls over with his arm covering his face. His perfect teeth his father the dentist has invested a lot in are stained red.

'Dad, stop!' I scream. It's like he can't hear me.

Dad reaches down and takes a fistful of Matt's hoodie in his hands. 'Why don't you answer me? I told you to stay away from my daughter! You dare to throw stones at her bedroom window in the middle of the night, trying to get her attention. Yes – I know that was you! How dare you come to my house after you've been warned?'

Matt manages to spit something out along with some blood. I'm sure I hear the words, 'Not your house,' amongst it.

These magic words seem to bring an end to the chaos. Dad freezes with his fist raised in anticipation above Matt's face. But now he stops. Suddenly, it's my dad's turn to look horrified.

I can virtually hear the wheels turning inside my father's mind. With frightening speed, my dad now lifts a wincing Matt to his feet and forcefully marches him down the driveway.

He says something in a low voice to Matt before pushing him away. Matt disappears behind the hedge that blocks the country lane from view. Dad promptly turns back towards the house. His face is thunder. I've never been more afraid of my father than I am right now.

He storms past the bag of shopping he dropped with the shock of seeing my guest.

His key is shoved roughly into the lock. The front door is slammed, locking the two of us firmly inside together.

Then there is silence. An ominous horrible silence that I wish he would punctuate with shouting orders, or some kind of criticism. But there's nothing. Just the horrible quiet where I'm left to wonder what on earth he will do next.

I find my courage. I use it to take a cautious step into the hallway where I find my father staring through the front door as though watching the past version of himself launching the attack upon Matt in third person.

Supposedly the replay is complete when my father places a hand on each side of his head and grips his bristly hair like a man possessed. 'What have I done?'

It's only now that I realise I have tears running down my face. 'We have to go and check Matt is okay,' I say to him. 'I think he is really injured.'

Dad shakes his head, muttering almost to himself rather than me. 'No. No, he could walk. He left under his own steam. Some broken ribs. Some cuts. That's all. It's me who is really in trouble here. I was the one who attacked him. Besides, he said...'

Dad groans and drops his hands. 'The boy will go running straight to the police. They'll realise who we are and then it's all over. For both of us.'

'I'm so sorry, Dad. I should have told him to leave straight away. I should have pretended I wasn't here like you told me to. Then none of this would have happened.'

Dad doesn't seem to be listening to me again. His eyes are glazed over. He is clearly thinking fast. 'One hour. Maybe two. That's all we've got. Then we need to be out of here. For good.'

'What?'

'You heard me, Chloe. Go upstairs and grab your backpack. Pack every photograph you own. There should only be a few. Take all the cash I gave you recently. Pack some underwear and socks and warm clothing. Put on as many layers as you can comfortably wear too.'

'But, Dad–'

'Don't argue! Just go and do it. Now! We are leaving in ten minutes. Move!'

I force my shaking legs up the stairs. I have to grab the handrail to stop myself stumbling. I'm shaking all over in fact as I grab the little old backpack I've had since I was little. I think it came from my first home. On the day Mum was killed.

I've never really had any use for it other than playing around in my room or, occasionally, on the walks Dad has taken me on. The smaller pockets are still stuffed with long dried-up conkers and pine cones. I shake them out hurriedly onto the threadbare carpet of my room.

I've dreamt for years of leaving this house. Now the idea of being forced out of it terrifies me.

Where will we go? Does dad have a plan? I grab the little tin at the bottom of my wardrobe and stuff it into the silly little girl's bag in my hand. I realise now it is adorned with a teddy bear print down one side. It's never seemed more ridiculous.

I can only fit enough underwear for a week and my college books won't go in, not even with me bending the corners as I am right now.

Dad appears in the doorway behind me. 'Leave those,

you stupid girl! Only take important things. We have to hurry! Do you have any idea what will happen to us if we are caught?'

He drags me from my room once he is satisfied I have the things he instructed. He leaves me in the hall downstairs with our backpacks whilst he runs out to the shed in the back garden.

He returns with a canister, sloshing the liquid deliberately around the place frantically as he goes. Strong fumes hit my nostrils as he splashes it up the stairs I meticulously dusted and polished just weeks ago.

'Dad, what are you doing? What is that stuff?'

He ignores me, giving the living room the same treatment, stopping briefly to snatch at a framed crayon picture from my childhood. He smashes it on the floor and slides the drawing from the shards, before stuffing it hastily into his pocket. 'Grab your bag.'

He pushes me out through the front door, and I almost step on a New York cheesecake spilling from Dad's bag of abandoned groceries. My favourite dessert. Dad was coming home to surprise me. Instead, he was the one who had the shock.

I catch sight of a bright glow of flame that erupts before my father slams the door shut.

I'm pulled by the arm to the bottom of our driveway, my over-stuffed backpack hanging from my shaking fist. It hits my thighs as we go.

When I look over my shoulder at the beginning of our lane, I see flickering orange behind the glass of the living room window where Matt and I had had our exchange less than half an hour earlier.

Then we round the corner and the home I've spent

twelve years hiding in is gone. I know I will never see it
again.

25

The real world is a shock, a vivid assault on the senses after my years in a quiet village where nothing ever happens. Dad rushes us to Bamford railway station just a few minutes from our home. We get on the first train that arrives. And then another.

Dad doesn't seem to care where we end up... unless he has meticulously planned this hypothetical journey without telling me. Either way, he is only intent on getting us out of the village. Away from the only home I've ever known.

I want to tell him that I'm sorry. But the words seem so feeble and useless in the harsh reality that we are now facing.

At the first train station, I think we are leaving and stepping into the city. It just turns out that Dad is stuffing something from his bag into the nearest public bin. It's a load of paperwork. Old bank statements and a driver's licence.

I catch sight of the image on the photo ID, but it's someone I don't recognise. An old man. Where did Dad get that?

He stuffs a few more items in with the rubbish: a wallet, some photographs and faded old postcards. I don't dare ask him about this. He shoots me a look that says I shouldn't dare question him.

We return to the station for more train-hopping. What overwhelms me the most is the sheer amount of people around. It feels too much. Dad and I are exposed without the protection of our familiar cottage where we have hidden for as long as I can remember.

There are people everywhere. Strangers with paper cups of coffee. In every direction, there is a new face.

Everyone has a phone in their hand, taking pictures of something or other or simply staring at the screens.

A young man almost walks into me in Sheffield train station, too intent on staring at the device in his hand and not looking where he's going.

Dad pulls me out of his way before a collision, muttering angrily to himself. 'We shouldn't be here.'

I blink back tears, not daring to look in the direction of a scary-looking security guard watching everyone as they file past.

We get on another train and end up in Leicester. There aren't any seats that aren't around a table, so Dad gets me to settle in a flip-down seat in between carriages. I feel like an inmate switching prisons. My jailor grips a bar as he stands over me, keeping a close watch on his charge, eyeing others as they pass by.

I try and fail not to cry. We have lost everything. It's all because of me. I bow my head so Dad can't see my tears.

When I glance up at the glass door to the carriage, I notice a smartly dressed woman watching me from her table seat.

At first, I think she has recognised me. *Please, no,* I think. *That's the last thing I need. Dad will go ballistic. I don't know what he will do.*

Then I notice the lady seems annoyed at my upset. She glances away and back a few times. Then she gets up. I pray she doesn't come in this direction to talk to Dad.

Luckily she isn't. Part of me thinks she is going down the carriage to speak to someone in charge. The driver maybe?

It seems she only wanted to switch seats, however. She slips into an aisle seat further down the carriage, facing the opposite direction. The realisation hits that she just wanted to not have to look at my distress, however subtle the sign.

My father's words ring in my ears. *People are cold in the real world, Chloe. They have no use for beings of integrity like us.*

My tears have dried by the time we get off the train. I think we will board another, but Dad pulls me towards the exit instead.

It's dark by this point and I'm freezing as we step out of the draughty station into the unwelcoming street. I couldn't squeeze into my winter coat at all before we left, so I've got a couple of thin jumpers on above my t-shirt. Plus the hat Dad had forced onto my head before we arrived at the first station.

Dad walks with purpose across the road and we disappear down the nearest street. I see the shadowy outlines of tall buildings in every direction. We couldn't seem any further from our small village than we are right now.

I have a surprise as I glance sideways at my father and see he has a phone in his hand. For one wild moment, I think that it's Matt's. But it looks different somehow. On the screen, I see a simplified view of the streets around us. It doesn't take me long to realise we are following a line on the map. It seems like we walk for an hour or more to reach the end, however.

Our destination seems to be, at first glance, someone's house. I want to ask who lives here but I still don't dare ask Dad any questions.

My father leaves me on a bench nearby as he enters the building alone, pulling a fistful of notes from an envelope in his hand.

Ten minutes later he returns to take me inside. I briefly glimpse an entrance hallway and a dining room with several tables and chairs set up, just like Mrs Turner's guesthouse. Except that this place is a lot more shabby and worn.

Dad leads me straight upstairs to a room on the top floor. It's already unlocked and has his backpack resting beside the larger of the two beds.

'This is where we will stay tonight,' he explains flatly as he locks the door behind us.

The room is small. It's musty, but somehow in a different way than our familiar house. There is a sink with greening taps and a little bar of cracked soap in one corner. I guess this place must be cheap, nothing at all like the luxury hotels I've seen in TV shows and films.

I nod. 'What about after that?'

He shakes his head. 'Don't ask questions, Chloe. Just sit down. We need to get some rest.'

I sink onto the smaller bed. It's hard and the duvet cover has stains on it. It's so far removed from the pretty purple and pink bedspread Dad bought me for my birthday last year. I imagine there won't be anything left of it by now, miles away at home. Poor Bunny too.

A tide of misery threatens to overwhelm me. In fact it

does, despite my attempts to stop it. I bury my face in my hands.

To my surprise, I feel the bed springs give next to me. A comforting arm winds around my shoulders and I sob into my father's chest as I consider everything we've lost. And it's all because of me.

26

I don't get much sleep. That's no surprise to me, but I don't know how anyone who stays here is expected to with a leaky tap dripping all night.

Dad leaves early in the morning, strictly instructing me to stay within the room. He returns close to lunchtime with a bag of food and a set of keys to a flat across the city.

By this point I'm ravenous, having not eaten since lunchtime yesterday. So much so, I actually feel quite sick. Dad hurries us out past the dining room, where the food smells are emanating from, which only makes things worse. I gobble a banana and croissant from the bag of food he bought instead as we walk.

We make the journey to our new accommodation on foot. The city doesn't look so bad in the daylight, or maybe I'm just grateful to have eaten something. Plus it's less of a shock than being abruptly dropped here in the darkness without knowing what was going to happen.

Dad pulls his smartphone out again a few times to check the route. I want to ask him how long he has had a phone without telling me. Matt must have been right. Everyone needs a phone to exist, he had said. Even my father has one, it turns out.

Poor Matt. I've been fretting about him all night. Is he okay? I can't be sure how bad his injuries were. Did Dad downplay them? I wonder what he thinks of me now that I've caused him so much pain.

I don't think it would be unreasonable of him to regret ever meeting me. I'm starting to, but not because I don't like him.

Will I ever see him again?

The flat isn't so bad, or maybe just not as bad as I was expecting it to be after the rundown bed and breakfast. It is one of two within a small converted house much like our own cottage in size. I expect vintage styling and antiques when I step inside the hallway but it turns out I'm wrong. It's more just an entranceway really. There is somewhere for coats and shoes, with black mould and a set of stairs leading to our new first-floor flat.

The main thing that hits me when we step inside is how small it is. In recent years, I'd come to think of our cottage as being small, especially when I saw the house that Matt's parents had renovated. Now it seems we have less than half that space to live in.

There is one bedroom only with a small single bed. It already has furniture, but it's all white and thin, not like the sturdy dark wood of home. Everything is grey-coloured and modern-looking, albeit jaded and uncared for. Pieces are missing here and there.

The lounge, kitchen and dining room are all one room. There is no bath in the bathroom. Just a shower, sink and toilet all crammed in close together. There is black mould everywhere I look in here too.

Beggars can't be choosers; that's one of Dad's favourite phrases. Although he refrains from saying it now. I suppose I should be grateful we still have our freedom. If you can call it that. This flat is making me feel claustrophobic, but I don't dare say it out loud.

My father seems at the edge of what he can cope with as it is. Then there is the air of all this being my fault hanging between us.

I'm grateful it remains unsaid at this point, however. Or maybe I'm not. Perhaps I would prefer it if my dad was to shout at me. Maybe that would clear the air between us? Wouldn't it be easier to resent and hate my father than to feel guilty for ruining everything, as I have done before? It's a much more familiar feeling.

But is that because I've inherited Mum's mental health issue? Whatever it is, something inside me has caused all this. There is no getting away from the fact that everything that has happened is because of me and my inability to do anything right.

Poor Dad. Poor Matt. They would both be better off without me. At least Matt is now. I can't see that I will ever see him again.

I flop down on the bed, exhausted despite the fact it's midday. I'm starting to wish I could find a way to rid the pair of them of me permanently.

Matt would be allowed to grieve and move on with his life and Dad would get his back. No more running. Would he be allowed freedom after keeping me in hiding all these years? Or would the police not care? Somehow, I think he might have to pay a price for being my loyal protector after all this time.

Everything is such a mess.

DAD PULLS the phone away from his ear and jabs at the screen angrily. 'Waste of time,' he mutters to himself as he shuffles with the papers spread over the coffee table. He does some furious crossing out.

'How did it go?' I ask. Although I can already tell his employment search hasn't just come to an end.

'Not good. They want someone with waiting-on experience. I lied, but they can probably tell I have never done that kind of work. Besides, I'm far too old. They want some airhead student they can pay peanuts to and treat like shit.'

Dad's unexpected use of a swear word startles me. I know it's swearing because I heard some just last week. An angry couple were screaming at each other in the street outside our flat. They were calling each other all sorts. Dad said Matt is immoral, but I know he would never talk like that to or about anyone.

'Why can't you find a job like your old one?'

Dad laughs bitterly. 'We lived in an area of outstanding natural beauty. This place barely has anything green. I can't exactly give walking tours around the dog shit park!'

I bristle at my father's use of language again. It doesn't suit him. It unsettles me. 'No, I meant when you worked at the law firm. As a solicitor.'

'I'm working on it. I expect a recruitment agent to get back to me with something more appropriate for my experience and skills. Ah. This might be them now.'

Dad answers the call and makes it so that he can hear the woman speaking even when the phone is on the desk. He wafts me out of the room as he scrambles around for a particular sheet of paper.

I catch sight of the name at the top of the page: William Hart. Dad told me firmly last week that this is his name now. He came back late on our second night with the passport to prove it. I am to forget he was ever called Albert Morris at all.

'What about me?' I asked him as he tucked me in beneath the duvet in the tiny bedroom on one of the first few nights. 'What's my new name?'

'You don't have one. It's not like you need an identity the way we are set up here. You don't officially exist.'

I was disappointed by this. Dad seemed able to become anyone he wanted. 'What if someone asks me my name? What should I tell them?'

'Don't tell them anything. Pretend you don't speak English. If anyone asks, I will tell them you only speak Swedish. That way, no one should talk to you. Don't say a word.'

So far I haven't left the flat at all since we arrived. Dad has been out a few times to get groceries, and I gather he has gone to look for work in person.

'Why didn't you tell me you had a smartphone?' I asked him as he said goodnight yesterday. He looked at me in surprise. 'What difference does it make? I only use it for important communication and things that can't be avoided. That's all. It is prepaid and untraceable, don't worry.'

I had never considered the fact a phone could be traceable. 'Why didn't you tell me you had such a thing?'

Dad cast around then. 'I didn't think I needed to. I hardly

ever used it. I kept it stored away most of the time until I needed it. It wasn't a secret.'

Was Dad's answer satisfactory? The thought bothered me for a while after he kissed me goodnight.

Now he is engaged in friendly banter on that very same phone with this recruitment agent. I've been shooed out into the bedroom but the door is open enough that I can still hear the conversation.

The woman asks Dad about his work history. What he tells her doesn't correlate with my knowledge of his life. I can't tell if he is talking about the time before I can remember, or if he is blatantly making the whole lot up to worm his way into the job.

She seems to be some sort of gatekeeper, this woman. Dad needs to schmooze his way past her, jumping through hoops to get the golden nugget of a job. Why is getting a job so complicated? My father has been going on at me about how expensive the rent is here. I don't know how much we paid for the previous house. I can only assume it was cheaper back in the village with its green, peaceful surroundings and the abundant fresh air.

Here in the city, there is always noise. There's always something going on. Always there is the sound of traffic outside, a car alarm or passing voices. The only bit of greenery I can see is the overgrown garden through the small living room window. The view from the kitchen consists only of the brick wall of the house next door.

I am forbidden from touching the curtains here in the bedroom so I suppose there may be something of an outlook from that room. I want to take a peep, but it's too soon after my biggest mistake ever to take the risk with my father.

I don't quite catch what the woman says on the phone now, something about the hours Dad is available.

He answers back earnestly. 'I'm available every weekday, nine to five.'

'Are you sure you can't extend that a little bit, be a bit more flexible? The company is looking for a finish time of six. With your experience, this job should be a walk-in. The salary is very generous too.'

'I understand that. It sounds great. I just know I'll be a great fit there. But I can't do longer hours than that, I'm afraid.'

'Okay, Will – do people call you Will?'

Dad falters. 'Yes – only my friends though!' he laughs. I can hear the falseness of his voice, and I cringe as I imagine the woman on the phone might be able to also. But maybe she doesn't know him well enough yet.

'Listen, Will. On paper, you are perfect for this job. It's everything you're looking for. I would love to send your details to them. But they are looking for these hours. They were quite particular. Do you have any particular commitments stopping you? Is it kids?'

'Yes, actually. I'm a single dad.'

'Ah, okay. Same! I'm a single mum to twins – a boy and a girl. It's hard, isn't it? Childcare is expensive. How many do you have?'

'Just the one, but she's quite a handful.'

'Awww, bless. How old?'

'She'll turn sixteen soon.'

There is a pause. 'Oh. Okay, Will. I'll tell you what I'll do. I'll have a little word with the company and see if they can arrange those hours for you. Also, I'll keep your details on file and I'll let you know if anything comes up for you. How does that sound?'

There is a pause from my father this time and it sounds like he has gritted teeth now. 'Great. Just great.'

My heart sinks. I don't need to be on the other side of the door to see the expression on my father's face right now. I can just imagine it.

What I don't anticipate is his reaction after he has ended the call.

I have to stifle a gasp as something hard gets launched across the room. I hear it hit the thin wall separating the lounge from the bathroom, followed by a groan of frustration from my father.

Yes, my existence is creating an inconvenience for him. Though I know he will never admit it.

27

D ad is clearly under as much stress as ever as we have breakfast a few days later. He is red and blotchy in the face as he sits at the dining table and sips his scalding hot coffee. He has wet patches under the arms of his polo shirt too.

None of the hobs are working in the kitchen. Dad can't have his usual boiled egg with toast. It's been his everyday breakfast for as far back as I can remember, aside from a couple of odd days recently.

Today could have done with not being one of those days, as Dad has a job interview this morning. He seems particularly nervous about it, stiff and upright in his chair as he waits for me to butter his toast.

'Right into the corners of the bread,' he barks out of habit, watching me with the loaded butter knife. It seems half-hearted; a habitual attempt at his usual rhetoric.

He mutters angrily through mouthfuls of food when his plate is in front of him. 'Breakfast is the most important meal of the day. That isn't my rule! It's always been said.

Haven't you heard that from other sources other than me, Chloe?'

'Yes, Dad.'

'Where have you heard that?'

I look up at him in surprise. 'I don't know. In one of my books, I think.'

'Which one?'

'I'm not sure. Maybe it wasn't a book. It might have been a cartoon, like Scooby-Doo or something. Or maybe Peppa Pig...'

He scoffs at this. 'I've been too liberal with you. Letting you watch all sorts of rubbish. I thought I was being kind. *Too* kind, I've been. Something went wrong somewhere. Look at how you turned out. Obstinate and defiant. Just like your mother.'

I find I suddenly can't swallow my toast very easily. It gets stuck in my throat as my eyes burn.

Dad abruptly gets up from his seat. So abruptly, some of his coffee spills over onto the dining table. Luckily there isn't a tablecloth. The scuffed and scratched surface could benefit from one, if not only to cover the graffiti here and there.

My father returns moments later, standing over me. He nods at my plate of food. 'I need you to finish your breakfast.'

'I will.'

'No, it needs to be down before I go out.'

I look up at him. 'Why?'

'I need you to take one of these.' He shakes a capsule from a white bottle in his hand. 'These should not be taken on an empty stomach.'

I stare at the bottle. 'What are they?'

His hand blocks the label from my prying eyes. A bold

warning about not taking too much is just about visible through his thick fingers. 'They are to help you relax whilst I'm away. I know you've been very anxious lately. Your behaviour is out of control too. I'm worried about you.'

'Well, I am stressed. But that's only to be expected. We left our home. I've left everything I know behind.'

'I know. That was through your doing in the first place, though, wasn't it? And all because you were too hyperactive to sit still. You couldn't stay in the one place where you would have been safe, despite my instructions.'

'I'm sorry, I–'

'Won't do it again?'

I nod. 'I promise. I won't go outside again without you.'

'You've made that promise only to break it again too many times, Chloe. I can't take that risk.'

'I don't need medication. You said you didn't want me to take anything.'

He sighs impatiently. 'That was before. I've realised it's more cruel to you to let you suffer with your problems. You told me you hated me leaving you alone at home, and that was before you even met that horrid boy. Supposedly.'

My father scrutinises me over his glasses.

'It was,' I say quickly, worried he might be trying to catch me out on a lie I haven't told. 'I swear. It used to feel like I was going to die.'

He winces. 'You see? What kind of father was I not to have given you something sooner? I was too busy trying to provide for us financially. I thought you were exaggerating. But I've watched you more closely since. I've noticed you are very distressed in your sleep.'

'Am I?'

'Yes. Do you have a lot of nightmares?'

I nod as I consider my nighttime torment. 'I was having one last night. I didn't sleep very well at all. I've been awake since four.'

'I thought so.' He presses a blue and white capsule into my palm. Just swallow this down with water.'

I hesitate, turning it over in my hand. I've never taken anything more than paracetamol for a headache. This medicine looks scary. 'What will happen to me when I take it?'

'Nothing untoward. It will help you relax. It should stop your mind from running away with itself. You have such wild ideas, sweetheart. I want to help you make them stop. You might feel sleepy at first and it's all right if you want to spend the day in bed. Your body will get used to the drug eventually and you won't worry about taking one every morning with breakfast.'

'I don't want to.'

He sighs impatiently, squeezing his eyes shut. 'There you go again. So defiant. Why can't you just do as you are told for once?'

I want to point out I did as I was told for twelve years without incident, but I think better of it.

He checks the time on his phone with a small groan. 'Come on, sweetheart. I need to get going. This interview is more of a trial. I won't be back until this evening. I absolutely can't leave until I know you will be okay.'

Reluctantly, I pop the capsule into my mouth and swallow it down with a big gulp of water. It leaves a sweet taste on my tongue. I turn back to my toast and chew.

Dad's shoulders visibly slump with relief. 'Good. That's better. I hope you feel better soon.'

'I don't feel any different.'

He laughs. 'You won't right away. It will take a while to

start working. As I said, you will likely be very tired today, so just rest.'

He checks the time again. 'Right. I'd better get going. Your arguing has cost me time.'

'I'm sorry. Will you be late?'

'Not if I hurry along now.'

I'm pulled into a firm hug. 'I love you.'

'I love you too, Dad. Please come home.' I want to add the word 'safe' or 'soon' to that, but I can't think which one, so I leave it at that.

Dad laughs. 'Of course I will. Take it easy today. Have a go at the puzzle book I got for you. I'll be back before you know it. Remember, don't answer the door to anyone. Don't go near the windows either.'

'I won't.'

'Good.'

Dad's keys jangle as they lock the door up tight. He pushes down the handle to be sure. Then I hear him run through the same procedure with the outer door downstairs.

Usually, I would descend into a pit of nerves upon my father's absence; I have done so every day since we got here. Today, however, I feel quite calm.

I wonder if the medication is starting to have an effect. I do feel quite tired now that I come to think of it. I yawn as I clear away the breakfast things.

I push myself to do the dishes and wipe down the table and then I take my father's advice and go to bed with my puzzle book and a pen.

I find I can't concentrate on any of the puzzles though. At lunchtime, I give up and stop fighting the wave of tiredness.

I lie back and pull the duvet higher up over me. It's not long before I slip away into the best sleep I have had for ages.

28

D
ad gets the job after completing his trial day. He
won't tell me much about it, just the hours, which
are shorter than before. He isn't happy about the
position, which makes me suspect it's low-paid and one he
isn't suited for. I appreciate he is doing the best he can for us
under the circumstances.

I suspect I would probably be more pleased about Dad
finding a job if it wasn't for the medication I now have to
take. I feel it is dulling my senses. My real thoughts and feelings are lost somewhere beneath the layer of drugs that must
be coursing through my system.

I express this to Dad over breakfast one day a few weeks
later.

He tuts impatiently as he attacks his egg with a spoon.
'Chloe, we've been through this. Your medication is doing
you so much good. I've seen such a big change in you lately.
You have been sleeping better. You have behaved yourself
too, haven't you?'

'Yes. I have done everything you have told me to.'

'What about nightmares? They have been better now that you take your pills, haven't they?'

I shrug. 'I suppose. I am sleeping much better.'

'Good. I'm so happy for you. Keep up the good work.'

'I want to. I just feel so tired all the time.'

'That's natural. You're a teenager. You have a lot of growing and developing to do. Completely normal.'

'But I wasn't this tired before.'

Dad tilts his head at me with a sceptical look. He doesn't believe me. 'Are you sure?'

'Yes, positive. It's the pills making me tired. I've slept so much lately. Maybe I could stop taking them.'

Dad nods. 'Of course, you can stop taking them if you think they are giving you side effects.'

'Thanks. They are.'

'Hmm. The thing is, sweetheart, you've been so much better since you started them. I wouldn't want to see you become unwell again. I can't in good conscience allow that.'

I tear off a piece of buttery toast. I didn't have a choice, did I?

Dad gets up and fetches the bottle of pills from the high shelf in the kitchen cupboard. 'Just take your medicine like a good girl, now.'

I take one of the pills from him reluctantly.

He rubs my back reassuringly like I'm a toddler who doesn't want to eat her vegetables. 'If you don't have the will to be better, Chloe, then please, do it for your father. What do you say?'

I pop the pill in my mouth as I have done for weeks and take a big gulp of orange juice. I look up at Dad and give him a reassuring nod back.

It's when Dad's gaze doesn't leave mine that I know I'm in trouble.

His tone changes. 'Open your mouth, Chloe.'

I quickly try and manoeuvre the retained capsule from beneath my tongue and swallow without him seeing, but he grabs hold of my chin unexpectedly and squeezes my cheeks.

The capsule lands in Dad's hand. He leaves his palm flat for what feels like ages to demonstrate my disobedience.

'I'm sorry,' I say finally to break the silence. 'I just want to feel like me again.'

He shakes his head with a bitter laugh. 'I'm only trying to help you. What do you think I'm trying to do, poison you?'

'No. I just want things to go back to normal. I want to go home and for everything to be like it was before.'

'Normal? We can't go back. Our home is gone, sweetheart. This is our life now. You made that decision for us. You need to get better if you want us to be okay. I'm doing a job I hate so that we have enough money to live on and I can look after you. The least you can do is take one tiny dose of medicine to help me. It's supposed to make you less disobedient, less unhappy.'

There is silence as I consider this. Finally, I can't take it anymore. I snatch the pill from my father's still outstretched hand and put it back in my mouth.

The outer shell is partially dissolved now and the contents taste sweeter than ever. I down my orange juice, not stopping until I can put the empty glass back on the table.

Dad bows his head. His voice is quiet. 'I have to go or I am going to be late for work.'

This wasn't a victory for him. It feels like I have turned this into a battle of wills. A war for moral superiority. My father wants to help me. I let him down. It's that simple. Why did I ever imagine there was more to it?

My dad goes downstairs to fetch his coat and shoes, then pauses with a hand on the door handle. 'I hope you will have a good hard think about your actions whilst I'm away today.'

I hear the lock on the door downstairs and know that he is gone.

I'm left alone with a guilty feeling sinking through me. It was foolish of me to try and deceive my father. He can see right through me, always.

I follow the routine of clearing up after breakfast. As I'm doing the dishes, my mind strays up to the high cupboard where Dad keeps the bottle of capsules. I want to find out more about them but I can't. Dad wouldn't like it.

I shake the thoughts away and move over to the small two-seater sofa where I arrange it for day use. Dad sleeps on this at night, as there is only one bedroom.

He keeps complaining about how uncomfortable it is. Another thing that is my fault. I'm always offering to swap places with him so he can take the bed, but he won't hear of it. He is too polite.

I fold the duvet up and place it over the back of the sofa; there aren't any large storage cupboards in this tiny flat.

It's not so quiet this morning in our first-floor flat. The sound of a television comes from somewhere below me. I hear the jingle of a TV show now and then. There is a set in our living room too, a thin one. Not like our big glass-fronted box at the cottage. Dad must have made sure this new one was disconnected before I arrived. There isn't a VHS player either. I so wish there was.

There is a sound like canned laughter and then a toilet flush from the flat downstairs.

In a way, it's kind of nice to think someone is close by, even if I never see them. Dad doesn't let me near the windows. I have to do what I am told from now on.

I suppose that is my medication talking, making me less reckless.

Although it's not like I didn't know how to be good before I started taking it. I just made some bad decisions, not knowing what the consequences could be. For anyone else, that wouldn't be a big deal. For me, it's been devastating.

My mind wanders back to the kitchen cupboard. I'm not feeling quite as tired today.

It's funny how I can change from one day to the next. I would have thought the medicine would make me tired all the time, not just when I first started taking it.

I still don't even know what the stuff is called. It wouldn't hurt to take a peep, would it?

29

I stand and listen at the front door for noises, in case there is a warning that Dad might unexpectedly reappear. I judge the coast clear after a good ten minutes or so and move a dining chair over to the cupboard.

The bottle of medication is on the top shelf. I am careful to note its exact position ready for when I replace it in a moment.

The bottle doesn't reveal much. Half of the label is missing; it's been ripped off. Only the back part of the label remains, the part with all the warnings. And there certainly are quite a few. The common side effects include; tiredness, dizziness, nausea, weight gain, and blurred vision. The list goes on.

WARNING: Not to be taken by those under 25, as they may experience worsening depression and/or suicidal thoughts. This medicine increases the risk of stroke, heart failure and fast or irregular heartbeat. Use with caution.

*In case of severe adverse reaction, seek immediate medical
help.*

Reading this label certainly explains a lot. No wonder
I've been so tired and out of sorts. Why did my dad hide this
from me? Is my behaviour that bad that he would take this
kind of risk?

Other words and phrases from the bottle jump out at me.

*Rapid speech, trouble sleeping, irritability, impulsive
actions, severe restlessness. Feelings of hostility and
aggression.*

Don't those all sound like me in the first place, before
Dad even produced this little white bottle? Are they doing
more harm than good to my mental and physical health?

Besides, it sounds like it should have been prescribed
under a doctor's supervision. Where did Dad get this bottle
from anyway?

A thought strikes me all of a sudden. What if Dad has
been giving me these for years? He didn't seem all too
concerned about leaving me unattended after taking the first
one at breakfast recently. It would explain everything if it
turned out I'd been dosed with this for years without even
knowing.

My father stressed these pills should be taken with food.
Dad is almost religious about eating breakfast at the same
time every day. What if this was the reason?

He could have slipped something into my morning juice
without me realising. These pills are quite sweet. They could
easily be slipped into orange juice without me noticing a
thing.

The only time I missed breakfast as long as I can remember was when we arrived in the city. And I had felt quite queasy on that morning. Had I been medicated without my knowledge on an empty stomach?

What if my impulsive behaviour lately has been down to this?

I replace the bottle exactly where I found it to the very millimetre. But I am no more reassured than I was before.

I feel more anxious than ever. The thing I get from time to time where my heart beats irregularly threatens to start now. Is that a side effect of the medication? Would it be happening naturally now anyway? It's really hard to separate the two.

I'm about to step down and replace the dining room chair when something catches my attention. On top of the kitchen cupboard, there is an old chocolate tin. It's not dissimilar to the one beneath my bed that once presumably held toffee, the one where I keep all my photographs and personal things.

Curiosity sparks in me. It might be what the bottle of pills describes as impulsive behaviour, but I decide to take the tin down and open the lid.

For a moment, I think that this must have been left here by a previous tenant. There is no mistaking my father's distinctive handwriting on various bits of paper, however; tight and neat, but jagged around the edges.

These must be the personal items he brought with him from the house. He doesn't have much else, just some clothes and toiletries. Everything else was left behind in such a hurry. Burned and turned to ash by now, probably.

These things must be very valuable to him. Part of me wants to return the tin and pretend I was never snooping here. The other part of me – an impulsive side, shall we say – wants to see what is in here.

Especially when I spot the edge of a birth certificate. It has Dad's new name on it. I've never seen a birth certificate before. There are more below it, faded and crinkled. The sight of a more worn document with a female name catches my attention. Ruby Adams. She has the same birthday as me, the 2nd of January 2008.

Has Dad prepared a false identity for me, after all? Perhaps he didn't mean what he said about me not officially existing. I can only hope it means he has plans for me to leave this flat one day and live under a different name. Maybe I could hide in plain sight too? The idea that I could one day go outside like a normal person gives me a glimmer of hope.

Then I notice the date of issue. It's March 2011. I must've been three years old at the time. Not recent. I don't understand. This must have been issued before everything went wrong. Mum was still alive at this point. I can never forget the day she died: the 16th of March 2012. Why would somebody request a birth certificate for me back then under a different name? Everything was above board in those days. We were free.

For a wild few moments, my mind comes up with all sorts of fantastical answers to this question. My heart pounds excitedly as I consider the possibility that I might have a twin sister out there somewhere, just like the siblings in the story of *Parent Trap*.

Then the reality clicks into place. Something stirs in my memory banks and I know immediately I'm right. Ruby is my real name.

Mum never called me Chloe.

'My name is Ruby,' I whisper out loud to reaffirm this fact. I have a flash of memory of being on a swing on a sunny day, a stunning blue sky overhead. Mum is in front of me, saying my name and laughing, one hand holding up a camera, the other resting on her stomach.

Dad never told me I had another name. Annoyance pounds in my head for a few minutes as I consider how my father could have kept something so big from me.

After a few moments, I decide it's not such a big deal. What difference does it make when all is said and done?

It occurs to me that my abrupt change of heart has to do with the medication rushing through me. Is it mellowing me out and dulling my sense of anger? Sometimes, I guess. Others, I'm on the other end of the spectrum.

At least Dad kept my birthday the same. This feels important for some reason.

I wonder why someone requested a copy of my birth certificate almost a year before Mum was killed though. What do people do with birth certificates anyway?

Dad seems to need one for getting a job, but why would a three-year-old need one? It's just another one of those questions I don't yet know the answer to. I'm starting to wonder if I ever will, being locked up in here.

The next item in the tin is a passport. This is the first time I have seen one of these in real life too. I have never seen the photo of me inside it before either. I'm struck by how young I am. A small child. I hardly have any pictures of me at all. I look at the details of the ID.

The date of issue is just two months after the birth certificate. Is that significant?

An odd-looking black-and-white photograph draws my attention underneath more paperwork. I lift a stack of paper, remembering how it went. My breath catches in my chest when I see what the subject of the photograph is.

It's a distorted black-and-white photograph of a baby. An ultrasound image. I've seen one before, in the medical textbook in our old attic.

This must have been me before I was born, I think. It's creepy to look at. Yet I can't stop staring at it. When I'm finally able to tear my gaze away from the baby's unborn face, I notice more of Dad's handwriting.

In remembrance of Emily, whose light still shines. On 16th March 2012, your memory is eternally cherished within me. Alongside your mother, Rachel, you will live on in my heart forever. I hope you two find happiness and peace. I wish you knew how loved you were, my angels.

I forget all about the exact positions of the various bits and pieces inside the tin. I'm still holding the dark photograph, but my fingers have gone numb.

Only one thing registers in my shocked brain. My mother was pregnant when I killed her.

I extinguished the life of my little sister too that day.

30

My heart pounds in my ears. On some level, I'm aware I'm getting dizzy. I seem to spend a long time staring at the ultrasound photo and the inscription underneath.

Dad is always calling me the light of his life. I had no idea there were once three of us in receipt of his affections. Two, however, have been snuffed out by my actions. One stupid moment. It's cost all of us everything. So much pain. Too much. There is something deeply wrong with me, I think.

The inscription haunts me, as though I can hear Dad reading it aloud. I know I can never forget the words he has written so profoundly. They will haunt me forever.

I can't bear to look at the ultrasound image any longer. It's causing my breath to catch in my chest. With trembling hands, I try and replace everything carefully in the chocolate tin. I can't remember where anything goes and I am shaking so much I can hardly get the lid on straight.

I get up shakily onto the dining chair and attempt to

slide the tin back on top of the cupboard. I lose my footing and the whole thing comes crashing down sending bits of paper and documents everywhere.

'No!'

I'll never be able to get everything back inside without Dad noticing something afoot. He is so observant. I can't breathe as I stare around at the contents of the old tin.

I fail to take a full breath in as I drop to the floor and start picking up the pieces. Three ruined lives. All because of me. I don't know how I can carry on after learning this.

I had thought that being ripped from the only home I've truly known was the worst thing that could happen. I was wrong. The cottage is just a physical place, after all. What I've just learned is devastating.

I wish I had never opened that tin. I couldn't feel more like a real-life Pandora.

I stop scrabbling around trying to gather papers for a moment and sit up straight, trying to take a full breath in. I'm rewarded for my troubles with a round of palpitations so bad, I must grasp the kitchen cupboard handle for support.

The room blurs around me. I still can't breathe.

I use the back of the sofa to pull myself upright. Then the thing that I've been fighting the last few minutes becomes unbearable. I rush to the bathroom just in time to vomit into the toilet.

My dizziness doesn't abate. The room spins around me. I stagger towards the bathroom sink and grasp the edge for support. I splash cold water over my face and hands as I hope to wash away what threatens to consume me.

The trouble is when I close my eyes, I can only see the face of my unborn sister and hear the echo of my mother's laughter in my ears.

When I open my eyes again, I see a scared girl looking back from the dirty mirror. She seems like a stranger, finally untangling the threads of a past woven in deceit. It makes me doubt everything I know.

The items in the tin aren't the only things troubling me now though. The list of side effects I read on the medication bottle alarms me too. I feel like I'm experiencing every one of them.

I certainly wish I had never been born now. That's a suicidal thought, right?

I'm dizzy, I've just been sick and I can't breathe. My heartbeat is irregular too. I resent Dad for forcing me to swallow today's pill despite my unwillingness. I know he was only trying to help me, despite everything I've done to ruin his life. I just wish I had never had to take those pills.

I clutch at my chest breathlessly and will my heartbeat to steady itself.

'Please,' I beg in a terrified whisper. It's never been this bad before. Not ever.

Water still drips from my face as I move back into the kitchen.

I reach up for the medication bottle, the contours cool beneath my trembling fingers and reread the warnings.

I'm reacting to the medication. There is no other explanation. The warning label says to seek immediate medical help if the side effects are severe.

What should I do? Dad never took me to see a doctor when we lived in our cottage. Not once. There is no way he would do it now when we have taken hiding to a new level.

There is nothing I can do. Either I blow our cover and try and get some help, or I stay here and let my heart slowly fail.

I wish Dad would come back. I don't care how much

trouble I would be in for looking through his things and investigating the medicine. I just want him to be here with me. I miss him so much right now.

I feel so helpless. In a desperate attempt to regain some control, I fumble with the bottle. It's a sudden wave of impulsiveness, the same one that got me in this mess, that causes me to unscrew the lid and tip the lot down the sink. The capsules hit the steel, bouncing in all directions like the documents. Some roll down the plughole, helped along by my fingers.

I'm going to have to stand up to Dad on this one. I don't know how, but I have to. That's if I survive the afternoon, anyway. I can't keep taking these things.

'I'm sorry, Dad,' I whisper, my face crumpling at last. The weight of everything presses down on me.

'Sorry for what?'

I gasp and spin around to see my father shutting the inner door behind him. He looks at me in surprise.

He stops dead. His eyes move from my tear-soaked face to the out-of-place dining chair.

Then they take in the vintage confectionery tin and the various bits of paper strewn all over the floor.

His mouth opens in horror. It is a few moments of horrible silence before he speaks. 'Ruby, what have you done?'

31

My breath is coming in large, heaving sobs by this point.

Dad's face has gone pale like the day he attacked Matt. He is rooted to the spot, keys in hand, as he stares around at the mess I have made.

'I'm so sorry, Dad,' I manage through ragged breaths. 'I didn't mean to. I just wanted to know what I have been taking. I'm having a bad reaction to them!'

Dad's mouth tightens at this. 'You silly girl. I was only trying to help. They were supposed to cure you. I wanted you to be better. Why can't you do as you are told? That was all I ever asked of you.'

'I know! I want to be good. Of course I want to be healthy. But I can't breathe! I think I'm having a heart attack.'

I expect Dad to soften at this, to spring into action and maybe even get me a doctor. Couldn't he arrange for one to come here and give me something to stop all this? I know he won't.

I've suffered through all sorts of illnesses at home. All I

had then was my father nursing me with simple medicines he seemed to acquire with ease. Something tells me this time I need something more complicated.

Instead, my father shakes his head. 'You aren't having a heart attack. There is no way what is inside those capsules could cause one.'

'I know you think they are safe, but–'

'Don't be so silly, Ruby. You were supposed to trust me. I've only ever done what is best for you. Do you think I would intentionally hurt you?'

'No. Of course not. But there is something really wrong with me right now!'

'That's just your anxiety. Trust me.' Dad comes closer to me, pocketing his keys. 'I think you are having a panic attack. I get them too sometimes.'

'You do?'

'Yes. I think you've inherited that from me. It's a case of nature versus nurture here because I've always hidden my attacks from you.'

'I didn't know.'

'Of course you didn't.' Dad takes hold of my hands. 'Now just breathe with me. Deep breath all the way in. Hold it for the same amount of time. Then all the way out. Good. Repeat.'

Dad guides me through deep breathing for a few minutes. I go through with it at first to humour him, to show him that it won't have any effect. It will prove it is the medication he forced on me that caused this. But then, miraculously, my breathing becomes more normal. My heart rate steadies too. The palpitations are becoming further apart.

'There you go, sweetheart. Better?'

'Yes. I can't believe it.'

Dad releases his grip on my hands. 'You are the light of my life, Ruby. I'm not going to snuff you out. Look.'

Dad reaches around me and takes one of the white and blue capsules from the sink. 'These pills were never going to hurt you.'

He twists the capsule apart and tips the granular contents out onto the draining board. 'What does that look like to you?'

I look at the clear crystals closely. I was expecting something more powdery and white, like painkillers. 'It looks almost like sugar.'

'That's because it *is* sugar.' Dad sighs. 'These pills are nothing but ordinary sugar inside a gelatine casing. No medicine. Nothing that would be harmful.'

I shake my head in disbelief. 'That can't be true. I've been... different since taking them. My... I've been so tired, for one thing.'

Dad shrugs. 'I've told you, teenagers get tired. They sleep a lot. You have done so for years. You only started analysing yourself when you thought it might be a side effect. I tried to keep the bottle hidden from you so you wouldn't read the label. But I still needed to make you believe you had something solid to cure your anxiety. It needed to look like real medicine so you would believe it. That's the power of the placebo effect.'

Dad drops the empty capsule into the bin. 'It worked too. You finally allowed yourself to relax enough to sleep at night, even in the day sometimes. It eased your fears. But only until you decided not to trust me. As if I would try and poison you. We've been through too much together. I love you too much.'

His voice breaks and he turns away. He lifts his glasses to wipe his eyes.

I stare at the side profile of my father's salt and pepper head with wide eyes. My calming heart sinks as I remember the overly sweet taste of each dose of so-called medicine. Nothing bitter or funny-flavoured.

Of course Dad wasn't drugging me. He had just declared weeks before that he was partly hiding me from the world so I wouldn't be medicated.

I shake my head. 'I'm so sorry, Dad. I should have realised the pills weren't real.'

'No you shouldn't. That would defeat the whole purpose.' Dad sighs heavily. 'We aren't protected here in the city by a sparse population and countryside. That cottage was like our bunker. I wanted you to think you were being given something to relax in this place, behave yourself. If you believed you had something suppressing your inhibitions, then they would be suppressed. People are more likely to come knocking the door here. Or you might be tempted to slip out again. The pills did work too. Obviously too well if you were fretting so much about the side effects.'

'I'm sorry.' It's those empty words again. They do so little as they fall from my mouth. Especially now.

Dad looks crushed. 'I don't understand why you are so determined to make me into a monster. All I have done is try to keep you safe, no matter what.'

'I just thought...'

'You thought what? I don't understand what you are accusing me of, Chloe.'

Dad winces. 'Force of habit. I haven't called you Ruby for years.'

He looks at me and nods towards the paper explosion

from the vintage tin. 'I suppose the cat is out of the bag, or at least the chocolate box.'

He gathers up the fallen documents and the ultrasound photograph. He pauses to stare at it, no doubt reading his own inscription. 'I haven't looked at this for a while.'

'Why didn't you tell me?'

'Tell you what?'

'That Mum was pregnant when she... When she died. I was going to have a little sister. Baby Emily.'

Dad pulls a face at my use of her name as he replaces the lid neatly. 'Let's not dwell on what could have been. Yes, Rachel, your mother, was pregnant. Six months gone, on that... fateful day.'

My eyes widen. 'That's so close to being born. I had no idea.'

'We can't change what happened. I don't want to add more guilt to your burden. I think you already have enough. At least you know why you must never go outside. You are old enough to understand at last. It was such a relief to tell you after keeping that from you for so many years.'

Tears stream down my cheeks silently. Dad fetches himself some tissue to dab at his face and hands me some without looking in my direction. It's like he can't bear to look at me. I don't blame him.

'Why didn't you tell me I had another name?'

He shrugs. 'What difference does it make? When I rescued you from your first ever home, I didn't have a clear plan. I just knew I had to get you out. I dread to think what would have happened if we had stayed.'

Dad stares off through the kitchen window, lost in thought. His eyes are glazed over and I know he can't simply be looking at our view of next-door's brickwork. 'It was a dark time for both of us. I didn't know whether to hide you in plain sight under a false name, or hide you completely.'

'You chose the latter.' I consider how hard all this must have been for Dad, uprooting his life on the spur of the moment to save me. Because of my recent actions, he has had to do it all over again. I wish I could just go back to taking the pills without fretting about them. I wish I could have been a better daughter – to both my parents.

'Yes. Life is hard. No one knows if their decisions are right, only in hindsight. I still believe I made the right decisions back then. I would do it all over again the same way if I had to. I just would have kept a closer eye on you, that's all. Especially lately.'

'Wasn't it hard, calling me by a different name for years without letting on?'

Dad puts a reassuring arm around me. It feels comforting. Not that I deserve to be comforted.

He nods. 'It was strange at first. I kept saying the name Chloe, to remind me. Saying it out loud made it real. At the end of the day, it doesn't matter what you are named. Just as long as you are safe and we are together. It was so important that we stayed together. I never wanted anyone else to get their hands on you. The real world is a horrible place, Ruby. We don't belong there. You are safe with me.'

32

In light of the latest revelations, I am on my best behaviour with Dad. He is on his too. We seem to come to a sort of unspoken agreement. I feel like I understand my father now that I know the truth he has been carrying around all this time. At least now he doesn't have to carry it around alone.

He has also started calling me Ruby again. My real name. It feels nice. Dad has always used my name to tell me off when I've been in trouble. I've come to associate it with being a black sheep, especially in more recent times. It is good to be Ruby again. I feel like it suits me more.

Dad and I have settled on the sofa one afternoon at the weekend. He has some time off work over Christmas, so he doesn't have to leave the house much, which I find a relief.

It's cosy in our flat. I'm starting to get used to it now. It's late afternoon. The lamps are on and Dad has procured a CD player for us to listen to. It's so much faster than the cassette tapes we had in our cottage. We can skip between the tracks with ease instead of having to fast-forward and rewind them.

Dad has managed to find some of his favourites. He sings along to a track with an upbeat melody, but lyrics that become increasingly at odds with the jaunty tune.

I'm going through the puzzle book he bought me and he is reading a gardening magazine. On his current page about growing your own vegetables, he has made a note:

Must do this with Ruby this year!

I look up at him for a second, wondering what is going on inside his head. It doesn't seem to bother him that we don't have a garden any longer, or that he never really did anything with it when we did.

I can't begin to imagine how he plans on doing this. The neighbour downstairs has rights over the tiny front garden and it is clear they have no intention of doing anything with it other than continuing to let their bins overflow into the grass.

I'm not sure how much of the text of the articles Dad is taking in anyway because he keeps leaning into me to emphasise a lyric now and then he is particularly passionate about.

Later on, the music has mellowed out and so has Dad, thankfully. I look up from a crossword I'm stuck on. My mind is still trying to process all the new information I've learned in the past week. 'Dad? What was Mum really like?'

He frowns at his magazine. He seems annoyed that I've interrupted his moment enjoying his music and reading. 'Oh, she was a lovely person. Warm. She tried her best, despite her troubles. It was difficult though, I won't lie, especially towards the end.'

I frown too. 'Why did you marry someone if you knew it was going to be difficult living with them?'

He rests down his magazine. 'It's not that straightforward. People can be different when you first meet them, showing a different side of themselves. They can charm and coerce their way into your life, and tell you what you want to hear. They make themselves seem perfect for you. The other person is likely to believe them. Especially, if they are looking for love when Mr or Mrs Wonderful comes along.'

'Do you think Mum deceived you?' I prompt Dad, who seems to have slipped into a reverie, staring at the black television screen opposite the sofa as though it is replaying his life.

'Hmm?' Dad looks at me, startled, as though he has forgotten I was here. 'Oh, no. Well, a little, I suppose. Our relationship was complicated. Things were good when we first met. Then, as I said, people change and become relaxed with the other person. They let their true selves show.'

I am quiet for a moment as I consider this. I frame this wisdom around the situation with me and Matt. Would things have played out similarly between us if it had been allowed to?

'How did you and Mum meet?'

Dad smiles. 'It was an interesting story, actually. You know your mother was a therapist, don't you?'

I nod.

'I had another partner before I met your mother. We were having problems. Her behaviour took a nosedive after a few years together.'

'Like it had with my mum?'

'Yes. So in a foolish attempt to salvage the relationship, I suggested couples therapy. I went ahead and booked it with Rachel, your mother. Marie never showed up. Not once. I guess, that's when I knew it was over between us. It wasn't a bad thing, however, because I met your mother. Eventually, of course, it led me to have you. Plus, Rachel helped me through some childhood trauma I had been carrying around. She taught me I could let it go. I was disappointed that I hadn't made more of my life until then, but that didn't matter anymore after a while. My biggest achievement was you and your sister.'

I consider this for a few moments. It seems my existence has done nothing but devastate Dad's life. 'Are you sure having me was worth it? I mean, don't you miss your old life?'

My father looks at me with a bewildered smile. 'Of course you were worth it! I told you, I would do everything the same way again. I miss your mother terribly. She and your sister have left a massive hole in my heart. They are gone and I will miss them forever. Being with you keeps my ticker patched up, if not healed. As long as I don't lose you, everything will be okay. I just know it.'

He reaches out and squeezes my knee. There is a slight crease across his forehead as he looks at me before returning to his reading. He hums to one of his lesser favourites on the music player.

I watch him for a few minutes more. Dad is so stiff and regimented. He has rules and likes things to be done in a very specific way. Aside from the mental health troubles my father describes, my overall impression of my mother is that she was more easy-going, happy and relaxed.

If she was a therapist too, wouldn't she be a master of her

emotions if she was dispensing advice to others and guiding them through hard times?

I don't have much to go on, of course. Just some vague memories and photographs. I suppose everyone is all smiles in those. It's more just a feeling I get when I think of her.

But this idea of a happy spirit, full of life and maybe even a little mischief, is something I'm finding hard to reconcile with my father. How did the two of them fit together as a couple?

The phrase chalk and cheese springs to mind. Perhaps I'm only seeing the side of Mum that she showed to Dad when they first met. Maybe I'm making the same mistakes as him? It wouldn't surprise me, as Dad and I have similar personality traits. I'm so glad he shared the fact he gets panic attacks too. All these years he had kept that hidden from me. It's a sign he trusts me now, on a more adult level. An equal. That can only be a good thing.

There is something else that bothers me though. 'Dad?'

'Hmm?'

'Where did you get such a convincing medicine bottle from? Did you buy those capsules already filled?'

'No.' He looks up from his magazine again. 'Why do you ask?'

'I just wondered.'

He seems to consider me for a second, before telling me soberly, 'They were a bottle of mine. I used to get a prescription in Hope. With all the upheaval and stress, I'd forgotten to take any recently. Since we moved, I haven't got around to getting registered with a doctor and jumping through all the hoops to get more. Besides, I found I don't need them.'

He raises his shoulders animatedly with an uncharacteristically carefree expression on his face. 'So that left me free to empty the capsules and fill them up with sugar for you. It's quite freeing to find I can manage my emotions myself these days without being dependent on a drug. I suppose you have done me a favour on that front. So no more pills for me. Just natural management. I have to say I feel much better. Much more free.'

I blink in the wake of another revelation from my father. 'I had no idea you were taking anything.'

'Well, you wouldn't. That's the point. They were supposed to make me appear normal. So I could slip in amongst so-called civilised society.' He nudges me with his elbow and chuckles.

'Were they just for anxiety?'

He nods as he returns to face his magazine. 'That's right. What else would they be for?'

'I don't know.' I shrug. 'I'm glad you don't need them anymore.'

'So am I.'

Dad begins singing enthusiastically again and rhythmically turning his head side to side. This is one of his favourites. I could write the lyrics backwards a hundred times over if I had to as I've heard it so many times.

I return to my crossword. I keep re-reading the same clue over and over, not really taking it in. I know the answer is something obvious. My brain is refusing to join the dots. I feel it is being just as uncooperative in other respects too.

Something about Dad's admissions trouble me. There is a missing part somewhere that I know would make everything slot together and make sense.

Just as I'm carefully considering another question to Dad, everything goes black. The music stops too, and we are left in silence.

33

I stare around in the darkness that suddenly surrounds us. It presses in on my eyes. 'What's happening?'

Dad swears. 'My music!'

I blink at Dad's use of a swear word. It's so unlike him.

My eyes are starting to adjust. The streetlight positioned right outside our flat allows me to reach out and put down my puzzle book and pen on the coffee table.

I manage to fumble my way to the light switch on the wall. I flick it a few times back and forth. I can hear Dad messing with the CD player too. The lack of light doesn't seem to bother him as much as the lack of music. Against the illuminated orange curtain, I see my father's silhouette. Just in time to see him snatch the CD player up, ripping it from the socket. He slams it hard down on the floor.

I gasp in shock. 'Dad! What are you doing?'

'I need my music! Why do people always want to take what's mine away from me?'

My heart suddenly ramps up in response to Dad's sudden change in mood, dizzyingly so. Even after all these years, I can never anticipate when a mood swing will occur. 'What are you talking about? Why has the electricity gone off?'

'The greedy parasites at the power company want their money. They act like I haven't paid my bills all my life! They could give me a break after the thousands of pounds I paid them, couldn't they?'

'What do you mean? Haven't you paid the bills here?'

'With what?' Dad snaps. 'I'm not made of money. I had all the finances under control in our real home. Everything was up to date.'

I try and swallow down my sudden anxiety. 'I understand. You have always done a good job of taking care of us. But isn't this place cheaper than the cottage? It's so much smaller.'

Dad scoffs. 'You don't need to tell me this place is a shithole! It only adds insult to injury. We were living rent-free in the cottage. That's a massive difference each month! I had to hand over two months' rent here upfront as a deposit. As if anything here is worth that much! I'm beyond outraged that I have to pay so much money to live in this shitty little flat! Not that you would understand. I bet you are disappointed you didn't get to go and live with Prince Charming and his parents in their nice expensive renovation, aren't you?'

'What? No, of course not. You're my family.'

'That's right. You remember that, Ruby. I know you are desperate to leave me. You don't trust me. That's why I caught you throwing your medicine away.'

'It was just sugar.'

'So? I worked hard to prepare them for you, to make you believe you were going to be better. And you threw it all down the drain, literally!'

'I'm sorry, Dad. I know you were just trying to help. I'm sorry I ruined it.'

'You've ruined a lot of things.'

'I'm sorry.' The rhetoric of my life lately. 'I know you had to take a low-paid job because of me. I know you chose fewer hours so you could take care of me.'

A high-pitched noise suddenly makes me jump. I look around for the source, then realise it is coming from my father. The shoulders of his silhouette shake and his whole figure slumps to the floor of the living room.

'Dad?' I say uncertainly in the darkness. His form has bridged the gap between the back of the sofa and the worktop of the open-plan kitchen. Now I'm not sure where any of it ends.

I reach out an arm and blindly make my way over to him.

His hand grabs me. He takes a fistful of my jumper and pulls me down to the floor with him. It's now I realise he is shaking with sobs.

'I'm so sorry, sweetheart. I should have told you about the money. You are so clever. You would have known what to do.'

'What's going on?' Suddenly I feel like I'm the adult comforting a child. It makes me uncomfortable. It's forever been the other way around.

'We don't have any money left.'

'That can't be right. What about the job you got?'

'I didn't get it. I did a whole day working for them only for them to turn around and tell me to fuck off.'

'So you haven't been paid all this time?'

There is a sudden movement I take to be my father shaking his head. 'They paid me for the few trial hours, but that was it.'

'I don't understand. You told me you got the job. You stopped looking for work.'

'I know. I'm a massive screw-up. I'm a failure. A parasite, just like my dad always told me. I've failed you so badly. You need me. You depend on me just as much as I depend on you.'

I'm lost for words for a few moments. 'You haven't messed up,' I say, desperate to reassure him. 'You'll find another job.'

'I don't think so. Things are hard here in this city. It's not the small village Hope was. It's quite literally the opposite of hope!'

Dad laughs in a way that scares me. 'My father always told me I wouldn't be able to make it in the real world. "You're far too sensitive, Mark!" he used to say. "You've got some serious growing up to do!" and, "All the other boys your age have got jobs. Get your backside out there and start earning!".'

'That's horrible.' I don't quite know what to say. Dad has never spoken about his parents before. 'Mark. That's your real name, then? I've got so used to thinking of you as Albert. It always sounded like an old man's name. I don't understand why you chose it.'

'That's because it is an old man's name,' Dad replies flatly. 'He was the legal owner of the house. Our cottage. That's how we lived rent-free for twelve years.'

'How?'

I feel Dad's shrug. 'You know how it is in Hope. Lots of abandoned properties. Old people die off and don't have any relatives to pass it to. It's the wet dream of greedy developers these days now that property is at an all-time high.'

I'm not entirely sure what Dad's phrase means but don't

feel like I should ask. 'We will sort something out. I'll help you. I have the money from my business. That will tide us over until we get things together. Maybe I can start running the business again here. There are more potential customers around, that's for sure. Maybe you can talk to the business owners around here, and set up something similar again?'

He groans. 'I'm sorry, sweetheart. I shouldn't have lied to you.'

'About what?'

'I didn't get your products in the local businesses. I made it up.'

'What?'

There is a pause. 'I'm sorry. You must understand that your business idea wasn't valid. It wouldn't have been worth either of our time for the amount of money it would make.'

Dad must have made a mistake. He isn't thinking clearly at the moment. 'But you had me making all those batches. They must have been selling.'

'Not one, Ruby. I'm sorry. I gave you the money myself.'

My mouth is open as I consider all this for a few minutes. I'm annoyed with him for lying to me. My anger fizzles, however, when I consider what a pathetic state my father is in at the moment. I just wish he could pull himself together and look like the man I recognise. I'm scared too. I need him to be strong.

'I don't understand how you could have lied to me. Where did you take everything I made if you weren't delivering it to local businesses?'

He exhales. 'I ate most of it, to be honest. You are a very talented baker. But it's a hobby, not a business.'

I shake my head in disbelief, foolish tears in my eyes. Thankfully, Dad can't see them.

He sighs deeply. 'I was going to ease you off the idea gradually, tell you things had stopped selling one by one.'

'You'd already started that, with the coffee cake. Matt said he hadn't seen any for sale. Now I know why.'

'I'm sorry. It went against my rules about keeping our heads down and not getting involved. I had to make sure no one found out about you. It wasn't worth risking everything we had worked for, for a few pieces of cake.'

I let this sink in for several minutes. I'm furious with Dad for the deception, but I understand why he did it. I get up and feel for the toffee tin in the bedroom. I know the contents so well that I can easily find the money in the dark.

I pull it out, feel my way back to my father and press the money into his hand. I feel regret at having to hand it back, despite the fact I now know it was never mine to start with.

Dad pulls me nearer to him and presses his wet face against mine. 'My sweet girl. I'm sorry. I've failed you in so many ways. Even in ways you can't even begin to imagine. I don't deserve you.'

My hair clings to him as he tries to regain control of himself. 'It's okay, Dad. We'll get through this together.'

His sobbing comes to an abrupt end when there is a banging at the door.

34

'H ello?' The banging comes again. 'I know you're in there!'

Dad slips quietly through the inner door and down the stairs. I hover behind him, a few steps up, uncertainly. It seems he doesn't recognise the man's voice either.

He leans forward and peers through the spy hole fitted in the external door.

Just as he does so, the letterbox opens and the voice comes through louder.

'Can you open the door, please? I need to talk to you.'

Dad slams the letterbox flap down again with a panicked glance up the stairs to me.

It's still dark in here. I highly doubt someone from outside could see much through the black bristles anyway, let alone up the staircase.

Dad gestures for me to go back inside the flat and draws himself taller to shout through the door. 'Who is it?'

'Hi, it's Alex. I'm your neighbour from downstairs.'

'What do you want?'

'Can you open the door, please? I want to have a quick word if that's okay?'

'It's not.' Dad's reply is too quick. I know he is startled. I don't know what the other person must think of this.

'Excuse me?'

'Look, I'm busy. I'm tired after being at work all week.'

'I appreciate that, but I've heard a lot of noise coming from upstairs all evening. First, it was loud music, then it sounded like something got smashed into my ceiling.'

'I'm sorry about that. I had an accident. It will be cleared up soon. Nothing to worry about. I'm sorry if the noise disturbed you. Thanks for checking up though. Have a nice evening.'

'Hold on – why are all your lights off? I can usually see through your curtains if they are on. Have you tripped a fuse or something during your little accident?'

'No. It's fine.'

'If everything is hunky-dory, then why are you sitting in silence in the dark all of a sudden?'

'I'm not.'

'It looks like it from out here, mate. You don't even have your hall light on. What's going on?'

'Nothing is going on. It's just a problem with my account at the power company. Please leave me alone.'

'I see. What about your daughter? Is she okay?'

Dad bristles at this. I can feel the air in the staircase change.

'What daughter?'

'The young girl you've got up there with you. I know she lives in there with you. I can hear her moving around when you are out. I mean, I assume she's your daughter...'

Dad pauses to think for a moment. His thoughts are

almost whirring like audible gears. 'What makes you think there is a girl living here?'

The man makes a noise on the other side of the door, as though surprised by Dad's response. 'I saw you sneak her in one day a few weeks ago. That was a bit weird, I admit. Looked pretty dodgy to me, the way you were looking over your shoulder and had a hat pulled over her head. Are you saying you don't have a daughter now? That would make me suspicious.'

'It's winter. It's not unusual to wear a hat. Have you met her?'

I cringe. Dad is messing this up. It's the same concept as when I say the wrong thing to my father and it leads me along a linguistic tightrope. One slip could lead to my doom.

Should I intervene now? Or will it make things worse? Normally, I wouldn't dare. Tonight, however, I can tell Dad isn't his usual self.

'You what?' The man laughs bitterly. 'No.'

'Have you spoken to her whilst I've been at work?'

'No. Why would I?'

'You might have been in here when I wasn't looking.'

'Are you accusing me of something? I've never spoken to your fucking daughter, mate!' The man's voice is deeper now, more aggressive. I have never seen him, but he sounds as though he might be well built.

'Fine.' Dad is forcing his voice to remain calm. I can hear the quiver in it though. 'I believe you. Just leave.'

'Hang on. I heard shouting and banging. Why are you and your daughter sitting in the dark? Something doesn't smell right here. I want to know what's happening in there.'

'Please leave, or I will call the police.'

'Yeah, go on, mate. Do it. Let's see what they have to say about all this.'

Dad falls silent. I hear his feet on the stairs and I back up into the flat to let him inside. He locks the inner door and we stand in the dark in our living room as the angry banging on our front door starts up again.

My eyes feel wide. 'Will he call the police?'

'He might.' Dad takes a deep breath. It sounds like he might be shaking. 'Let's go out for a bit, just in case.'

'Now? At this hour?'

'It's not even 9 p.m. yet. Cities don't sleep. This is as far from village life as you can get out here. Pack a bag, make sure all your personal things are in it. Just in case.'

35

'Pack a bag? Are we moving again?'

'No. It's just for a few hours. Just in case the police have been called. Watch your step and don't make any noise.'

I swallow in fear and do as I'm told, gingerly treading across the carpet in case the man from downstairs hears me. I'm forcefully reminded of a game I used to play, pretending I was jumping from stepping stone to stepping stone over a pit of imaginary lava, or crocodile-infested waters.

I pack my things into my small backpack again, frustrated they don't seem to fit in as well this time around as they did before.

I still don't have a winter coat, so I pile on another jumper or two. Dad meets me in the living room, however, and bundles me into his oversized wax jacket. He pulls a hat over my head as he did when we arrived in the city. How unlucky the neighbour was watching out the window as we approached the building that day.

I'm not sure if my father is thinking of keeping me warm or if he is simply focused on disguising me.

Either way, I'm grateful as I follow my father's footsteps out into the cold December night.

Dad puts an arm around me and glances towards the illuminated square of the downstairs flat window before we walk briskly together, steps matched down the street.

Dad seems to relax as we round the corner a few streets away. We walk for a little while through endless rows of houses. Christmas lights adorn many of the buildings. I see trees inside each postage stamp of light, decorated and colourful. Some real trees are out, discarded in the street here and there.

I spot ripped wrapping paper in more than a handful of bins. Christmas Day must have been and gone. I must have lost track of time. I thought it was yet to come. Dad didn't mark it at all this year.

I guess if he didn't have the funds for food or presents, there would be no point in mentioning it. It's not like we have much to celebrate. Nor do I deserve to receive gifts. Maybe Dad thought I was too old for the festivities now. Christmas is for children, I suppose.

It isn't long before we make it to some hustle and bustle. Dad was right. People are milling about everywhere like it's the middle of the day. It should be reassuring to be lost amongst the activity, but I just feel lost and scared. Dad is angry and erratic. He isn't currently the loving parent I want to cling to.

There are Christmas decorations and colourful lights in the shop windows, many of which are still open. I'd love to go inside some, but Dad would likely deem it unsafe.

To my surprise, he steers me towards a building nearby

and pulls open the door. A wave of noise hits my ears, even through my hat.

Inside, there are old wooden tables and squashy leather chairs. There are so many people moving about and chatting loudly. It makes me uncomfortable. I just want to be at home, somewhere safe and away from people. It's what I'm used to. New and different scares me now. I've had enough of it. I glance up at Dad with wide eyes.

'It's all right,' he mutters back. 'This is what you call hiding in plain sight. This is a busy pub. No one will notice us. We will stay here for a while.'

Dad leads us to a table away from the bar where people are receiving drinks, money in hand.

I seat myself in the booth he gestures me into. 'At least it's warm in here.'

'Do you resent not having heating at home?' he shoots back immediately. 'I suppose you want to live in a home with someone who has the heating cranked up twenty-four seven. Do you imagine it was like that at your boyfriend's house?"

'I didn't mean...'

Dad sighs impatiently. He rotates his shoulders as he looks towards the bar. 'Wait here. Don't speak to anyone. Remember, you can't speak English.'

I nod. When he leaves, I chance a few glances around me.

A girl not many years older than me is at the nearest table. She doesn't pay me the slightest bit of attention. She is entwined with her boyfriend, a similar age. They are both deeply involved, kissing and giggling.

I look away. I hope they don't do that the entire time I'm here with Dad. Seeing the couple reminds me forcibly of Matt. Has he recovered from Dad's attack yet? I dread to think what his parents thought of the incident. They would blame me, I guess. I would imagine at the very least Matt is banned from seeing me ever again, even if somehow we were to meet once more. Even with my limited real-world knowledge, I know that it will never happen.

Dad returns after a few minutes with two steaming white mugs. A coffee for himself and a hot chocolate for me.

'You never have caffeine this late,' I say to him as he adds little packets of sugar to his drink.

'I need to stay alert this evening.' He glances up and sees my worried expression. 'Just in case.'

'What's going to happen to us?'

'Nothing with happen to you, sweetheart. I won't let it. I'll kill anyone who comes close to you.'

I look at Dad's serious expression. The hardened look in his eyes scares me. I know he means it. But should he be willing to do such a thing? After all, I'm the one in the wrong. It turns out I always have been. I'm the one that should stop running.

Dad is just getting himself deeper and deeper into trouble for me. I should hand myself in and spare him. I just know he won't let me.

We sip our drinks in silence. The sweetness of mine is so intense it almost makes my tongue burn. I've never had something with so much sugar in it at home.

My father orders us another round each after a while. We don't really want them, of course. It's just an excuse to be here out of the cold. Hiding in the hubbub and chatter. My head spins with the rush of the sugar in my veins. I want to run and hide.

There is one of those flat TVs mounted on the wall behind my father. I don't point it out. Dad wouldn't approve of me watching unauthorized programming. I guess in this unconventional situation he hasn't noticed.

It's only a news program. I try not to stare too interestedly in that direction for fear of arousing his attention, despite the fact I am fascinated.

Headlines roll across the bottom of the screen, some worse than others. Scientific breakthroughs, photos of stabbing victims smiling, oblivious to the attack in their near future, and images of war seem commonplace.

Other people in the bar hardly glance at the screen. I can't tell if the set is muted, or just on too low to be heard above the noise of this place.

I try and lipread what the various people say, but it's not easy. I don't have much experience talking to anyone else than Dad and he seems to pull his lips stiffly as he speaks. Usually, anyway. He seems a little more animated tonight, and I know it's not just down to the caffeine.

My father keeps looking around him, quick sharp glances that I worry will lead him to the victim he has yet to identify. His forehead is sweating, despite the fact he walked here without a coat. I'm still wearing his. Along with the hat he pulled over my head it's making me uncomfortably hot.

I move to take them off.

Dad's arm is on me immediately. 'Leave it on! You are less conspicuous with it.'

His eyes are wild now as he watches me shrug his jacket back over my shoulders.

'Dad,' I say, voicing what has been troubling me all evening. 'What were you prescribed that medication for? I don't think it was just anxiety. Can you tell me what it was?'

My father gapes at me with an open mouth. I flinch, managing to detect the eruption before it happens this time.

'Why are you obsessed with what is inside that little bottle?' he hisses across the table. 'You are just like your mother, always questioning me. If you must know, it was allergy medication in that bottle. I only needed it because you don't clean the house well enough. You've kept us living in filth for years. I hope you are happy. Now let it go! I've warned you.'

I'm aware the nearby couple has pulled their faces apart to stare at us at Dad's raised voice.

'Fuck off,' Dad says to them.

I expect them to get aggressive, like the man from the flat downstairs. They don't. They just look at each other and at me a few times, down their drinks and get up and leave.

It's a relief when they step out the door and into the street, even if they throw us a few glances before they finally disappear.

Dad looks around us a few times. 'I need the toilet. Wait here. I'll be two seconds. Again – don't speak to anyone.'

'I can't. I don't speak English.'

Dad hovers, as though wanting to judge whether my tone is sincere enough, but then he blinks and leaves me for the back of the building somewhere.

I pick up a long spoon and squash the collapsing foam at the bottom of my lukewarm drink for something to do.

Dad says you shouldn't make eye contact with people. They remember you less.

When I look up again towards the television, I have the shock of my life. I even gasp out loud, without meaning to. My own face smiles uncertainly back at me from the screen.

36

M y mouth drops open.

The rolling news has the photo Matt took of us on our first and only date. It's displayed proudly on the screen for all to see.

I glance around and see that no one pays it any attention, apart from a shrivelled old man sitting alone. He is at a table closer to the television set, holding a large beer in one hand. He is facing away from me, however.

Unless he turns right around in his seat and picks me out of the crowd, there is no way he can tell that the subject of the current news story is yards away.

I can't hear what is being said, but I suddenly notice the headline at the bottom of the screen:

Ruby Adams Disappearance – New Breakthrough In Decades-Old Case

Disappearance? That's a strange way to word it. Manhunt

would be more appropriate. I'm a fugitive in hiding. There is no mention that I'm a murderer.

Then a middle-aged couple appears on-screen. I can't hear what they are saying. They pause as the interviewer in the studio asks something. I've seen them before. The house behind them too. It's the renovated house. Our only neighbour back in Hope. These are Matt's parents.

'No,' I whisper. I feel like I've swallowed something cold. Matt. He didn't make it. He must have died from his injuries after we left. Why else would his parents be interviewed on television and not Matt himself?

I'm suddenly aware of a dark figure stopping right beside the booth. For a moment, I think the police have finally caught up with me.

Then I look up and realise it's Dad back from the toilet. He stares at the screen with a horrified face. His dark eyes are wild behind his glasses. He looks possessed. There is a split second where I forget my fears of being caught and wish I wasn't anywhere near my father.

He stares at Matt's father as he speaks and gestures angrily off-screen. Only Dad and I know that he is motioning towards our house. Then it appears on the screen instead. A burned-out shell of a building with broken windows.

I put my hand to my mouth as I see what has become of the only real home I remember.

Dad blinks and seems to come to, looking down at me fearfully.

Suddenly, I'm snatched from my seat. My eyes are torn abruptly from the broadcast. He drags me painfully by the upper arm to my feet, grabs our bags and pulls me out through the bar.

Then we are out into the cold night once again.

He looks left and right towards various dark streets like a rat in a maze as I scramble to pull my backpack onto my shoulders. My arm throbs painfully. I know it will be bruised tomorrow.

I know why Dad looks as white as a ghost. The full weight of what he has done has hit him. He realises now he has killed Matt. He has joined the murderers' club with me, just as unwittingly it seems. Although I doubt I would have struck out at my mother with such deliberate aggression as my father did with my boyfriend.

Now we both have a reason to run.

37

D ad grips my small hand in his sweating one tightly as we dash down one street and then another.

'Where are we going?' I pant at him. He doesn't reply. I have the feeling he has somewhere in mind, however.

I suspect we won't be going back to the flat again, not even to destroy evidence. Flames won't be there to erase our fingerprints and skin cells. It won't consume the measly tinned dinner we were planning for tomorrow, or our respective handwriting in that puzzle book and magazine we both put down so abruptly just hours earlier.

Are the police crawling over the place, dissecting our life of the past few weeks as we run out here in the dark?

Dad can't keep up the hurried pace for long. He slows to a brisk walk, his free hand clutching his side as he wheezes. As we pass a public bin, Dad drops his smartphone inside with a loud thud. I thought he said it was untraceable.

I'm sweating beneath my father's heavy coat. Not just from exertion either. I don't know if we will ever stop running – not just right now, but for the rest of our lives. I can't see into such a bleak future. I'm not sure I would even want to.

The grand railway station building comes into view as we round another corner. It seems familiar, despite the fact I only came here once upon our arrival in the city. It seems so long ago even though I know it wasn't.

Walking through these doors tonight feels as though the past few weeks have been a dream I am now waking up from.

It's much quieter here than when we arrived that day, yet there are still clusters of people milling about.

It's one of the latest times I have ever been awake and out of bed.

I shiver as we hurry across the stone floor. It doesn't seem any warmer than outside. We cross the foyer with its grand glass ceiling high above us. Dad pulls my hat further down where it had been slipping upwards after the hurry here.

He checks the sparse departure boards. There is a train leaving any minute on platform 3.

I open my mouth to ask Dad if that is the one he is going for, but he leaves me standing on the spot and approaches the ticket office.

The shoulders of the woman behind the counter slump. She was in the process of leaving her post and shutting up shop after a long day. She serves Dad quickly with a tight jaw and pulls the blind down promptly without thanking him when he has turned to leave.

She must be tired, I think. I certainly am. But is that a reason for such outward hostility to a stranger? Dad was desperate for tickets. It's not like he could put the cash I gave him into the machine nearby, and we can't get through the barriers without tickets. We would have been trapped.

People are so cold in the real world. It makes me sad. I want Dad to get us somewhere without any people. I'm exhausted. But where can we go that would be safe for us?

'Where are we going next?' I ask Dad as he rushes over.

He ignores my question. Instead, he pulls me by the already bruised arm and hurries us up some hard steps and over the bridge.

My heart skips so many beats as my bag bounces off my back. I fear it might just give out, leaving Dad dragging my limp form along for a good few steps before he realises.

We finally slip in through the train doors just before they hiss shut behind us. The engine rumbles loudly and the station slips away past the windows.

My father pulls me past a congregation of drunk men singing and cheering sprawled around a pair of table seats. He nudges me into the least crowded carriage. Finally, he gestures me into the window seat and wedges himself in beside me, stuffing our bags at our feet.

It's quieter in here. The occasional person gets up and sways their way to the toilet through the automatic doors behind us. A few people here and there doze off in their seats, or are on the verge of it, swaying with the motion of the train.

The person in the seat in front of Dad scrolls idly through their phone, white earphones trailing from one ear. They flit between various videos of cats and dogs doing funny things. I find myself staring at the images, not in the least bit amused.

It's a shock when I glance up after a while and see Matt's parents on the screen. I glance sideways at Dad. He is staring at the back of the person's headrest and is shaking his head, muttering quietly to himself, 'We've got to get somewhere away from people. Too many people here. My father always said I can't handle people.'

My father can't see what I can from my angle. I don't tell him the news broadcast is in the palm of everyone on this train if they so choose to tune in. I wonder how many others are watching as we speed along away from the city.

The broadcast moves onto our ruined house as it had earlier. This must be a repeat. The news goes round and round, nothing new to report. Does that mean we got away from Leicester in time? The police might not yet have realised we were there at all.

Yet.

A man is standing outside our house now, a presenter in an expensive-looking outdoor coat. He gestures to the charred building behind him with a circular motion, glancing back at the camera now and then. I've still no idea what is being said.

The presenter turns back to face the camera, his hands clasped in front of him. He stops talking and it's back to the news anchor in the studio. He talks for a few moments, then pauses.

Then another segment of video fills the screen. This one has a whole room of people sitting in plastic chairs. They face a long table where a man and a woman take a seat. Matt's parents. They seem to be giving some kind of speech. Cameras flash all over the place like lightning as they sit down.

The camera shot changes to a close-up of the couple. Then I realise they aren't Matt's parents. I can't imagine who they are.

I squint at the headline at the bottom; it's much harder to make out on a smaller screen. The story doesn't seem to have morphed into a different one. I can still make out my name in the headline.

The couple hold hands as they listen to a question posed by someone offscreen. The woman starts giving her response. She has sandy-coloured hair. The warm tone shines through, even in the harsh camera lights that keep firing. Her round face shines, emphasising the dark circles under her eyes.

There is something familiar about her. Something tugs in the recesses of my weary brain. Is she something to do with Matt too? Perhaps she was a business owner in Hope? I wouldn't have seen much of her or anyone else on my monthly walks with Dad.

He never encouraged anyone to get too close. He wouldn't usually stop for a chat if he was out with me, briskly moving past with a, 'Lovely weather we're having, isn't it?'

Or a, 'Terribly rainy lately, isn't it? Nice weather for ducks!'

I went out so little that the increments between the interactions were hard to judge, time-wise. Seasons would pass in the blink of an eye when I could only experience a few hours of them here and there. Yet at the same time, the hours dragged on.

Was this woman a witness to Matt's injuries? Perhaps she was the one who found him collapsed in the country lane between our two houses.

She might have stayed with him as he died, holding his hand as his eyes slipped shut for the final time. Now she has taken to the world's stage to tell her traumatic story.

A lump forms in my throat. *I'm so sorry, Matt. I never meant for you to get hurt.*

The woman's partner puts his arm around her shoulders protectively, stroking her upper arm in a comforting gesture. He has a more square face and chunky features. Nothing about him rings a bell.

He lifts a photograph from the table in front of him. It's a photo of me, clearly taken from the one Matt took of the two of us together. Happier times.

They've cropped Matt out though, allowing for a clear image of the Pandora who led him to his death to be enlarged.

Camera flashes ripple around the room again as the image is raised. I'm never going to get out of this alive, I realise. There won't be anyone left soon who doesn't know my traitorous face.

The woman presses a tissue to her mouth as her eyes crease, changing their shape. This action causes something to click in my brain. The confused pieces slot together to create an epiphany.

No. No, it can't be.

I lean forward to squint at the bottom of the phone screen. The headline has changed slightly now. It reads:

Live Earlier Today: Missing Girl Ruby Adams's Mother Speaks Out.

A rush of recognition leaves me breathless. Mum.

My mother was speaking somewhere live earlier today. She isn't dead.

She is very much still alive.

38

I blink in confusion at the screen through the gap between the seats. My head is pounding. I think I might be sick.

I can't label the main emotion I'm feeling right now. It lies somewhere between terror and elation, panic and despair. Or maybe all of them. I swallow down my feelings.

The headline changes again. A subheading scrolls across the screen:

Rachel Adams pleads again with former husband Mark Adams for the safe return of their daughter Ruby. The missing father-and-daughter pair were revealed to have been living secretly in a small village in England until mid-November, when Mark violently assaulted a local boy. Police are asking witnesses to come forward.

My confused brain tries to piece this shocking information together, but it's like it is being deliberately uncooperative, joining the dots slowly.

Mum is alive. I didn't kill her. Dad couldn't have been the perpetrator either. The crime he insisted happened was an utter fabrication.

There was no murder at all. Mum is fine and well all these years later.

It just won't sink in. I've spent my whole life in hiding because of my mother's murder.

I thought Dad had killed her to save me until recently. Then he turned the tables and told me I was the guilty one. We had to run from the scene of the crime, all the way to Hope, when I was so young, hadn't we? We are still running, right this minute, for that very reason. What the hell is going on?

Only one thing registers in my confused thoughts: Dad has been lying to me.

He has kept me trapped in a contrived prison of deceit all my life. I don't understand.

I've spent my childhood locked up and kept away from the whole world. Not allowed to go outside. Not allowed to speak to people.

My father didn't even let me go to school, though I begged him on so many occasions.

Why would he have done this? I just can't believe it.

Tears run down my face. Hot, angry tears of confusion and betrayal.

My father continues to mutter to himself in the seat beside me now and then. He is oblivious to what I have just seen on a fellow passenger's smartphone.

Between his large frame and the bulk of our hastily stuffed backpacks, there is no getting out of my seat. I want to get as far away from him as possible. I need some air, some time to think away from his presence that I've had to live with all these years.

I stare at the phone of the passenger in front of me. He shifts in his seat and I have to move slightly too so I can continue to see the screen in his hand.

At the last second, I feel Dad adjust position beside me too. I glance sideways, just in time to see him follow my gaze. He cranes his neck between the seats.

Foolishly, I throw my arms up, blocking the gap. I have no idea why I do this. Why am I trying to hide what I have learned from him, even now? As if it will change the cold hard facts.

He looks at me in bewilderment. 'Ruby!' he hisses. 'What on earth were you looking at? Why are you crying?'

I shake my head, lost for words.

He wrestles my hands down and stares through the gap with determined interest. He must have a shock to see his own face staring back at him.

He freezes in horror. The photo now filling the screen was taken when my father's face was younger and fuller, free from glasses. His hair is completely dark, long, and drawn back into a ponytail. He looks almost genial, so much more approachable than the man I know.

The current version of my father is somehow more sunken. I can't determine in what way I think that. Only the eyes behind the glasses are the giveaway that he is the same person. Even those have lost the sparkle from the photograph.

Dad is suddenly a lot paler than I have ever seen him. His lips have taken on a white tone. The broadcast returns to the press conference with Rachel, my very much alive mother.

She shakes her head, squeezing her wet eyes closed in regret. Instinctively, I just know she is saying something about Dad.

A teenage girl reaches out now and takes hold of Mum's hand. She and Mum's partner sit on either side of my mother, visibly offering their support.

This girl has tears running down her face too, I realise. I hadn't noticed her at all before.

She looks a lot like me, with Dad's dark features and hair, but with Mum's round face. She looks younger, however.

It takes me a split second to realise who she must be.

This is Emily. My little sister.

She didn't die either. She wasn't killed by proxy when I accidentally snuffed out Mum's life. Because none of that ever happened.

Oh, Dad. Why did you lie to me?

The poetic memorial words Dad wrote on Emily's ultrasound image must have been a lie. How did he know I would find that photo one day and read what he had written?

Dad slowly turns from the phone screen to my tear-stained face. I expect him to explode, or snatch me away from the screen. He doesn't do either.

He knows the game is up.

39

Even Dad can't lie in the face of such raw facts when they have been laid out like this in front of us. He eyes me carefully, cautiously gauging my reaction.

I am the first to speak, alarmed by how much emotion shakes my voice. 'Why?'

He doesn't answer my question directly. 'I love you, Ruby. I love you more than life itself.'

He reaches out to take my hand but I snatch it away from him.

'No! You need to tell me why. Why have you lied to me all these years? You told me Mum was dead. You told me I did it! How could you?'

Dad's face creases uncharacteristically across his forehead and chin. He gives a great sniff to steady himself. 'She was going to take you away from me.'

'Who?'

'Rachel. Your mother. She wanted a divorce when you were so small. She told me she was going to take custody of you. I was to be allowed weekend visits only, she said.'

'I don't understand. She was pregnant when she d–' I sigh impatiently, as Dad has so many times when something has annoyed him. Now he is the source of my fury. The truth is going to take some getting used to. Everything I know has been shaken.

I gesture bluntly. 'When we left, she was having another baby. Emily. Why would she be having another baby with you if she wanted to divorce you?'

'She– I...' Dad's dark eyes are wild, darting around, down the train and back to me.

'I couldn't let her just leave me!' he whispers angrily. 'I loved her so very much. We were supposed to be together. She had no right to even think about leaving me.'

This all sounds so very familiar, I think.

Dad pushes himself higher in his seat and starts talking quickly, as though all this has been on his chest for years. His movements, his speech. It's all too fast. 'I had to try something, to stop her devastating our lives. You meant the world to me, sweetheart. I loved you so much. Even more so now. I couldn't bear to only see you for a few hours on a Saturday whilst your mother moved on to some other man.'

I press my hands to my cheeks. 'I don't believe this.'

Dad leans closer. Too close. His breath is on my face. 'I knew someone else would worm their way in sooner or later. Your mother was very attractive. She still is. I know full well she has replaced me with someone else. Jack, his name is according to what I've read over the years in the news. Not that I care! Rachel certainly doesn't give my well-being the slightest bit of thought anymore. The vicious bitch.'

I blink. 'So what did you do? How did you stop her from leaving you?'

Dad purses his lips. 'I switched her birth control pills for sugar tablets.'

'What's birth control?'

Dad laughs hysterically. 'Oh, Ruby. This is why I wanted to keep you away from the world. There is so much out there to pollute your mind. You were so much safer in the village cottage with me, away from harm. I wanted to keep you innocent and happy, away from immorality.'

'Well, you failed,' I say bitterly. 'You should never have kept me prisoner for no reason. What were Mum's tablets for?'

'I suppose this talk is overdue.' He sighs, as though I am asking a schoolwork-related question and we're not on the last train of the day trundling away from a safe house that can no longer hold its title. 'It's called contraception. It's what women take to stop themselves getting pregnant.'

This sounds familiar. Dad seems to like to exert control through medication, real or otherwise. 'So you made her believe she was taking something to help her. All the while, it wasn't. You gave her a placebo, just like you did with me.'

He raises his palms, as though feeling under attack. 'Yes. It's not the worst thing I could have done. I wanted to keep our family together. I tried my best. I didn't know what else to do, my angel. At first, it worked. Your mother just assumed the pills had failed her. They don't work one hundred per cent of the time anyway, you know.

'I convinced her it was a good thing. I told her it was fate. "A baby is a blessing," I said, "and we should embrace it." We already had a child together, after all, and plenty of room in our comfortable home for another. "Ruby would benefit from having a sibling," I said. And I meant all of that. It's my biggest regret that I never got to meet Emily.'

I stare at him for a few moments. 'That's what you meant when you wrote that message on the ultrasound photo. You told them they would be forever loved. You did lose them that day. On the day we left. But they didn't die. You left them behind.'

Dad squeezes his eyes shut and bows his head. 'Yes. That was the day we left the house we all lived in together. No one died.'

The weight of his confession washes over me like a tsunami. 'I just don't understand. I was so convinced Mum died. I remember blood.'

Red on white streaked all over the bathtub. Seared into my memory forever. I'm sure I didn't imagine that. Or was it another trick of my father's?

I look at him with suspicious eyes. 'I didn't imagine it. You planted the memory in my head. You made me believe the lie. How did you do it? Did you use fake blood? How did you trick me?'

'I didn't! Of course I didn't set out to deceive you. I wouldn't do that to you, Ruby. Think about it. I only ever wanted to keep us together!' He swallows hard. 'Think! Do you remember there being blood anywhere else other than the bathroom?'

I scan the recesses of my mind. 'No. Just in the bathroom. That's all I remember.'

He nods and waits for a man to stagger past us to the toilet, swaying with the motion of the train. 'Your mother went into labour early with your sister. That was the source of the blood you saw. Emily was born too soon. Far too soon. She was born at thirty weeks. The papers made a big thing of that afterwards. It added to the drama of your disappearance.'

'The papers? You never went back to see Emily, or check on your wife.'

He winces. 'That's right. That was the day we left for good, as you have already guessed. March the sixteenth 2012. That's Emily's birthdate, not the date of her death, as you assumed after reading my writing on her ultrasound image. Writing that message to them both helped me deal with the loss. I knew I would never see them again one way or another.'

I let all this sink in. The shock of it all is almost too much. 'But what made you do it? Why did you abduct me at the moment your wife went into early labour? You ran out and left her! She must have been so scared. You only made it worse.'

'No!' Dad shuffles erratically in his seat, gripping handfuls of his trousers at the knees. It's somewhat satisfying to see this is causing him distress. He should be tormented by this, I think bitterly. He deserves it. Just like I have been in turmoil all this time because of him. No doubt Mum and Emily too.

I've spent my whole childhood thinking my mother was murdered violently and it was all my fault. Then Dad twisted the knife further and told me I had been the one to do it.

My father looks at me imploringly. 'I didn't mean for it to happen. I tried to be a good husband and father. I wanted nothing other than to be by Rachel's side and for us all to be a family.'

I swallow down a lump in my throat. 'So what happened that day? What went wrong?'

'Rachel realised what I had done. She had her birth control analysed. That was the day she confronted me. She knew I had made the switch. To say she went ballistic would be an understatement.'

'I'm not surprised. It's a terrible thing to do to trick someone into having a baby if they don't want one. You said she wanted to split up with you, not have another child.'

He nods erratically. 'You are right. I wouldn't ever have dreamed of doing such a thing normally. Your mother left me no choice, however. We had a terrible fight. She got herself so worked up over the whole thing and acted as if I was trying to harm her!'

Dad grips the armrest as he leans in again. 'I only did what I thought was right. She didn't see it that way. She was going to leave. Your mother started packing your things, hers too. She was going to take off and go and stay with her parents whilst the split was all arranged. She told me to be gone by the time the two of you got back.'

He shakes his head as he watches the events of the past unfold in his mind. 'It didn't work out that way. She never finished packing her things into her suitcase. She started having contractions. That's when we knew the baby was coming that day. She was going to drive herself to the hospital and take you with her, but the pain became too much. She was bleeding heavily too. I helped her climb into the bathtub to contain the blood whilst I called an ambulance.

'She was screaming – from the pain and with anger at me. She told the paramedic she wanted to keep you with her. But I told him I was your father and I would look after you whilst Mummy was getting better in hospital.'

He looks at me suddenly with such concern. 'You were very distressed, crying and clutching your bunny in the doorway. I didn't think you should see your mother go through that. The ambulance doors shut and she was taken away. That was the last time I saw her.'

'Didn't you want to go to the hospital with her?'

'Of course I wanted to! She wouldn't let me. I've never seen her so adamant. She kept screaming at me to keep away from her. I knew then our marriage was over. There was no going back from that.'

'So you took me.'

'Not at first,' Dad says earnestly with wide eyes. His skin is clammy now, his hairline damp. 'We were at home alone for hours. I received a call from the hospital informing me your mother was being taken into theatre for a caesarean.'

Dad sees my look of confusion. 'That's an operation a woman has, to have her baby taken out of her. Your mother's body wasn't ready to give birth naturally at that point. It was too early.'

The train rocks us back and forth. I'd almost forgotten we were on a train. 'What did you do then?'

'Your mother was a determined woman. Strong, unrelenting. I knew as soon as she was able to, she would see to it that she made good on her promise to take you from me. She wouldn't just forget what I'd done. I knew I had a choice. It was a crossroads. I could allow myself to be walked all over, only seeing you for one day a week. Some other father figure would move in on my marriage, stealing your affections with gifts, taking what should have been mine – precious moments with you. Or I could stand up for myself for once. Be proactive.'

'By abducting me? You took me away from my mother. You denied me a normal life!'

'I know you must resent that, Ruby. I never meant it to be that way. Things just spiralled out of control so quickly. I didn't know what to do – I panicked. I am your father, but abducting a child is a serious offence. It wouldn't have worked out well for me if I had been caught. Even though you morally belong to me, the law doesn't see it that way. I took a child. I needed to hide us. It was a desperate time.'

'You didn't have to do it. You could have left me with Mum. It would have been all right.'

'No, it wouldn't! I didn't want anyone coming between us. Think of all the time together we would have been denied. We have an affinity, you and me, that I didn't have with your mother. Not anyone. You are part of me. All my life no one has ever understood me. My own father couldn't wait to be rid of me. My mother only did what he told her, always. He shut her down if she objected to anything.

'I had no one for most of my life. I could only make rela- tionships last so long and they would drift away. Your mother was the longest love affair I had, and even that... Well, it wasn't based on the best foundation. But you, my angel, I could tell you are just like me. We are so alike.'

I open my mouth to protest, but he points a finger at me.

'No – you know that is true! Don't deny it. No matter what happens between us, you can never just cut me out. You can never get rid of me, Ruby, for as long as you live.'

I turn away from my father's intense stare just as we go through a tunnel. I'm faced with my reflection in the dark glass. I pull my woolly hat off... I free myself from Dad's over- sized coat now too. I'm boiling hot. Both my jumpers are soaking under my arms.

Dad protests, looking around the train carriage, but I don't care. I've gone beyond caring. I've always followed Dad's rules for fear of the consequences. Now I'm not even sure what they are supposed to be.

My reflection is hard and angry. Dad is right, we are alike. My face is tainted with his, dark brows and eyes, right down to the same shape of the bones underneath. Parts of my personality are inherited from him too. I hate the fact. I wish I could scrub him from me, but I can't. He is in my blood, my DNA. Every time I look in the mirror, I will see him looking back. For as long as I shall live.

I'll never be free of him, one way or another.

40

It scares me to see the hardened look on my features now as the train moves through this tunnel. My face is thinner than I've ever seen it. I look so much older. My heart has never felt as heavy as it does at this moment.

I turn back to my father, who watches me in a way that scares me. 'What possessed you to take me? How could you ever think that was the answer?'

Dad winces again. 'As I said, I didn't intend to. Your mother was being taken for an emergency caesarean. She would be home before I knew it. I was alone in the house with you when I put the phone down from the hospital.'

He leans his head back against the headrest as the train rocks us back and forth. 'I remember so vividly. I walked into the living room. You were so small then. So adorable and perfect. You reminded me a little of my mother when she was younger. You have an infinitely better personality though. I credit myself for that. It's a testament to how you have been raised, along with your natural warmth.'

Dad smiles sadly. 'You were traumatised after seeing

your mother carted off screaming. You were bleeding a little too – you had dug your fingernails into your hand. That's how you got that scar. I put your favourite television program on – Peppa Pig. You were clutching your bunny so tight and smiling, all curled up on the sofa. I knew I couldn't leave you at the mercy of your mother's decisions and whatever suitor she decided to bring home. What if he turned out to be a monster who hurt you?'

'It's unlikely.'

'Not as much as you might think! You don't know the world as I've seen it, Ruby. I couldn't take the risk. I didn't want to leave anything to chance, not with something as important as your life. Your bag was ready-packed upstairs. Your mother had finished it for me as she went into labour. So I picked it up and packed my things too. You were in the bedroom doorway by this point, watching me with your big eyes. You came with me so willingly as we left your first home. In one hand you held mine, in the other, you had your precious bunny.'

We sit quietly for a few minutes as we both contemplate the horror of what Dad has done. I'm struggling to slot together everything he has said with everything I have found out recently. It's just so much to process.

Someone down the carriage laughs raucously. It seems amazing that those around us are carrying on with their everyday lives when mine is falling apart by the very fabric I thought it was built on.

I suddenly remember something. 'Hang on. There was a passport and birth certificate in your tin of documents. The issue date was late 2011. That must have been before you even thought of getting Mum to have another baby.'

He nods. 'Yes, I remember. That was Plan A. I had

thoughts of taking you abroad with me. I don't know, maybe starting a new life in the sun, just the two of us.'

'I thought you said abducting me was a spur-of-the-moment thing?'

'It was! I didn't follow through with that original plan. It was just more of an idea, really.'

'You got a passport though. You started the process.'

'But I didn't go down that road. Don't you see? I tried to make things work with your mother. I really tried, Ruby. I promise. It was Rachel that was the problem. Not me. I told you, her behaviour became so difficult.'

I am quiet for a moment, studying Dad's face. 'So Mum was the problem, because of her mental health issues? Not you?'

Dad nods earnestly, eyes wide. 'That's right. It was her. Not me.'

'So why is she the one holding a press conference with the whole world behind her whilst you are the subject of a manhunt? Why are we on a train so late at night?'

Dad blinks and mumbles. 'You don't understand.'

He looks dazed and defeated. He isn't all here. I've never seen him lost for words as I have this evening. It's like he is crumbling. After tonight, there is no way I can believe he didn't benefit from whatever the true contents of those capsules was.

'Sweetheart, I love you. You are my world. You can't ever leave me. You'll die without me. I'll die. We need each other.'

He wraps his strong hands firmly around mine. His palms are slick with sweat. 'We belong together. Forever. I'm going to make sure of it.'

I feel my own eyes widen. 'Dad, what are you going to do?'

'Whatever I have to, to make sure we are never parted again. We can't let other people decide our fate. Nor can I let you face this world alone, my angel. It's too cruel. Both the people and everything in it.'

Dad leans closer and rests his moist forehead against mine, still keeping a firm grip on my hands. 'Don't worry. I won't let anyone hurt you. Don't be afraid of what happens next.'

41

M y insides pulsate with electric fear. 'What are you talking about?'

Dad pulls back from me and nods placatingly. 'It's okay. We will find somewhere quiet.' He pulls something from his backpack. A sandwich bag of white powder.

'What is that?'

'My medicine. There's enough here for both of us. It's powerful stuff, you know.'

'Enough for what?' I say slowly.

Dad smiles sadly and reaches out to stroke my face. His touch is so gentle. It's almost like he is his true self for a moment. 'We are going to put ourselves to sleep. We don't need other people interfering with our relationship. No one should ever come between us.'

Dad wants to end things, right here. I'm not going to step off this train.

Tears form in my eyes. I feel sick. 'I don't want to die, Dad. I don't want you to either.'

'This is what we are doing, Ruby. Don't fight me. Don't make our last moments a struggle. Don't be like your mother. My last memory of her was a terrible one.'

He reaches down again and rummages in his backpack. There is a bottle of water inside. Dad pulls it out. It's empty.

He frowns at it and pulls a fistful of wet clothing from his bag too. The water bottle has leaked.

'Shit.' Dad twists in his seat and looks down the carriage. 'There must be a drinks trolley somewhere. They might have your favourite orange juice. Or maybe I can fill this up in the toilet sink? I don't suppose it matters much if the water is labelled as safe to drink or not.'

My heart thuds as I realise my father is serious about what he is planning. He has lost his mind. He doesn't even plan on us leaving the train alive. He feels he has reached the end of the road. There is nowhere left to run. The warning on the label about not taking an overdose is vivid again in my mind.

'Dad, please. Let's just stop for a while and think. Maybe we should get some sleep? You're tired. We've been running for ages. Let's not do anything crazy.'

I raise my voice at the end, hoping Smartphone Man in front of us will pick up on what I'm saying. Then I see he has his earphones in both ears now.

I glance between him and my father, wondering if the man might be quick enough on the uptake. Would he respond to a subtle shove through the gap in the seat?

Or would he do nothing at all? I remember the woman on the train on our journey to Leicester. She switched seats so she wouldn't have to look at my tear-stained face that day when I was upset. I think of the angry neighbour threatening my father and the woman who sold our tickets tonight; she couldn't wait to leave her post. People don't want to help others. They don't want to get involved, and if you force them to, they get angry, uncooperative.

The only person who was nice to me was Matt. And I will never see him again. Maybe another young person might help me? Maybe people only become hardened as adults?

Who knows what might happen if I tried to involve someone else? Dad would see it as a betrayal. He might forget the pills and strangle me on the spot. Or he would talk himself out of trouble and disappear with me again. Then what would happen?

My father stands up now, peering down the carriage in both directions, supposedly still looking for the drinks trolley. It leaves a gap through which I think I can squeeze.

If I don't go, I am going to die. I know that.

My heart pounds, missing beats. I can't think what else to do.

In a split second, I make a decision. Dad takes a step one way and I make a sudden move in the other.

42

I dart up and tear down the carriage before Dad can register I am out of my seat.

I don't know where I'm going. The train sways and I lurch into the wall hard.

The toilet is vacant. I bolt for it on the spur of the moment and slam the door shut behind me. My shaking fingers fumble with the lock and it slides across.

Just in time it seems. The handle is forced down from the other side.

At the same time, pressure is applied to the other side of the door. It creaks. I think the flimsy thing will give under the force.

I cower back until my calves are pressed right into the metal of the tiny steel toilet.

Then there is banging. It's Dad. 'Ruby, why did you run? That was very badly behaved of you. Open the door!'

'No!' I shout back, my voice out of control with terror. 'I don't want to die, Dad. I just want to go home!'

'Sweetheart, you can't. Your home is wherever I am. I've

told you what we need to do to stay together forever. Just the two of us.'

I look around the tiny room. There is nothing to defend myself with. Everything is locked down or attached. The only things that can be moved freely are the toilet tissue and paper towels. And they can hardly be weaponized.

I can't breathe. I'm gasping for air.

'Come on, sweetheart. Daddy won't be cross if you open the door right now. I'm going to count to three! One! Two–'

Suddenly, I hear another voice. A man's. I can't hear what is being said. There seems to be quarrelling.

I put both hands to my cheeks in panic. My heart is pounding and missing so many beats I think I might pass out. I grip the sink for support as the train sways again. It's greasy. What will Dad do next?

I want to scream out to the other man. I want him to help me, but I can't. I can't form any words. Terror causes tears to run down my face as I hyperventilate. I can hardly breathe.

'Sweetheart?' My father's voice is gentle and understanding. I get the feeling he is being watched by the other person nearby, whoever they are. 'Daddy is going to sit back in our seats. Come out when you are feeling better, okay?'

After a few minutes more, it's gone quiet. I can't hear Dad's voice. I press my ear to the door gingerly. There's something unpleasant splashed up it.

I can't hear anything at all above the noise of the train.

Now what?

I can't hide in here forever. Someone else will surely want to come in. I would surely be ushered right into the arms of my waiting father. It seems as though he has already invented a story to get rid of the other person concerned about the disturbance. Perhaps he already has them primed, telling them I am disturbed and in need of psychiatric help, as he always told me about Mum. I know one of us is.

I have visions of the conductor or another member of staff forcing me out when we come to the last stop in some distant scary place.

The next moment, I realise that isn't going to happen. At least not the distant place part. An announcement is made. 'Ladies and gentlemen, the next stop is Birmingham New Street. The train terminates here.'

'No!' I whisper. This is it. The final destination. I'm going to have to open the toilet door soon. Or could I possibly stay in here, evading my father until everyone else has been shepherded off?

What if Dad manages to dodge the conductor and we are both left on the train alone all night? This is the last one of the day. Are trains simply left where they are overnight?

What would the staff come back to in the morning? I'm too terrified to consider that possibility. It's looking less likely than ever that I will see my sixteenth birthday.

The train slows and comes to a shuddering stop. The engines cease. Now the only sounds are of voices and footsteps – not many though.

I need to get off. I'm more terrified than I've ever been in my life. I put my hand on the sticky toilet door handle.

I count in my head, working up the courage to open the door.

One. Is my father right outside the door?

Two. He is most likely waiting for me somewhere nearby.

Three.

I let out an involuntary whimper as I yank the door open. I catch myself on the cheekbone in my fumble. I hardly feel the pain. It's just another bruise for later.

If there is a later.

I see a flash of uniform slip out of the train doors. The conductor shrugs his bag further up his shoulder as he waits for the other passengers to file out the doors. What if I run to one of them, anyone, and explain my father wants to kill me?

How would they react? Would they help? Matt would have. Or would they shrink back from the hysterical girl and be taken in by my father as he pulls me away and apologises? I don't want to make him angrier.

I can't see him. Where is he?

Maybe I can make it out of the station? I can find some police. How do I find the police station in the dark of an unfamiliar city?

I hold my breath as I slip behind a trendy couple in long coats. They step down onto the platform and I follow. Dad isn't anywhere nearby when I glance around. My heart pounds incredulously, hardly daring to believe it.

Then it happens.

43

M y breath is taken away when something is thrown around my shoulders. It's Dad's coat.

He bundles me up in it, pulling my hat over my head too. He pulls his arm around my waist roughly and holds me to him tight. He has collected our bags. They hang off his other arm.

I'm drawn along the platform, trapped and pressed against him as we loosely follow the sparse smattering of other passengers.

To anyone else, it looks as if he is a concerned father, protecting his daughter against the draught in this dark and cold station. We seem to be underground. But I know better. The strength in his grip is a warning.

Dad mutters to me, his voice low and threatening. 'Keep your head down and don't say a word.'

I'm pinned to his side, catching glimpses of the backs of heads and hurried footsteps as they move to leave the station.

I long to break free from the grip my father has on me.

My instinct is to scream out, but I'm paralysed by fear. What if my father follows through with his threats right here on this cold station platform? Could he have packed a knife or some other kind of weapon in that bag of his?

Tears sting my eyes again. 'Dad, please! Don't do anything crazy.'

'Shhh, Ruby,' he says soothingly. 'It will all be over soon. I promise.'

'It doesn't have to be this way! We don't have to keep running. We can go home. We can see Mum and meet Emily. I bet she would be fascinated to see us.'

'That can't ever happen. You must know that, Ruby. You're far too clever to believe what you're saying. You are trying to deceive me. I don't like it when you are insincere. Too many people in the world are like that.'

I shake my head frantically, willing my father to give me another chance at life. 'I do believe it! We can walk out of here alive and start a new life somewhere! We can choose somewhere abroad, somewhere in the sun.'

'Shhh,' he hisses again, shaking his head.

I can understand how I might sound to him, desperate and feeble. I certainly feel that way right now as I plead for my life. It doesn't stop me from trying, as we walk a distance behind the other passengers. The group is becoming more sparse now.

I look at the side of Dad's face imploringly. 'That was your idea, wasn't it? To start a new life in the sun? I want to do it. It's a good idea. You can choose the place.'

'It's too late for that now. We would never make it out of the country.'

I nod. 'All right. Why don't we go and see Mum and you can explain to her why you did what you did. Just tell her what you told me. Everyone will have to see things from your perspective.'

'It's too late for me!' Dad hisses. 'I've already done too much. I will never see the light of day again if we are caught. I'm a murderer.'

My heart sinks. Matt. I wish I had never unwittingly drawn him to his death.

It breaks my heart to think it, but I wish I had never met him. At least he would still be alive.

'You didn't mean what you did to Matt. I'll tell the police you didn't know what you were doing. We could tell them you thought he was an intruder or something. I don't know... I'll protect you, Dad.'

The lies taste bitter on my tongue as I utter them. It makes me realise how little I mean what I'm saying. I can hardly bear to utter Matt's name.

There was probably a time when I would have done anything to protect my father, but it's over now. As soon as I am away from him, I'm not going back. I struggle against his arm, but his grip is strong. He holds me firmly to him still. I can't take him by surprise and make a break for it. I wouldn't even make it one step away.

The anonymous faces here and there are all preoccupied with their own thoughts and lives. I'm hoping for a miracle as I glance around, hoping someone will notice my distress, but they don't. Of the few people left, everyone is either looking at a phone screen, has earphones in, or is otherwise absorbed in hurrying out of the station.

'Dad, think of Emily. She is your daughter too. She looks a lot like me and you. She is probably just like us. She might have a lot in common with us. I bet she would love to meet

you. We should be with her, even if you don't want to see
Mum again.'

I think I see a wobble across Dad's chin, but he is reso-
lute. 'No. You belong with me.'

I see ticket barriers up ahead. There is no way out but
through them. I know once we are on the other side, my
chance to escape will have passed.

This is it.

I look up at Dad again. 'There is nothing to run from. We
can work everything out. You'll see.'

Dad's eyes bulge momentarily. 'We can't! I've broken so
many laws just to keep you with me, to make you a home –
especially to make you a home. The real Albert Morris is
buried in the back garden of our cottage. I stole his identity
and his home. It's only a matter of time before the police find
the body. You have no idea what I've done for you, Ruby.'

44

M y stomach contracts in horror. I feel I might be sick again. 'You killed someone else too?'

Dad nods hurriedly. 'He was the old man who had lived in the cottage before us. He is the real owner. It still legally belongs to him. I killed him so we could have somewhere to live. We squatted there rent-free for twelve years. Albert had no relatives. He made the mistake of telling me so when we got talking. I simply told locals he had died and we were his only family when we moved in. No one questioned me. But it will all come to light now that the police are crawling all over our house. It was that damn boy! He ruined everything.'

I stare at the man beside me, hardly able to recognise him as my father now. 'You killed the previous owner of our house?'

Dad lets out a hysterical noise. 'It was never *our* house, you silly girl! Don't you see? I killed him. Then there is the identity theft, fraud and abduction of my own daughter. You can't even imagine the trouble I'd be in if I was to get caught.

You can't allow that, Ruby. Don't let Daddy get caught. You don't want to see me hurt, do you? I wouldn't survive being locked in prison with all those immoral men.'

I shake my head, lost for words. My gaze falls on the ticket barrier up ahead. The gateway to my demise. Police officers are hovering nearby, yawning and bored-looking, hardly glancing at any of the passengers.

I get an idea. Dad seems to know this, however, before it's even properly formed in my head. He knows me so well. My every move is watched.

'Don't try anything!' he whispers angrily. 'I know you want to run and leave me. That is a mistake. You'll die. We both will if you make any kind of attempt!'

'Don't talk like that.'

'It's always been us, Ruby. As you grew up, I realised you were the companion I'd been searching for all my life. I can't lose you. I've done so much for us to be together as a family. Stay with me. Please!'

It's the pleading note in my father's voice that reaffirms my plan. He is desperate. He has lost. I know he is in the wrong now, not me. I have hope that I can walk away from this.

I just need to play this right, or it will cost me my life. I pray Dad doesn't have a concealed weapon of some kind in his pocket. It isn't his style to carry a knife. Although, he has done some things to surprise me lately.

I force my feet to a stop. Dad is still trying to steer me, however, so we stumble a few paces.

'What are you doing?' Dad's wild eyes dart from me to the police up ahead.

'I can't go with you. Not this time.'

He turns to round on me, unwittingly releasing his grip.

'Yes, you can. We belong together. Where would you go without me?'

'I don't know. But I'm not leaving the station.'

'Yes, you are, young lady!'

'I can't stay with you, Dad. Not now I know what you have done and Mum is still alive.'

'You don't know what you are saying!' he hisses. 'You're confused.'

'I want to see her again. I want to meet my sister. If you loved me, you wouldn't deny me that.'

'If you loved me, you wouldn't talk to me like this! Making silly demands when we have something important to do.'

'You can't kill me. Not when Mum has been told that I'm still alive. How would she feel if she found out I didn't make it after coming this far all these years later? I have to leave you here. I'm sorry.'

'No – you have to stay with me. Where do you think you will go without me?'

I take a deep breath to steady myself. 'Home.'

Dad splutters and shakes his head. 'I'm your home!'

I keep my voice steady, despite the fact I'm shaking all over. 'I'm going to give you a chance, Dad. You can have your freedom. You are right – I don't think you would handle prison. I have no idea what it is really like, of course, because everything else you have ever told me could be a lie. I don't know which bits might be real anymore. But I bet it probably isn't nice and I don't want you to be locked up for the rest of your days. It's awful never being allowed outside to do normal things and see people. I'm not going to see you treated the way you have treated me. It wouldn't be right.'

Dad gapes at me open-mouthed as he struggles for words.

I nod towards the police, who peer in our direction now, hands on hips, curious as to why we haven't gone through the barriers with everyone else. 'Listen, they will clock any second who I am. My face is all over the news. Yours is too. I'm going to make a run for it in the opposite direction. You take the opportunity to get out of the station alone. Do you think you can do that?'

I don't get the chance to wait for an answer from Dad's white and shocked lips. The police are approaching from behind him at this point. I see it now – the recognition in their eyes as they scan my face. They look between me and my father. I can only hope that all three of them decide to chase after me.

I turn and dart; the image of my immobile father staring after me will be forever burned in my mind.

I just hope he has the sense to run while I am causing this diversion.

45

D ad's coat leaves my shoulders as I dash away. Its weight leaves me within a few paces.

My trainers squeak on the floor beneath them as I dart back around the twists and turns and onto the dark and draughty platform. There are less than a handful of people down here now. They lift their gaze from their phones as I pass, with what I hope is three police officers in my wake.

It isn't much of a chase. I've long crashed from the sugar in the hot chocolates at the bar in Leicester. My weak and tired legs give way from under me and I seem to trip over myself before long. At least Dad is out of sight now; I hope he ran.

I'm surprised at myself. I would have thought I would be more bitter about what Dad has done to me. Perhaps I will be less compassionate in the morning. Now I just feel so very numb, tired and cold.

I so want to go home. I wonder if this is where they will

take me. This is my thought as I hit the hard surface of the platform.

Where is home, anyway? I have no idea. What part of the country does Mum live in with Emily? I don't know. I just long for the feeling of warmth and comfort that I'm sure I truly knew once.

Authoritative footsteps hammer around me. Black boots and fluorescent tactical vests press in on my weary senses. I hear the crackle of a radio nearby. Pulling off my woolly hat seems to amplify the chatter.

'I think it's her,' comes a male officer's voice. 'It's Ruby Adams.'

I want to erase the doubt from their minds. I want to shout the truth, even if it's only me hearing it. I want to say out loud my name and have someone hear my voice who isn't my father. I learned from Matt what a liberating experience that was. It was so nice to be heard.

'I'm Ruby Adams,' I say out loud, my voice breaking into a sob. 'And I want to go home.'

46

SIX MONTHS LATER

My eyes spring open. For a few moments, I'm confused about where I am; this certainly has happened so many times.

Then I remember. I'm at home. My real home in Peterborough.

It's warm and bright in my bedroom. Summer sunlight filters in through the damask silver curtains each morning. The modern styling is so far removed from the yellowed old curtains in my old bedroom.

It was never truly that bright in Albert's cottage, even before Dad decided to board the windows up. Matt can attest to that, having seen how dingy it was when we touched hands through the glass of the living room window that one time.

At the thought of my boyfriend, I turn over and reach for my phone. I press the power button and smile when I see he has sent me a good morning text. He does this most days.

> Good morning, beautiful. Can't wait to see you for bowling this weekend. Tell Emily her reign as champion isn't going to last long! xx

I text back my reply.

> She is enjoying her title on borrowed time! It's not just you that she has to worry about though. Mum took us for a bonus practice session last night. Brace yourself for some serious skills! Can't wait to see you too. xx

I tap about looking for a cute heart emoji to add to the end of my message. It was easy to get used to the smartphone Mum bought me. Matt was right about needing one. I can't imagine being without it.

Matt has recovered from his injuries now. It turned out Dad left him with broken ribs, a fractured arm and a chipped tooth the day we left Hope. You wouldn't know it now though.

Matt's father managed to repair the damaged tooth. And his bones had fully healed by the time we met again in spring, following my escape in December.

Matt was astounded to learn who I truly was. His parents had suspicions about my father, but they hadn't expected that their son had stumbled into such a famous disappearance case. Apparently, they had done a full land registry search on both properties before they purchased the neighbouring cottage to renovate.

As a result, they had been expecting someone much older to be the new neighbour to their holiday cottage, not Dad. My father couldn't have been the real Albert Morris. As the records stood, my father hadn't even been born for another twenty years when the cottage last officially changed hands.

Not for the first time, I load one of the many news reports on my phone and look at the photographs of the true owner of our cottage. These photos were recovered from the boxes in the cellar. All the things in boxes down there had belonged to Albert and his wife. The image of him and his wife I look at now was taken in the back garden.

Albert Morris was in his thirties when he purchased the house to live in as a newlywed with his wife, Rose. The pair had never had children. Albert was widowed in his seventies and had no other relatives, just as Dad had said. That left him to live alone in that building until the day my father showed up at his door.

I shiver every time I think about it. What did Dad do with me whilst he carried out the crime? He couldn't possibly have left me with someone else. He never trusted anyone, aside from me.

I must have been nearby when that poor old man's life was brought to an unnatural end. Did my father talk his way inside the cottage at first? He must have had some way of finding out how isolated the man was, how he had no remaining family to check up on him.

The news articles say the cause of death was suffocation. Was I left upstairs whilst Dad did that? That memory is buried inside me somewhere. I hope it never resurfaces.

Albert's body has been recovered from the back garden now. He has been given a proper burial. I would quite like to visit his grave and place some flowers on it one day. I don't quite feel ready yet. I'm still cringing about the times I must have walked over that shallow grave unwittingly, excited to be allowed out for an occasional look at the stars. Is Albert the reason Dad didn't want me venturing out into the garden? He isn't here to ask. I regret not gleaning more from him when it was possible.

The once-peaceful cottage has now been stripped of its dark secrets. The building is ruined after Dad's hasty attempt to burn it to the ground. Matt tells me his parents are purchasing the plot. They want to turn the space my prison occupied into an extension of their own property.

Matt's mum has designs on turning it into a landscaped garden, with a koi pond, beds of colourful flowers and a summer house.

It sounds lovely, but I'm not sure I will ever be able to set foot in that area again, no matter how much remodelling goes on. Matt doesn't have any plans to live there, so I hope it never becomes an issue.

I shudder at the very thought of returning to the place where I lost my childhood.

47

After sending the message to Matt, I get out of bed and open the curtains. I'm keen to do this each day, appreciating that I can. It's a hard concept to understand that I can do whatever I choose to now, within reason. I finally have the freedom I so longed for for years.

June sun is already strong on my arms and face below my short-sleeve pyjamas as I stare across the garden.

It's so beautiful. My stepfather, Jack, works so hard in the garden. It's his trade. He runs a landscaping service alongside his own blog.

He is out there now, all plaid and denim, watering and weeding. I can just see the back of his sandy head.

He doesn't notice as I open the window and let in the sweet air. Mum has chosen well in her second marriage. Jack is a good man. It takes me by surprise almost every day how laid back and easy-going he is, leaving decisions up to Mum and going with the flow. He reminds me a bit of Matt.

Our strip of shallow garden leads to a view of the marina.

Small white barges drift about lazily on the mirror-like surface of the water, which today reflects a perfect blue sky.

I turn away from the window and face the room. It's at least twice the size of my bedroom at the cottage, light and airy. The warmth of the sun reaches into the corners. No dark spaces, or worn-out areas.

This was my childhood bedroom, the one I slept in until four years old, anyway. It's not like I consciously remember it. It's changed a lot since those days. Mum admitted she had kept my room intact and untouched for almost ten years, finally relenting and updating it a couple of years ago when she listed the place for the sale that never went through.

Tears formed in her eyes and she looked terribly guilty as she told me this. It was so difficult to maintain a room frozen in time. It was hard for Emily too. When she was younger Mum found it heartbreaking when Emily would ask when her big sister was coming home.

My mother admitted part of her couldn't bear to look at my abandoned room in its state of perpetual infancy with its soft toys, colourful character bedding and matching curtains. I told her it was okay, I understood.

Since then, she has bent over backwards to make other changes, and encourages me to choose things for myself – something I'm not accustomed to. Most days, I don't know what to do with such freedoms. I've humoured Mum by selecting some colourful pink and blue cushions I was drawn to in a homeware store.

And I got to choose the pale wood bookcase for all the brand new books Mum has gifted me. As soon as I told her I liked reading, she hasn't been able to stop herself, coming home most days with the gift of a good story, amongst so many other things: clothes, games and gadgets, like my smartphone and a laptop. I wonder if she will ever get used to the fact I'm home again.

I inhale deeply, breathing in the room. It may be cosmetically different now, but it's so familiar and comforting in a way I can't explain. Quite a contrast from Albert's claustrophobic cottage with its dark wood and vintage everything.

I can forgive Mum for not wanting to keep my bedroom a shrine forever. Who would want to look at a silent testament to a childhood cut short forever? I'm finding it hard to send out the same feelings to my father, however.

It wasn't forgiveness that I felt for him in that cold railway station that night. It was acceptance. The damage he has wreaked upon my life is unforgivable, but some part of me is empathetic towards him. Sending him to prison seemed unimaginable that night. I was tired, emotionally and physically exhausted. I wasn't thinking clearly. I can't help but wonder if I did the right thing letting him run for it.

My plan worked. He managed to evade the police at the station. The three officers gave chase to me, as I expected. Dad took his opportunity to turn and run too.

I've had mixed emotions since. Part of me is hurt that he did leave me for the first time in my life. It was the first time he left me behind.

I tell myself that it was only because he knew it was over. The genie was out of the bottle and there was no way of ever putting it back inside.

The police haven't caught up with him. Dad knows how to stay hidden, I told them that. He is like a silverfish, slipping beneath the cracks in the blink of an eye. I would be surprised if he ever surfaced again.

As I dress and get ready for the day ahead, the scent of freshly brewed coffee and crispy bacon wafts up the stairs. I don't know if I will ever get used to having food prepared for me. My life with Dad was such that if I didn't cook, we didn't eat.

48

Emily is engaged in animated chatter as I enter the kitchen diner. She is dressed the same as me this morning, in a black school blazer over a white shirt and tie. It's the uniform of the local secondary school, the one I should have attended for the last few years.

It's my final month now. I've mainly spent my lessons revising alongside my classmates. I'm sad I didn't get to enjoy the school experience for longer. But it is what it is, I suppose. As Mum says, we can't change the past.

The schoolwork is easy, as I already completed it myself at home in my bedroom prison, passing every test Dad gave me with ease. The result is I'm not as stressed as my classmates about the upcoming end-of-school exams. The possibility that I might become a vet seems realistic now. It's exciting.

The hardest thing about starting school was dealing with the stares of the other pupils when I first arrived. They've got over it now though.

Mum smiles as I enter the kitchen. Even now, her round

eyes linger every time she sets them on me. It's like she can't quite believe I'm really here after all these years.

She admitted to me recently she thought I was gone forever when she discovered Dad had taken me. He had made all sorts of threats towards the end of their marriage, apparently. She had believed he may well have followed through with them. Especially when it had been so long since my disappearance without any word or sightings. There was no sign he had left the country with me either. I don't blame her for thinking that way.

Emily looks around as I join her at the breakfast bar. Her hair isn't quite as long as mine, only reaching past her shoulders. Her energy for everything is infectious.

'What's up, sis?'

She grins at me and passes me a plate of bacon and eggs. 'I was just saying to Mum, we could go shopping later when I've finished school. I'm still looking for the perfect pair of jeans.'

Mum nods and pours me a glass of orange juice, cold from the fridge. 'We can pick up anything you want, Ruby,' she smiles at me kindly. 'Is there something you've had your eye on?'

I shake my head, overwhelmed and feeling very much like the poor relation, out of sorts from these two people who buy whatever they want whenever they want as if it's nothing. 'I think I have everything I need. I've never owned so many clothes in my life.'

My words darken Mum's face a little. Her eyes take on a watery sheen and I regret opening my mouth.

I'm walking on a new variety of eggshells in this house. Not one where I'm afraid of an angry explosion, but one where I fear hurting anyone's feelings by saying or doing the wrong thing.

Mum says not to worry. She is a therapist, and she knows about trauma and how to deal with it. She has helped me process everything a lot since I've been home. She says healing is a journey, not a destination.

'Take each day at a time,' she said. Which is basically what my officially appointed therapist told me too. I see her once a week still. I have a lot of issues to work through, but I'm not diagnosed with anything other than PTSD.

Emily clucks her tongue in mock disapproval now. 'Rubes, you have so much to learn. It's not about how many clothes you own, it's the thrill of the chase when you buy them.'

She winks, her dimples creasing in the same way mine do when I smile. She has my father's dark eyes, brows and hair too. There is no mistaking the fact that we are sisters. I wonder what Mum thinks when she looks at her two girls and sees the husband she so regrets.

Mum's phone buzzes.

Emily stretches up in her seat to look at the screen on the kitchen island. 'Urghh! It's that bozo from the TV again. He wants to know if you will reconsider that documentary. He says he can increase the interview fee. What do you think?'

'No!' Mum says forcefully. 'The last thing I need is the press inside our home. It was bad enough at the time.'

It was. At first when I came home, there were cameras following our family around everywhere. For the first few months stories would emerge every few days as Dad's deceitful trail was unwoven and picked apart for the public to devour with interest.

Then Albert's body was found. After that, a story surfaced of the police closing in on my father. From an anonymous tip, they found a bedsit he had been using down in Dover. There was strong evidence he had left the country for France. The police over there are on the lookout for him now. We were told they will let us know when they catch him.

Anyway, the stories seem to have died down a lot now. The papers run stories of others' misfortune instead.

But I can never shake the feeling of being watched.

49

Mum looks between us as we gather our things in the spacious entrance hall that stretches to the back of the house.

She has on a colourful floral dress, much like the one in my baby photo I've had for years. 'Are you sure I can't give you girls a ride?'

Emily smirks at me as we shrug our school bags over our shoulders. 'Mum, it's a fifteen-minute walk to school. I think we can just about make it.'

'I know, but I don't have my first client until eleven. I've got some time to kill.'

Emily rolls her eyes. 'You've always let me walk to school alone before. You never used to trail behind me in the car either. Anyway, the walk is good for our precious growing bones.'

'Yes, I'm sorry.' Mum fiddles with a brooch on her dress. She looks through the glass doors at the back of the house at a flicker of movement. A pale heron swoops in to land gracefully, striding with his long legs along the jetty beside the picturesque water. 'I just want to know you are safe.'

My sister snorts. 'Our crazy father is in France. That's miles away in another country. Don't worry so much.'

Our mother moves forward to hold us tight. 'I can't help but worry about you two. You're my little ones.'

Emily makes a noise like she is being strangled and pulls back, ending the moment. I'd have preferred it to last a touch longer, although I won't admit it.

'I think we'll be okay,' I say, trying to put her mind at rest.

I smile and try to pretend the tender embrace wasn't making my eyes water. 'It's lovely weather outside. It will be a nice walk.'

I mean it sincerely. Mum knows how controlling her husband was. I've explained how I was never allowed out alone. So she backs off now with a nod, albeit with pursed lips, knowing how important my freedom is to me. The last thing she wants to do is remind me of Dad.

Besides, I know Emily has felt restricted by the new level of security she has faced in the last six months. Just when she was starting to gain some independence in their own life as a twelve-year-old, I arrived. It meant she experienced something of a clampdown on the freedoms she had taken for granted.

We step out into the sunshine and start the journey to school. I enjoy the feeling of the hot sun on my face. I don't mind that it is bringing me out in freckles. I welcome them.

The little dots of melanin on my hands and cheeks are a testament I can walk outside in the glorious summer light.

Emily and I pass gardens in full bloom, birds fluttering in and out of the many suburban hedgerows in front of the large detached houses. I think I even spot a fish rippling the surface of the water of the marina as we stroll away from our quiet residential street.

I'll never take something as simple as being allowed out for a walk unchaperoned for granted. Ever. We are halfway to school, stepping onto the familiar footbridge that crosses the busy motorway when I explain this concept to Emily. How even being allowed outside in the back garden is such a novelty to me still.

Emily snorts. 'Our dad sounds like a right nutjob. I can't believe we are related to him. You're so normal. I'm so glad you got away.'

She hooks her clasped hands over my shoulders suddenly and presses her cheek against mine in a playful embrace. 'You belong with us. I know you're the big sister, but I'll always look out for you.'

I laugh and hug her back. 'Same.'

This sentiment still rings in our ears when something unexpected happens a few minutes later.

We are most of the way along the footbridge when we spot a figure emerging from the trees up ahead. Somewhere in the back of my mind, an alarm goes off. It tells me something is wrong.

Only when the figure grows near enough to spark a jolt of recognition do I realise we made a mistake in turning down Mum's offer of a ride this morning.

I stop and stare at the man as he draws closer.

He may look dishevelled, but there is no mistaking who he is. Not to me anyway. Not after having spent so much time in this company.

It's mine and Emily's father.

He has come back for me.

50

The anxiety I thought I could finally move on from now returns as though it has never been away. I'm that same oppressed girl again. My breath catches in my chest. My heart misses those same familiar beats.

I stare at my father as he draws levels with us. He shouldn't be here.

That's the only thought that goes around my head at this moment. My brain is stuck in a loop.

This man shouldn't be here. It looks wrong to see him on such a beautiful sunny day, silhouetted against the bright blue sky. There is nothing but a single cloud around us.

He just shouldn't be in this place, miles away from where I last saw him in that dark underground station. Most of my memories of Dad have been in the darkness, whether it was the night sky or hiding in a dull environment away from prying eyes.

Now here he is.

Emily stops beside me too and frowns. 'What is it, Rubes? Why are you staring at that old tramp?'

Emily can be forgiven for thinking that the man coming our way across the bridge is a homeless person.

Dad certainly looks like one with his long raggedy hair, beard to match and shabby, torn clothing. They look like the same ones he was wearing when I saw him that night. His cheeks are sunken and thin. He has lost a lot of weight. I wonder how he has survived at all without me there to look after him.

His glasses are missing too, giving him the reverse Clark Kent effect. I guess he ditched them in response to the stills released of him at various railway stations when he ran with me.

If he had simply walked by briskly now, there is a chance I wouldn't have noticed him.

'Hello, Ruby. Daddy's here now.' His voice is coarse and rough, as though he hasn't used it for a while.

I'm shocked and speechless. Emily is quicker on the uptake than me, taking half a step forward. 'Get away from us, you freak!'

Dad blinks. His intense eyes leave mine and he looks at his other daughter for the first time in the flesh. 'I'm sorry I couldn't take you with me too, Emily. I hope you don't think it was favouritism. I had no choice, you see. I'd have loved to have got to have known you too.'

He blinks slowly, taking her in. 'It would have been much different in the cottage with the three of us, I expect. Ruby wouldn't have become so lonely. A little sister to keep her company would have been perfect. Things might have worked out. Wouldn't they, sweetheart?'

He looks at me again, his dark eyes ablaze, and nods fervently.

I'm still speechless. My brain has gone numb.

Emily jabs a finger in his direction. 'The police are watching us. So you'd better disappear quick!'

Dad smiles wryly. 'No, they are not. I've been watching you for some time now, Ruby. You and your new little family. There hasn't been a police presence at your nice comfortable house for five weeks. And no doubt that isolated visit was to officially let you know about the anonymous tip. The one that led to the discovery of my bedsit and the evidence inside indicating that I had left for France.'

I flinch. Dad set that whole thing up. I told the police in all the various statements and interviews I have given that my father was cunning. Wasn't there a clue somewhere in that bedsit that the scene was staged? I guess not. After living with Dad for so long, he could still surprise me. Even in those last few months together.

'You shouldn't be here.' I'm impressed by my ability to keep my voice steady. I certainly don't feel this brave as I stand and face my father. 'Just let us pass.'

'I can't, Ruby. I've come to take you home.'

A beam of understanding passes between us as we stand on the bridge.

The noise of the fast traffic suddenly seems deafeningly loud. The bridge vibrates beneath my school shoes as a huge lorry passes below.

If I had thought that Dad's last stand was the railway station, I was wrong. It's now. I know exactly what he is planning to do as I glance down at the unrelenting current of traffic on the motorway beneath our feet.

Dad's face is desperate. He has never missed a day of being clean-shaven in his adult life. Not even with the stress and upheaval of us leaving Hope. He has always taken such pride in his appearance. The fact that he has abandoned it now for an unruly beard speaks volumes.

He is only here for one purpose – to take me down with him.

'I've missed you, sweetheart.' He takes a step closer. 'The days have been so long without you. So dark and lonely. This is what it would have been like if I'd let your mother force me out of your life when you were so small. I know I did the right thing all those years ago, even if you don't think it now.'

He takes another step forward. 'I don't want you to have to go through the world without me. You must have seen how immoral it is by now, haven't you?'

Emily stares at him in horror, just as I do. She grabs hold of my sleeve all of a sudden, pulling me backwards.

Another lorry rattles the concrete below us. People in the stream of traffic below must glimpse us as they shoot past at seventy miles an hour or more. The image would only be fleeting, however.

Even if it wasn't, there is nothing they could do to help us. They wouldn't be able to react in time.

I have to make a split-second decision. I don't have time to think it through. I know our only hope is to get away from here as fast as we can.

'Run!' I hiss out of the corner of my mouth to Emily.

51

M y sister doesn't need telling twice. She grabs my hand and turns rapidly, planning to tug me off the footbridge the way we came.

Dad is right behind us, however. He snatches at my arm, dragging me backwards. Emily is right by my side. She aims a kick at Dad. I'm not sure where, but I feel it connect. He makes a sudden movement and crumples.

Then Emily turns and runs, my hand in hers.

It seems I am two steps behind her all the way. A few months of walking isn't enough to reverse twelve years of confinement. My legs aren't as weak as they were, but I can't seem to keep pace with Emily.

'Come on!' she shouts, yanking my arm.

Terror fills my senses. It's one thing Dad dragging me to my death. It's another entirely if he hurts Emily too. I don't want my sister to suffer because of me.

Emily gives me another tug with surprising strength. She has inherited Dad's broad frame. 'Quick – we'll lose him in the trees!'

I realise too late that this is probably a mistake. We are already running through the wooded area and I'm gasping for breath, unable to speak.

We can't stop running. Or we'll die.

I have no idea where we are. Emily's superior knowledge of the area is what we rely upon now. I can only hope Dad isn't as well versed. Although, I'm fully aware he used to live here with Mum before the idea of Emily or even me entered his head.

I pray he is confused, disoriented or out of sorts with the patch of land he used to frequent all those years ago.

I'm certainly bewildered as we run through this cluster of trees and bushes. The brambles are dense, scratching at my legs and ruining my tights.

Emily slows and doubles back. My heart pounds with terror at the thought we are lost. She drags me into a thicket of trees. We are hidden behind the luscious green foliage. She presses a finger to her lips as she looks at my face. Her eyes are wide and frightened too. She has as many red cuts on her legs as I have.

There is a crashing up ahead. Thudding footsteps. Dad is searching for us. I grasp a handful of my blazer, bringing it up to my face to pant into. I just don't dare make a sound.

I'm so out of breath I think I might be suffocating. The line between fear and physical exhaustion is blurred as we crouch in the overgrowth.

The sound of my name from between the trees startles me.

'Ruby!' Dad wails. 'Come on, sweetheart! Don't let Daddy be all alone again. It's not good for him. It's been a nightmare without you. I can't eat. I hardly sleep anymore.'

He disappears out of sight, oblivious to our hiding place,

but I can still hear him. His voice becomes quieter as he treads off somewhere else. 'I miss your cooking and your sense of humour... Your smile...'

After a few minutes, Emily deems it safe to guide me from the thicket. 'I think he has gone,' she whispers, looking this way and that with wide eyes. The terror I feel is reflected on her face. 'What a nutter. We need to go home, quick. Mum can call the police. Come on. We'd better call her.'

Emily pulls out her phone as we emerge from the woods, but I put out a hand to stop her. 'I'll do it. It's better if she hears it from me.'

I tap my phone and hear the ringtone. Thankfully, Mum picks up almost straight away. 'Ruby, is everything okay?'

'We're okay now.' I glance over my shoulder at the quiet streets as we hurry home. I'm very aware our father can't have gone far. 'But Dad was here. He chased us.'

'What! Where are you? I'll come and get you in the car!'

'There's no need. We are just turning back onto our street now.'

Mum dashes from the driveway of our detached house before we can get there.

'Oh my god,' she says again as she reaches out to us, her summer dress flowing around her ankles. 'Get inside the house, quickly!'

'Where's Jack?' Emily asks as Mum ushers us inside the front door and locks it firmly.

'He went out on a job across the city. He won't be back until late.' She grabs the cordless phone in the hall and dials the police.

Emily reaches out and wraps her arms around me, pulling me close. Her skin is damp with sweat beneath her white school blouse. Her heart still pounds hard.

I hug her back, glad she is safe.

Then there is a flicker of movement through the tall glass door behind her. I tense.

Emily must sense this, as she pulls back from me and looks at my face. 'What's the matter, Rubes?'

'I thought I saw something out there. At the end of the garden, near the water.'

We both tread closer to the tall glass doors that lead out to the garden and marina beyond. Mum rushes forward, the phone pressed to her ear and checks they are secure.

'Jack locked them when he came in. I just thought I'd check, though. Sometimes he forgets–'

Mum doesn't finish her sentence. She shrieks in horror.

I don't have to ask what has caught her attention. Emily and I can both see it too.

It's our father.

52

T he three of us stare as he makes his way slowly along the path that separates our garden from the glassy water of the marina. His movements are awkward and fumbling. He looks exhausted. He must have headed straight here when he lost us in the woods.

'That's my school bag!' Emily says suddenly. 'What's he doing with it?'

She is right. Dad has the backpack she hastily dropped on the footbridge as Dad gave chase.

'I don't understand. What's he doing with it?' I watch my father's juddering movements as he stops to adjust the straps on Emily's purple rucksack. He then slides it with difficulty over his shoulders. He must have filled it with something heavy. Rocks or soil or something.

He teeters backwards almost comically as he turns to face the house. He stares through the glass at Mum, Emily and me. Even from this distance, I can feel the intensity of his eyes.

'This is what you've driven me to, Ruby! And you, Rachel! You've both made sure I have nothing left!'

Emily looks uncertainly towards me and our mother. 'Mum, what's he going to do? I don't get it.'

Mum reaches across for her other daughter, turning her shoulders away from the glass. She does the same to me, but I can't pull my gaze from the scene by the water. 'Come away. Don't look at him!'

She presses the phone back to her ear, talking to the police in a more terrified voice than she did a few minutes ago. 'I need you to send someone over right away! My ex-husband is here. He is threatening to drown himself.'

All the windows in the house are on the vents. Mum had hopes earlier of tempting a summer breeze into the house to cool the stifling air. As a result, we can hear Dad perfectly well as he shouts again.

'Ruby! I'll kill myself if you don't come back to me. I mean it! Don't make Daddy go into the water now, will you?'

'Please don't!' I scream at him. 'I told you I don't want you to get hurt!'

Mum talks hurriedly into the phone nearby, pleading for an officer to turn up.

Dad's voice shakes with emotion as he turns towards the water. 'You don't love me any longer, Ruby. What choice do I have? I can't stand to live without you. The light of my life has gone out!'

I reach out for the glass door hurriedly, fumbling with the lock.

Mum reaches out and stops me. 'Don't unlock the door! You can't go out there, Ruby. He will kill you.'

'No!' My lips tremble now. The first time in a while. 'I have to go to him. It's himself he is trying to hurt, not me.'

Mum nods frantically. 'This is just another way your father is abusing you. Only, it's his body he is using, not yours.'

'I didn't think of it like that.' I blink in confusion. 'But he is going to get hurt if I don't go out there. I can't allow that to happen. I don't want someone's death on my hands, especially not my family. I know what it's like to live with that kind of guilt. I did it for twelve years, thinking I'd killed you, and later on Emily too.'

Mum blinks back tears. 'I understand. I can't let you go outside, however. For your own safety.'

'Ruby! Where are you?' Dad is making his way along the wooden jetty towards the water. The pain in his voice is intense.

I put my hands over my head, grabbing fistfuls of hair. 'I can't stand it! I can't let him do it.'

Mum puts her warm hand on my back. Her comforting touch is what I've craved for as long as I can remember. 'It's his last weapon to wield against you. He has lost you. He knows it's over. You have to use one last bit of strength to break free from him, as I planned to.'

'I don't want him dead though!'

'I thought that once too. He used to threaten me with self-harm often, especially towards the end of our marriage.'

My blurry eyes find her face. 'He did?'

She nods sadly. 'In the end, I decided I needed to be free. It's his choice what he does with his health and wellbeing. Not yours. You aren't responsible for what he does. You haven't been for a long time.'

I blink as Dad calls again. His feet are nudging the end of the jetty now. 'Ruby, can you see me? You can stop this! Just come to me, sweetheart. Daddy needs you more than ever!'

'Don't listen to him.'

Mum must deem me stable enough to move away and shut the windows completely, blocking out her ex-husband's shouting. I'm not out of the woods yet. The temptation to run out to Dad is almost overwhelming. I wish someone would hang on to me.

There is another shout, somewhat more muffled now. 'I won't give up on you, my angel. Not like you've given up on me!'

I look up to see Dad staring in my direction. There is a haunted look in his eyes that is most unfamiliar as he takes a step into the water. He is fully clothed and makes no attempt to look away as he wades further below the glassy surface of the marina. My father doesn't even seem to blink. I feel like he is staring into my very soul.

Mum is occupied with shutting the windows. I look again at the door handle in front of me. Maybe I can just go and calmly talk to my father, make him see sense.

Emily's arm comes out of nowhere. She forcefully turns me from the glass doors with a strength that surprises me, tearing my desperate gaze away. She leads me through to Jack's study at the front of the house and shuts the door behind us.

Emily pushes my shoulders down so that I collapse into our stepfather's squashy leather chair. She settles herself cross-legged onto the desk beside me, shoving paperwork and a succulent plant out of the way as she does so.

It's quieter in here. Emily puts Spotify on Jack's laptop. It's a song by Katy Perry that I'm not familiar with. The now-familiar sound of the singer's voice is soothing, however.

Emily wraps her arms around my shoulders, clinging like a Koala bear. She rests her head on mine. 'Everything will be okay, Rubes. You've always got me. I'll always be here for you.'

53

After a few minutes, Mum enters the office, shutting the door behind her. She looks pale and stern, nothing like her usual self. With the usual warmth, energy and light she exudes, it's not hard to see why Dad became so fixated on her once.

Emily and I watch her cast around the room. The fact she hasn't told us what is happening outside is significant. We follow her lead and don't mention it.

She takes a seat on a box of A3 paper beside me and intertwines her fingers with mine, her other hand on Emily's knee. 'I know he can be convincing. I was in your shoes once, my every move controlled by him and his moods. I feared what he would do next a lot of the time.'

She sighs and closes her eyes. 'Your father didn't want me going out when we were together. That was the first sign there was something wrong. That wasn't until long after we were married, however. I felt committed to him by that point. I was pregnant with you shortly after. I didn't realise that wasn't a coincidence. He wanted me to quit the work as a therapist I loved. He had ideas of me staying in this house with him so I could follow his plans for the day instead. I had to break free. You should too Ruby. You don't need his permission to live. You don't need his approval for anything.'

My mother's words take the weight from my shoulders. My throat is too constricted for me to tell her this, however. I simply nod.

I think she understands. She has an intuition with me. Like Dad always did, I guess. Except Mum uses this super-power for good, not as a way to catch me out or as a weapon against me.

Mum keeps talking. 'Did I ever tell you how your father and I met? I was a couples therapist back then too. Mark led me to believe he and his partner, Marie, would be attending the sessions together.'

It feels good to talk about something else. I realise Mum is using all this as a distraction. It seems to be good for her too.

I nod. 'Yes, he told me that. He said Marie didn't show up.'

Mum smiles sadly. 'No, she didn't. Week after week your father would turn up alone and we would wait for Marie to attend after work. But she never showed, not once. In hind-sight, I should have realised something was wrong at that point. But Mark was convincing.

'Besides, it's not unusual for only one-half of the couple to show up for therapy. He must have known that. He played on it, always the victim. Oftentimes, the other person doesn't agree to air their personal problems to a stranger. I see it a lot in my work, even now.'

Mum stares at the carpet as she remembers. 'So there we were alone for these weekly therapy sessions. I had been lonely for some time when Mark arrived in my life. He said the right things. It appeared we liked the same things too. We seemed perfect for each other.'

Her lip wobbles. 'I didn't read the obvious signs. I see all the red flags now that I look back. I'm always looking out for them in therapy sessions when couples come in to see me for the first time. I let my guard down with Mark since they weren't true sessions. His partner hadn't turned up but he had paid to be there anyway. It was a foolish mistake for me to make.'

An idea suddenly occurs to me. It's twisted and horrible, but I know as I voice it that I can't put it past Dad. 'Do you think he lied about having a partner just to meet you?'

Mum shakes her head. 'No, Marie was real. She got in touch with me once the story of your abduction was in the news. She told me about his behaviour when they were together. It turns out, she was the one who suggested therapy. But not for the two of them. She wanted him to get help for his own problems. She had concerns about his welfare.'

'What kind of things did he do?'

'There were a lot of control issues, apparently. I saw them myself during our relationship, so I know exactly what Marie means. Mark would want everything to be done his way. He has all these rules and habits and would get upset if they weren't done. She was constantly treading on eggshells.

'Mark wanted us dependent on him. He convinced Marie to give up work, just as he had tried to pile on the pressure with me to be a full-time mum. I loved you, but I also loved my job. It was a big part of who I was. Who I still am. Besides, I couldn't afford this house on his wage as a cleaner.'

'I thought he was a solicitor back then.' Even as I voice

the words, I realise how foolish I have been to still believe anything Dad said. I already discovered he lied on several occasions about his job. No wonder we never seemed to have any money.

Mum shakes her head. 'No. His father was one. He wanted Mark to follow in his footsteps. He was so disappointed when he didn't. Mark opened up to me about it during our sessions together. Marie said there had been unpleasant interactions between Mark and his parents when they were together. She was too concerned with getting her life back on track to get involved. She had moved house and not told anyone where she had gone in an attempt to shake him off, apparently.'

'Why didn't Marie call the police?'

'She had. She went to a police station before she got away, but there wasn't anything they could do as Mark technically hadn't broken any laws at that point. The things he did were difficult to prove. So she decided to run away to survive. The law has got a little better since then, but not much.'

We fall quiet again as I consider the horror Dad has caused. Not just to me, but to two other women and Emily. She can't have gone through all this unscathed, what with the knowledge of my father and what he has done to her mother and sister and all the attention from the press.

I don't like to admit it, but it's somehow comforting to consider Mum and Marie have been through the same thing.

Something clicks inside me and I realise I can let Dad go. Finally, I can give myself permission to be free of him.

EPILOGUE

It had gone ominously quiet outside by the time the police showed up that morning. I didn't need the police divers to confirm what the three of us already knew.

Dad was gone. He had followed through on his promise in the end.

He hadn't managed to take me down with him though. That gives me a sense of pride, of freedom. I survived, despite everything my father put me through. Dad always said pride was a sin. Maybe it is.

I'm strengthened every day, though, by the knowledge that I managed to break free from Dad ultimately through my own actions. In the end, my mother and sister gave me the last push. They are exactly what I needed.

We are a family now. Jack too. He turned up later that day to find police cars, boats and divers swarming around his home. Typical Jack, he'd left his phone inside his van as he had worked on his client's garden. He had missed Mum's calls throughout the day. It was all a shock for him. He rushed to Mum and held her tight, stroking her hair. Something about the image unsettled me, though I can't identify why. Was it because I realised then he had effectively assumed Dad's role? First and foremost Jack is Mum's husband, but he is also Emily's and my stepfather. I know how dangerous father figures can be if they are allowed to be.

I had almost forgotten about Jack before he got back, despite the fact it was his office we huddled in for most of that eventful morning.

Part of me was disappointed when he arrived. I had been appreciating the time with my mother and sister. Just the three of us.

I watched snippets of the scene in the marina unfold from my bedroom window over those next few days – when I could slip away from Mum, Jack and Emily, that was.

Thankfully, I didn't have to see Dad's body recovered from the water. As it is though, I'll be haunted forever by the look in his eyes moments before he stepped into the water, ruining the glassy surface.

A few months later, I was looking out my bedroom window at the place where it had happened. The window was open, letting in the cooling late summer air.

I was due to start college later that week after receiving great grades from my end-of-school exams. My future looked bright, happy and full of promise. I was going to start studying for my dream career path. I wondered what Dad would say if he knew I really was going to become a vet and one day step out into the world alone.

Jack was pottering around in the garden somewhere.

'Penny for your thoughts,' he said, straightening up with his trowel in hand and flicking sandy hair from his eyes.

I smiled. 'You can't afford all of them.'

He laughed and then looked at me thoughtfully for a second. 'You know, I admire you, Ruby. Your resilience is remarkable. Not everyone could go through everything you did and come out the other side so strong.'

'I guess not.' I shrugged at the unexpected compliment. Wait, was it a compliment? 'I suppose Mum is the same. She is strong too,' I told him.

'Yes, she is an amazing woman. But I think you've inherited more from your father than you realise.'

I stared at Jack. 'How's that?'

He shrugged, as though to dismiss his statement. He lowered his voice slightly and glanced through the glass. Was he making sure Mum and Emily weren't back from shopping earlier than expected?

'I don't know really. I just wanted to tell you that you've inherited the best of your parents. Your mother's kindness and the unyielding determination of your father. Those are good traits. They are what make you unique.'

Jack smiled then warmly and returned with ease to his precious garden, as though he thought he should have made me feel better with his words. All they had done was unsettle me.

Did Jack just want me to be comforted by what he said? Or did he identify something in me that I couldn't see for myself, something that echoed the darkness inside my father?

Dad always told me how alike we were. Is that what he meant too?

I watched Jack as he pulled out the weeds he deemed to be ruining his coveted flower beds, tainting the perfect pink blooms. The fact that I broke free from Dad meant that I was free from his influence, didn't it?

So now I am left questioning the complexities of the bloodline connecting me to my father. The one Emily shares too. Are there any nuances from my father's legacy I am still yet to understand? Can I ever be truly free?

ABOUT THE AUTHOR

Did you enjoy *The Guilty Girl*? Please consider leaving a review on Amazon to help other readers discover the book.

Ruth Harrow was born and raised in England and graduated from university before embarking on an unfulfilling career in an office job. She eventually put pen to paper and her debut psychological thriller, *In Her Footsteps*, was published in 2018. It quickly became a bestseller. Following the success of her first novel, her second and third books followed shortly afterwards. She lives in the UK with her husband, two children and chocolate Labrador, Rolo.

Want to connect with Ruth? Visit her at her website.

https://ruthharrow.com/

ALSO BY RUTH HARROW

Made in United States
Orlando, FL
01 July 2024

48517885R00189